CURSES!

CURSES!

A F***ed-Up Fairy Tale

J. A. KAZIMER

KENSINGTON BOOKS
www.kensingtonbooks.com

KENSINGTON BOOKS are published by

Kensington Publishing Corp.
119 West 40th Street
New York, NY 10018

ISBN-13: 978-0-7582-6912-6
ISBN-10: 0-7582-6912-9

First Kensington Trade Paperback Printing: March 2012
10 9 8 7 6 5 4 3 2 1

Printed in the United States of America

For John & Jacquie:
You raised me to believe in fairytales.

For Jennie:
You taught me that there are
no such things as wicked sisters.

For Dave:
You proved that there are.

For Jon:
You are my favorite little villain.

Acknowledgments

Once upon a time, a lot of people helped me get this book into your hands. Now I feel like I owe them something. I'm sure they expect cash . . . joke's on them.

Foremost, thank you to Peter Senftleben, editor extraordinaire, for making my happily-ever-after come true. Thank you to my agent, Sharon Belcastro, for believing in me even when I didn't. Thank you to my wonderful friends—Lisa Birman, Jennie Kazimer, Cindy Miller, Regina Rivera, Kathie Seyforth—who gave up hours of their lives to read the manuscript in its very worst form. Thank you to the amazing writers in Pikes Peak Writers and Rocky Mountain Fiction Writers—without you this book would not be here today. Truly. And a huge thanks to you, dear reader, unless you're a villain and you've pilfered this book. Then you should probably turn yourself in. Or not. Enjoy.

Prologue

Once upon a time (about nine minutes and forty-seven seconds ago) in a land far, far away (the corner of West Fairy-Second Street and Sugar Plum Lane, to be precise) stood a beautiful princess, a woman without compare in beauty or sweetness. Every man, woman, and child in the land loved her, from the most villainous villain to the wickedest of witches.

"Hello there." The princess smiled at the bluebird pecking at a bit of cocoa on the sidewalk. "Aren't you a pretty bird?"

The bluebird chirped, dancing around the beautiful princess. Its tiny claws scratched against the pavement as it bopped figure-eights around her trim ankles.

The princess laughed a high feminine laugh of pure delight. The bird paused, and then continued its acrobatic tricks. The princess bent down to run her manicured hand over the brightly plumed bird. The bird fluttered its wings, edging closer to the busy avenue. A taxicab blaring a bibbity-bop version of "Some Day My Prince Will Come" whizzed by, a little pig at the wheel.

What a lovely day, the princess thought, watching the bird rise into the cloudless sky as it chirped a familiar tune.

Yes, it was a lovely day.
Too bad it was also her last.
Sadly, the princess never saw the crosstown Fairy-Second
Street bus.

Chapter 1

A delivery kid stood in front of me in the pastel hallway of my four-story walk-up on the edge of the Easter Village. His hands juggled a grease-stained bag. My own arms juggled a week's worth of junk mail. I shoved an official-looking paper toward the kid. "This is bollocks."

The kid shrugged.

I waved the paper under his nose. "The union thinks I need a vacation. That I'm suffering from some kind of post-villainous-related stress." My eyes bulged and spit flew from my lips. "What kind of crap is that?"

"Whatever," the delivery kid said. His spiked green hair and facial piercings gave him a clownish appeal. The aroma of red curry noodles from Villainous Van's Corner Bistro wafted in the air between us.

"What are they thinking?" I shook my head, counted to ten, and ran a hand through my already rumpled black hair. "Mandatory mental health leave? Are they afraid I'll go postal or something?" This made little sense since I didn't even work at the post office. "Come on. I've suffered greater defeats and managed to pull through."

"Listen, Mac," the teen said to me. My name wasn't Mac, or anything that resembled Mac. Some people called me RJ, at least to my face.

"The total's ten bucks," the kid said. "Either pay me or

I'll feed your dinner to the rats." The kid motioned from my dinner to the furry creatures dressed in tiny felt hats that roamed my darkened hallway like a demented version of *Dancing with the Villains* rejects. I rolled my eyes, muttered something about kids today, and dug into my jeans for some cash.

"Don't forget my tip," the kid added.

I'll give the little shit a tip. I smashed two fives into his palm and snatched the bag from his hand. My boot kicked the door closed with a loud bang. The kid yelped, sending me into a fit of villainous laughter.

A few seconds later, the kid said, "Thanks, mister."

He sounded happy, which made me unhappy.

Shit.

Yanking a wad of bills from my pocket, a wad considerably smaller than it had been a minute ago, I pulled open the door and watched the teen practically tap-dance down the hallway, a hundred-dollar bill clutched in his hands.

My crisp hundred-dollar bill.

"Darn it," I yelled, booting the door closed again. "I can't take much more." I'd been out of work, suspended without pay, for six days. Six long days. Six days of fluffy bunnies and happy thoughts. All due to one little slipup and the union's subsequent curse. The worst part was, now, no matter what I did, it turned out . . . good . . . nice.

Take yesterday, for example. I'm walking down the avenue, minding my own business, when a little old lady calls out, "Son, would you mind helping me carry this package? It's a basket of cookies for my granddaughter. She's five. . . . "

On and on she went.

Rather than telling her to shut up and snatching her cookie basket, I found myself lugging twenty pounds of pastries four blocks up Avenue XYZ while exchanging recipes with the demented old dame.

What kind of villain does that?

I hated being nice, even more than I hated helping people. And I hated that more than curds and whey. But the union had voted, and I would remain cursed, forced to be nice to any idiot around, until they deemed me mentally stable enough for bad-guy duty.

Feeling sorry for myself and hungry to boot, I stalked across my living room and dropped down in my favorite chair.

My favorite chair screamed in response.

"Wha—?" I jumped up and flicked on my lamp.

A redhead in tight black leather glared at me from my seat. Her vivid emerald eyes sparkled with anger, and just a hint of something else. Something not very nice, but infinitely more interesting than a basket of cookies.

"Don't you look before you sit?" The redhead's lips curved into a frown, which only added to her beauty. She looked like sin, the dirty kind with plenty of sweat and saliva. Long copper hair curled down her shoulders, clinging to the outline of her C-cup breasts. The rest of her body was smoking with long, toned limbs and lots of pale skin.

"Who the heck are you?" I pointed the greasy bag in her direction. Before I could stop her, she snatched it from my fingers. I watched in amazement as the interloper dove into my curry noodles with the gusto of Goldilocks during a bout of bulimia.

"Hey." I stabbed my hand in her direction. "That's my dinner." I would've snatched the carton back, but I was afraid of losing a finger.

After a few minutes of gluttony, she paused to glance my way. "Sorry, but I'm starving. I haven't eaten since five."

I glanced at my watch and frowned. "That was like forty-five minutes ago."

"Really?" She cocked her head to the side, showing off the pale skin of her throat. "It feels like an hour at least."

"While I'd love to chat more about the relativity of

time, I'd prefer you tell me exactly who you are and how you got into my apartment." With each word, my voice grew louder and my tone grew more dangerous. While I might have lost my villainous powers, I could still make one little redhead cry.

Or not.

"Do you have any soda?" She smiled up at me. "Maybe a Diet Pepsi? All that MSG makes me thirsty."

With an eye roll I started for the kitchen, pausing to berate my treacherous legs for obeying her command. But I couldn't help it.

Literally.

I did whatever anyone asked, my own will completely ignored, as long as the requestor's intent was pure. Twenty-eight years of bad luck guaranteed any request made by a knockout redhead in black leather was as pure as Sleeping Beauty. Damn it.

Reluctantly, I opened my refrigerator and popped open the last can of mead. A rush of bubbles rose to the surface, foaming over the can and dribbling down my fingers. I sucked the foamy goodness from my thumb and grinned. The mead would have to appease my uninvited dinner thief. I returned from the kitchen, sat down on the edge of my coffee table, and handed her the can.

She glanced at my saliva-soaked fingers and then at the can. "Thanks," she said after taking a long drink. Tilting her head, she studied me for a moment. Her eyes examined every inch, from my scuffed boots to the top of my hair. "You're not what I expected."

"Oh, and what exactly did you expect?"

"Someone a bit shorter." She frowned. "What are you? Six foot?"

I nodded.

"What do you weigh? Sixteen stone?"

Again, I nodded.

She shook her head. "Puny."

"Hey—" Six foot, two hundred pounds was not puny, not by a long shot. Moreover, I was as fit as Hey Diddle Diddle's fiddle. In my line of work, it paid to be, with all that running from angry mobs with pitchforks and such.

"No offense." Her lips lifted into a smirk. "Maybe you could bulk up for the job? Eat more."

Rage flashed through my bloodstream like a boiling cauldron. "Eat more?" I strangled out, my eyes burning into my nearly empty carton of curry noodles and back at the redhead with a dollop of curry on her upper lip. What I should've said was, "Job? What job?" But I didn't. I blamed my dropping blood sugar for the mistake.

The redhead grinned, lifting the nearly empty carton my way. "Oh, was this your dinner? There's an egg roll left." As she said those words, her eyes locked onto the greasy cabbage roll, as if debating eating it.

I grabbed the egg roll, crammed it in my mouth, and spewed leafy green strands at her as I repeated my earlier question. "Who the heck are you? And why are you here?"

"My name's Asia." She paused, her eyes boring into mine. Don't say it, my brain begged, but just like a woman, she said it anyway. "I need your help."

Chapter 2

"Asia . . ." I tapped my finger to my chin. The vaguest of memories flickered at the edge of my mind. "Your name's familiar somehow. Have we met before?" I doubted it. She wasn't a Villain Vamp, as we called the girls who lowered their standards enough to date my kind. So how did I know her?

She blew out a long sigh. "My full name is Asia Elizabeth Maledetto." At my blank look, she added, "My stepdad's King Maledetto." She paused long enough to roll her eyes. "King of the land of Maledetto. You know, the kingdom that borders the northeastern part of New Never City?"

"Doesn't ring a bell." I shrugged. What the fuck was with the geography lesson? If I wanted to learn, I would've stayed in Charming School.

"Fine." Her hands lifted to her round hips and she glared at me. "My stepsister's Cinderella. Striking midnight now?"

Holy crap. I leapt from my seat on the table and paced around the room. Not that there was much room to pace. In fact, my whole apartment could fit into one of the three kittens' missing mittens. "You're the ugly stepsister!" I said with a frown. Yet this chick wasn't ugly, not by a long shot.

"I'm one of them." She shrugged as if the nickname didn't bother her, but the look of hurt in her eyes spoke more than words could. The villainous, still hungry part of me took satisfaction in her pain. It served her and her princess-stuck-in-an-ivory-tower kind right.

"I'm sorry about," I winced, "your sister's accident." Smashed under a bus was a bad way to go. I should know. I'd run over quite a few jesters and even a prince or two in my time.

"Thanks," she said. "But it wasn't an accident."

I scratched my chin, not liking where this was going. "I have an alibi. I was at my mother's in Queens of Hearts."

Asia arched a flame-colored eyebrow. "Why would you need an alibi?"

"No reason." I tried to smile, but it came off more like a grimace. "You were saying?"

"My sister's death wasn't an accident." Her eyes met mine. "She was murdered. And I need your help to prove it."

Damn. There was that word again. I started to say fuck no, but instead, the following string of words flew from my stupid lips: "Of course. Whatever you need."

God, I hated myself. In an act of revenge, I chomped down on my treacherous tongue until it bled. Served it right.

"Are you eating your tongue?" For a brief second Asia appeared terrified at the prospect. "I'm so sorry. I didn't realize you were that hungry." She shoved her hand into the pocket of her leather pants and removed a lint-covered breath mint. "Here. Take this."

Before I could stop her, she shoved the mint into my mouth. I wanted to yell "Are you fucking nuts," but it came out more like, "Thanks."

Damn it.

She smiled. "So you'll help me track down her killer?"

"Why the heck not?" I stared into her green eyes, losing

myself in their beauty. If a woman's eyes were a window to her soul, I was in big trouble. Because the only image inside Asia Elizabeth Maledetto's eyes was my own evil reflection.

"I'll come back in the morning," she said, "and we can begin our investigation."

I nodded, watching her heart-shaped butt walk out my door and disappear down the hallway. Ugly stepsister, my ass. Hell, even the gayest of the rats surveyed her strut down the corridor.

"I'd do her," said Tate, a pink felt hat-wearing rat with a lisp and a pronounced swish. The other, straighter rats rolled their beady eyes. To which Tate replied: "What?"

I closed the door before things got ugly and dropped into my favorite, now-empty chair. A cloud of dust exploded from the fabric and the sweet scent of pumpkin pie floated around me. I picked up the remnants of my dinner, surprised to see Asia had left a fortune cookie. I smiled at the plastic-wrapped goodie, picturing Asia's emerald eyes.

Peeling the cookie open, I licked my lips in anticipation of its sugary goodness and informative, if not valuable, summation of my future. The cookie read:

THE DELIVERY KID LICKED YOUR EGG ROLL.
HAVE A NICE DAY!

Damn! Foiled again by a teen with more metal in his head than Snow White had sugar midgets.

Hi Ho, Hi Ho . . .

Off to scrub delivery-kid spit out of my mouth I go.

Chapter 3

I woke the next morning to the taste of dead toad (don't ask) and turpentine, the only fluid strong enough to kill delivery-kid germs. My head ached, my eyes burned, and I coughed up something resembling Mary's little lamb.

Outside my window songbirds chirped in chorus, slightly out of tune, but with the gusto reserved for flat-chested strippers. I picked up my boot and threw it at the window. My boot, of course, missed and instead of shutting the damn birds up, it tore a hole in my centerfold poster of Pamela Hans Christian Andersen.

"Hello?" Asia pushed open my bedroom door.

I blinked, stunned by her beauty in the early morning light. Today she wore a red leather miniskirt and a black sweatshirt. Her hair was pulled away from her face in one of those girly buns held together by some magic combination of dulled #2 pencils and fairy dust.

"Oh." Asia covered her mouth. "I'm sorry. I didn't know you weren't," her other hand waved in my direction, "dressed."

I glanced down at my nakedness and shrugged. Like her not-so-ugly highness had never seen a nude villain before. Hell, naked villains were a dime a baker's dozen in Easter Village.

"Rough night," I said. "Too much turpentine."

"I see." Asia paused, patting her flat stomach. "I'm starving. Do you have anything to eat?"

I shook my head and pointed to the kitchen and its nearly empty cupboards. Not a bone in sight. Old Mother Hubbard I wasn't. "Help yourself."

I didn't have to say it twice. Asia disappeared down the hallway, leaving me staring after her. While my morning improved upon her arrival, I still felt the niggling fear that she wasn't what she appeared. Not that I minded her appearance in the least. Literally. Spending time with a not-so-ugly stepsister in red leather beat the hell out of languishing away in my apartment.

Stumbling from my bed, I headed for the shower. The cold water did wonders for my chemically induced hangover, as well as my overheated libido.

Once I was squeaky clean, I tossed on a black "Your Lair or Mine?" T-shirt and a pair of faded Levi's. I even took a moment to run a comb through my shaggy black hair. It paid to impress the client. Halfway presentable, I headed toward the distinctive scent of beautiful woman and coffee grounds.

Asia stood in my bare kitchen with my World's Greatest V (the dishwasher had erased the rest of the word "villain") coffee mug in her hand and a skillet of scrambled eggs cooking on the stovetop.

"My refrigerator had eggs in it?" I frowned, trying to remember the last time I went to the corner Fey grocer. A month at least, and that trip, I only bought a pack of Trojans. Fairy-dusted for her comfort.

Asia shook her head. A few stray ends of hair danced across her cheek. A hundred fantasies, all involving her royal ugliness, flickered through my head. Each one dirtier than the next. Most illegal in the Southern Fairy States.

"No eggs," she said.

"What?" My eyes narrowed. None of my fantasies involved eggs, well, not the edible kind, to be sure.

"You didn't have any eggs," she repeated.

"So what's that?" I pointed to the yellowish scrambled substance bubbling inside the pan. It smelled like eggs. Looked like eggs. Therefore, given my talents of deduction, it was in fact eggs. Yet I'd been fooled before. Mostly by my bitch of an ex-wife. The very woman responsible for my current cursed state.

Asia grinned, crooking her finger in my direction. I leaned in close enough to hear her whisper, "Do you really want to know what's in the pan?"

"Nope."

"Smart man." She winked, filled a plate with an egglike substance, and handed it to me. I grabbed a fork from the drawer and dug in. It tasted like eggs too—buttery, light and fluffy. I couldn't remember the last time a woman cooked for me. Hell, even my mum had ordered take-out.

I took a second bite. Warm. Tasty. Needed a little salt. "Ow!" I pulled a piece of concrete from my mouth. "What the hell's that?"

Asia wrapped her fingers around mine, eyed the offending bit of gravel, and smirked. "Looks like a piece of brick." She shrugged and tossed the debris into my sink. It smacked the stainless steel with a ping.

"Brick?"

Before she could answer, sirens echoed from the street below. I gazed out the kitchen window. A crowd had gathered. Fairy godmothers, rats in hats, and a little boy dressed in blue stood on the sidewalk, eyes wide as they took in the scene in front of them.

A man in a rumpled suit stood behind a string of yellow crime scene tape. He stooped down and picked up a goo-covered brick that lay next to an egg-shaped chalk outline. The cop's eyes darted from the front porch of my walk-up to the brick in his hand. Another cop nodded to my window. I jumped back and glared at Asia.

Her lips trembled and tears rolled down her pale cheeks.

After a few seconds, her tears dried and she crossed her arms across her chest. She mumbled, "I was hungry."

"While you were getting dressed," her drawn-out sigh reverberated around the room, "I noticed this egg just sitting on the brick wall outside. He looked so sad."

"Uh-huh."

"And I was so very hungry."

"Uh-huh."

"So when I saw him fall, I immediately ran to help him up, but I was too late." She shook her head, glancing up from lowered lashes. "All the king's horses and the king's men couldn't have saved him."

"Uh-huh."

"Poor little egg." A tear glistened in the corner of her eye. "I'm sure it was suicide. He had nothing left to live for."

"Fair enough." I dropped my plate of Humpty Dumpty into the sink and grabbed her arm. "But, sweetheart, in Easter Village eggicide gets you twenty to life."

"Oh." She eyed the evidence in her hand. "Maybe we should go."

"You think?"

She sighed, grabbed a fork from the counter, and gobbled down the rest of Humpty as if it was her last meal. When she finished, we left my apartment through the back door, arm in arm, partners in a deviled deed.

Chapter 4

"Nice ride," I said, motioning around Asia's Ford half-pumpkin, half-chariot hybrid. While the interior smelled like Thanksgiving Day throw-up, the vehicle handled like a dream and was surprisingly roomy. Asia shifted gears like a NASCAR driver, twisting in and out of the early-morning traffic.

"Thanks," Asia said. "Cindi wanted me to have it."

Cindi, as in the famed Cinderella, I deduced. Already I played the part of a PI, or rather a dick. Give me a couple more days and I'd unmask Cinderella's killer.

But anyone who knew my villainous past would ask: Why?

The answer was surprisingly simple and seated next to me—one egg-murdering princess. I wasn't planning our fairytale wedding yet, but I wouldn't mind finding out if not-so-ugly girls really did work that much harder in bed. If I solved her sister's killing, Asia would reward me, hopefully until I was limp and putty in her hands.

And if not, I'd kidnap her, lock her in a tower, and force her to weave knock-off Gucci handbags for the rest of her days. Because that's what villains did, and I, current mental health leave aside, was one hell of a villain. I'd crushed princes, made my share of maidens cry, and even stolen a golden goose or two.

I smiled, eased my seat back, and closed my eyes as Asia drove us through a snarl of commuter traffic to the heart of New Never City. Next to me, she hummed a familiar song.

But I couldn't place it.

Oh well, it will come to me, I thought as I closed my eyes.

A few minutes later Asia shook me awake. "Get up."

I opened one eye and snarled. The afternoon sun blinded me, searing my innocent eyeball. During my brief cat-and-a-fiddle nap, my legs had cramped up under the dash-board, twisting me into a villainous pretzel without the salty parts. No rest for the recently-cursed-used-to-be-wicked.

Yawning, I peeled open my other eye and glanced around at the city in front of me. It was a beautiful sight. Sky-scrapers and exhaust filled the sky. Pigeons dressed in pink dive-bombed passing tourists waiting in line at the falafel stand. Buses and cars sped past, as did the Pied Piper and a string of felt hat-wearing rats, coffee cups and the early edition of the *New Never News,* New Never City's num-ber one source of news, gripped tightly in their tiny, mani-cured paws. Shiny windows reflected the scene like a warped version of reality TV.

"We're here." Asia exited the Ford Pumpkin.

Here was Fairy-Second Street, the place where another chalk outline lay on the exhaust-stained blacktop. This one, however, told the story of Cinderella's final moments.

I followed Asia from the compact and scanned the crime scene. In death Cinderella appeared much smaller, her chalk outline merely a speck on a busy city street. For some unexplainable reason wetness gathered at the corners of my eyes. I wiped a tear away.

"Spice." A guy in a dark rumpled suit joined us on the sidewalk. He looked as worn as his clothes and just as outdated. Like a member of an eighties hair band once male-pattern baldness settled in.

"Spice?" I tilted my head, noting every detail about the man from his sagging jowls to his overly big nose. No wonder Asia needed me, if this was the best the New Never City PD had to offer. I mean, really, we stood in the middle of a crime scene discussing recipes, for fuck sakes.

"The reason your eyes are tearing up." The cop nodded to my salt-smeared cheeks. "Sugar, spice, and everything nice. Half a city block got coated in the stuff when the bus... well, you know." He waved a tobacco-discolored hand in the direction of the chalk outline.

I must've continued to look confused because Asia came up to stand next to me, her hand on my arm. "Sugar, spice, and everything nice. That's what little girls are made of." She shrugged. "And it tastes pretty good on toast too."

"I see," I said but really didn't. The chicks I knew weren't crafted from anything nice, let alone sugary sweet. I glanced at Asia. "What was Cinderella doing in New Never City? I thought she and Charming were to be married in two weeks."

"She was here to see me," Asia said. "I left home a month ago, for a...job...in the city." I noted her pause, but decided not to press her. Not yet. Asia continued, "On Monday, Cindi called me. She said she had something important to tell me. Something she couldn't tell me over the phone. We agreed to meet for lunch. But Cindi never showed. I waited and waited at the Quite Contrary Buffet..." Her lips dipped into a frown. "Until the owners tossed me out. All you can eat, my ass."

"So you never saw her?" I frowned, not sure if I believed her. Instead of Asia taking offense at my tone, the cop did.

He stuck out his chest and tucked his fat arms under his armpits. "This here's an official accidental death investigation," he said. "Just who the heck do you think you are, asking these questions?"

I grinned, ready and willing to go mano-a-villain with the good detective. In fact, I wanted nothing more. Cops rubbed me the wrong way, sort of like a brand-new shirt made by Geppetto himself. "Why don't you guess?" I waggled my eyebrows. "Come on, I dare you. Guess my name."

The detective stepped closer, invading my personal space. I exhaled deeply, wanting to hurt him, to punch him in his bulbous nose and spit on his scuffed shoes, but thanks to the union, my Humpty breath would have to do. I blew another burst of fetid egg breath in his direction.

His nose scrunched up, but he didn't drop dead as I had hoped. Instead, he jabbed me in the chest. "Let's see some ID."

"Stop it." Asia pushed herself between the cop and me. She grabbed his arm and held on. "Please. I requested his help to investigate my sister's death."

"Stepsister," the cop said.

Asia rolled her eyes. "Yes, stepsister."

The detective frowned and pulled Asia to the side. In a stage whisper, he said, "Who the hell is he? He looks like a bum."

I tried to look offended. It worked for a half of a second, but then my gaze fell on the chalk outline on the cement and I forgot everything else. Something about the outline bothered me. I peered closer.

"He's not a bum," Asia said in a near whisper of her own. "He's the most famous inspector in all the land."

For a second the detective looked as if he didn't believe her, his eyes narrowed and he frowned. Not unimaginable, since I wasn't buying it either.

Asia stomped her foot. "Inspector Holmes of Fairy Yard is responsible for catching some of the most dangerous criminals of our time. He busted that trespassing bitch

Goldilocks, and Little Pigs #1 and #2 for shoddy home construction. He's caught every villain he's ever been after."

Damn! Asia wasn't looking for me, RJ, master villain, when she magically appeared in my apartment yesterday, but rather, the famed Inspector Holmes. The same inspector who had resided in my apartment before me. The very same famed inspector currently stuffed into my chimney.

I shook my head. He wasn't that great a detective. After all, I'd managed to cram him in the fireplace, and it took me less than five minutes. Three minutes of that I spent playing inspector origami, a fold here, a tuck there, and voilà, a crane-shaped detective. Oh well, if Asia wanted a Fairy Yard Inspector, that's what I'd damn well be.

"He doesn't look like an inspector," the detective was saying. "In fact," he squinted in my direction, "he looks like a villain to me."

"He's undercover," Asia said.

The cop raised an eyebrow. "Is that true?"

"If Asia says so." I grinned. "So tell me what happened. How'd a pretty princess wind up smashed under the crosstown bus?"

The detective grimaced, but did as I asked. "An eyewitness swears Cinderella just stepped in front of the bus. The driver tried to stop, but ..." He waved to the chalked street. "It was too late. We see it all the time around here. A small-town hick princess comes to the big, bad city. She takes one wrong step, and kablam, she's roadkill." Asia winced, and the detective added, "No offense, ma'am."

"And the bird?" I asked.

"Bird?"

"Yeah." I pointed to the ground and the tiny bird droppings on the sidewalk. "A bluebird, by the look of it."

The detective frowned, but stooped down to examine the birdy-doo. Asia peered over my shoulder and down at the fecal matter. "How do you know it's a bluebird?"

"How do you know it wasn't?" I winked at her and

waited for the detective to rise from his crouched position. When he did, the look on his face suggested my deduction was dead-on. Hell, this investigation stuff wasn't so hard. Maybe when I retired from a life of villainy I'd take it up. That and knitting. I loved a good cross-stitch.

"What do you think the bluebird means?" Asia gazed at me expectantly. Her lips were parted, her eyes alight. How I wanted to snatch her up and carry her to the nearest tower. She was so beautiful standing in the middle of midtown, the sun reflecting off her auburn hair. "Ummm..." She snapped her fingers in front of my face. "The bluebird?"

"Right. Two things." I held up my index finger and paused for dramatic emphasis. A pause that neither Asia nor the detective seemed to appreciate. "I'm a damn good detective." I held up a second finger. "And Asia's right, Cinderella was murdered."

Chapter 5

Asia gasped, but the detective just raised an eyebrow. Everyone's a critic. I motioned to him and waited. His accusations weren't long in coming.

"Now wait a damn minute," he sputtered. "How does a bluebird equal murder? You're insane. We have eyewitnesses who saw the whole thing. Cinderella stepped off the curb. Nobody pushed her."

I shrugged. "You're right. She wasn't pushed. The bluebird distracted her, and she, being a princess," I glanced over at Asia with an apologetic smile, "followed the bird into the street. It's a typical villain ploy."

"A villain did this?" Asia's hand flew to her throat. "But why? How?"

I winced, unsure what villainous codes I violated by repeating the age-old "trick a stupid princess into the street" ploy. But since she had asked, I had no choice but to tell her. Everything. Damn it. "It's simple, really. Princesses cannot resist bluebirds. It's a widely known fact." I looked to Asia for agreement. She nodded, and I continued. "So a villain buys and trains a bluebird, and voilà, the princess steps into the street."

"But how do you know she didn't just follow some random bluebird into the path of the bus?" The detective scratched his whiskered chin like a chimp. "How can you know for sure it was murder?"

I raised an eyebrow. "What month is it?"

Asia answered for him. "October."

"What's that got to do with anything?" the detective said.

I raised my finger to my mouth, licked it, and held it up to the cool afternoon air like I'd seen the fake thick-mustached PI, Belle, and her effeminate boyfriend, the Beast, do on TV.

What can I say? I'm a product of the television generation. Plus, villains had a lot of downtime, and TV reruns helped us pass the time while recovering from broken limbs, busted facial bones, and the occasional hernia. Villainy wasn't anything like they promised in the recruitment brochures.

Asia looked at me and then at my finger, which was still hovering in the air. "Well?"

"What?" I frowned. "Oh, right. Cinderella's murder. In answer to the detective's question, bluebirds, like their blue-winged counterpart, the peacock, leave New Never City for the outer kingdoms at the first hint of fall. Usually sometime around September first."

The detective stared at me, his wide mouth open big enough to catch fairies. "So it's true. A villain murdered the sweet princess."

"No."

"What?!" The detective wagged his fist at me. "You just said so."

"No, I didn't." I turned to face Asia and whispered loud enough for the detective to hear. "Someone should IQ test these guys before giving 'em a badge."

Asia bit her lip. "In all fairness, you did imply a villain was responsible for Cinderella's misfortune."

"Oh, all right. I'll spell it out for him." I faced the detective and smiled before explaining, very slowly, in short sentences. "Cinderella's killer wasn't a villain. But he is a . . . jerk. One who wants to smear the bad name of villains everywhere."

"I get it." Asia nodded when I finished. "A villain would've boasted of his dirty deed, not tried to pass it off as an accident. So if it wasn't a villain, who was it?"

"I don't know." My eyes roamed over her face, sliding lower, cupping the curves of her body. When my gaze reached the glob of dried egg yolk on the strap of her gold slipper, my eyes lifted to hers. Her irises sparkled with hidden, dark knowledge, and a shiver ran up my spine. "Why don't you tell me?"

Her hand fluttered to her ample chest. "What? You think that I had something to do with my sister's death?"

"Step—" I started to correct her.

"How dare you!" She spun on her heel, and then must've thought better of it, because she turned back to face me. Tears welled in her eyes. She wiped them away with the back of her hand. But when she spoke, her voice lacked any emotion. "If I killed Cindi, why would I ask for your help?"

Good question. One I didn't have the answer for just yet, but I suspected I'd find out soon enough.

An hour later, I shoved the last of my clean T-shirts into a duffel bag and tossed the bag over my shoulder. Asia stood highlighted in my apartment doorway, her eyes shifting up and down the hallway. Probably waiting for the egg cops to show up and arrest her.

She took a sip from the steaming cup of Wish Upon a Starbucks and grinned at me over the rim. "I really appreciate your doing this," she said. "Not many men would help a damsel like me solve a murder, let alone travel across the land in hope of catching a killer."

"What can I say?" I shrugged my shoulder, jarring the duffel bag. "I'm dedicated." That and I hoped to see her naked sometime in the near future, which, of course played the bigger role in my decision to travel to the kingdom of Maledetto. But if I happened to catch a murderer while there, so be it. That's what henchmen called multitasking.

"Do you honestly think someone from Maledetto killed Cindi?" Asia asked. I nodded, and Asia shook her head. "But why? Everyone loved her. And that's not an exaggeration."

Even though her words sounded right, Cinderella's pancaked body gave me the distinct impression a few people in the kingdom weren't in the everyone category. After all, someone had crushed the pretty, pretty princess so widely loved under a bus.

"Exaggeration or not, when you're looking for a killer," I grinned, tapping my heels together, "there's no place like home."

Chapter 6

Asia and I arrived at the kingdom of Maledetto around two in the afternoon as the sun started to duck behind the pointy turrets and gleaming gold of the castle. I glanced at Asia for an explanation for the incoming darkness surrounding only the castle. The rest of the kingdom appeared unaffected by the setting sun. Odd, to say the least.

"Cursed," she said.

Fair enough.

I grabbed my bag from the trunk of the Ford Pumpkin and followed Asia up the yellow brick path to her childhood palace. The place reeked of wealth, from the golden doorknobs attached to every door to the diamond-encrusted chandelier, bigger than my apartment, hanging in the foyer.

I gazed up at the shining diamonds and thought, my kingdom for a ladder. I brushed off my thieving instincts when a butler dressed in black stepped from the shadows. He resembled a troll, but without the dramatic flair, his face small and round with large eyes and an upper-crust sneer.

"Sir? I'm Winslow, the butler." He gestured to my duffel bag with a snicker. "May I take your things?"

I nodded, ignoring the desire to scream, "The butler did it." Hell, for all I knew he did kill Cinderella, which would leave me out of a job or any chance of getting into Asia's chastity belt. And I really, really wanted to unlock that particular mystery.

"Thanks, mate. We'll chat later." Shifting my burden to Winslow's capable arms, I followed Asia farther into the castle. My lust for her increased with her every step as her leather-clad hips strained against the material. To take my mind off their sway I studied the palace hallway. Paintings lined the walls, as did antique furniture and polished suits of armor. The thick carpet swallowed our steps. A girlish golden harp sat in the corner of the hallway, her eyes watching me with suspicion. This place was a villainous fantasy come true—riches beyond compare and a princess to boot. The scent of wealth and pie drifted around us. I smiled happily.

We drifted farther down the long golden corridor, Asia leading the way, her legs just as long and golden. I watched with true reverence. The kind reserved for the Sunday afternoon hare races. When she paused outside a large ornate door, I asked, "Why'd you ever leave here? This place is amazing."

Asia's eyes burned with something I couldn't decipher. Something dark and dangerous, and not at all appealing. I shivered in the temperature-controlled palace.

"Wait for it," Asia said, and a second later, a woman screamed. The noise was followed by a loud crash. I winced, the pitch grating on my nerves. The noise didn't appear to bother Asia, though. She took my hand, plastered a smile on her face, and pushed through the door.

"Time to meet our number one suspects, or as I call them, Mom and Dad."

The door opened and we stood in the center of a large, dark room filled with books. Unread books, by the look of them. They sat on the shelves in perfect alphabetical order, not a spine out of place. Tomes as old as time, but maybe not as old as the lady in the painting over the fireplace. She made the old woman who lived in a shoe look young.

The framed portrait glared down at us, passing judgment. If the look on the woman's face was an indication, she was also passing a kidney stone the size of a golden goose.

"The first Lady Maledetto and Cinderella's mother." Asia pointed to the painting and then gestured to the couch in the center of the room. "My mother is the king's second wife. The second Lady Maledetto."

I gazed into the shadows where Asia had pointed, finally noticing the two people on the couch. Asia closed the door behind us, and a cloud of dust shifted around the room.

I sneezed.

"Bless you."

"That's just what I need," I muttered to myself, my eyes studying Asia's parents. A wolf pelt lay at their feet, its eyes fixed. Sharp rows of teeth gleamed in the dim light.

But that wasn't the weird thing.

Nope, the housecoat and hair rollers attached to the wolf's fur won that honor, hands down. I frowned, my eyes narrowing. The wolf in drag looked an awful lot like my nana.

Next to Grandma Wolf sat a pile of shattered hand mirrors. My face reflected back to me in the thousands of shards of glass on the floor. Suddenly I wanted nothing more than to grab Asia and run from this place.

"The Big Bad one himself." King Maledetto jabbed a finger at the pelt on the floor. The king's grey beard shook with each word. "Got him right between the beady eyes. One shot."

"Congratulations," I said, unsure of what else to say. I wasn't much for shooting animals, especially fellow villainous ones. Now, give me a clean shot at a white knight . . .

"Dad." Asia gestured to the brave hunter / king, and to her mother seated so primly next to him. "Mother. I'd like you to meet a friend of mine. A duke," she motioned to me, "Duke..."

"RJ. I go by RJ," I said when she paused.

"Yes." Asia grinned as if we shared a secret. "Meet Duke RJ."

Asia's mother, Lady Maledetto, rose from the sofa with a regal air, the look of welcome vanishing from her face at my assumed title. After all, a princess, even an ugly one, needed a prince, not some duke with delusions of grandeur and initials for a name.

I smiled my most charming smile and studied Lady Maledetto. Asia resembled her in many ways, the red hair and pert nose, not to mention the smoking-hot body. By all accounts, King Maledetto had married up. How had Cinderella avoided her true mother's ugly genetic fate? It wasn't like the king was anything to look at, with his grey hair, beard, and mead gut that spilled over his belt like a muffin.

"Duke RJ." Lady Maledetto held out her hand. "It's a pleasure to meet you. My daughter's," she glared at Asia, "told us so much about you."

Liar, liar, pants on fire. I checked to make sure her nose hadn't grown before clasping her hand in mine. "Thank you, madam." I slowly bent to kiss her knuckles like I'd seen plenty of princes do. Somehow, I slipped into the role of Duke RJ without even trying. Must have something to do with the "nice" clause. Fucking union. "It's a pleasure to be here, but under the most tragic of circumstances." Lady Maledetto stared blankly at me, so I added, "Cinderella's death. I'm sorry for your loss."

"Oh. That." She waved her hand in the air between us, probably calling her legion of killer bluebirds. "Yes, it's a sad time for us all. Honey," she pointed to the king, "say hello to Asia's friend."

The older man shuffled from the couch. "Duke, was it?"

"If Asia says so." I nodded, my eyes never wavering

from his face. "But feel free to call me RJ, or whatever you like." I grinned. "Most people do."

"So what brings you to our fair kingdom?" Like any good father, the old king regarded me with suspicion through narrowed eyes. The kind learned by men at a very young age. We were not to be trusted around beautiful women. Ever.

"Daddy," Asia started to interrupt.

I held up my hand to stop her. "Well, sir, Asia asked me to, so here I am. Your daughter—"

"Stepdaughter," the king and his wife said in a freakishly similar manner.

"Stepdaughter," I corrected, "is very persuasive."

The king nodded in apparent male understanding of the inner workings of the illogical female brain. Asia looked as if she wanted to scream. On the other hand, her mother just beamed at the clueless king, and then her attention returned to me.

"You must be starving after your long journey," the queen said. "I'll ask Winslow to ask Cook to have one of the maids deliver some sandwiches to your room."

My stomach growled, reminding me of my aborted breakfast attempt. The thought of bread, meat, and a selection of cheese excited me much more than it should. "That sounds grea—"

"No, thanks," Asia interrupted. "RJ's not hungry, and I'm on a diet."

"Of course you are, dear." The queen nodded as if the shapely princess next to me needed to lose a hundred pounds. If anything, Asia was far too thin. I preferred my victims a tad meatier, but I knew, perhaps better than anyone did, how mothers could be. Mine, to this day, insisted on holding my hand when we crossed the street. Nice at ten. A bit creepy at twenty-eight.

"I promised RJ a tour of the kingdom." Asia nodded in my direction. "So we better get started."

Lady Maledetto beamed. "Have fun."

"Thanks," I said, bowing at the waist like a fool. "It's been a pleasure—"

"Yes, well...," Lady Maledetto interjected, catching Asia's eye. "Make sure you stop over at Charming's place."

I raised a questioning eyebrow at Asia. She responded with a drawn-out sigh. Lady Maledetto ignored her daughter's look, and instead patted Asia's arm, causing the poor, un-ugly girl to wince. "Maybe you should wash up first." The queen fingered a strand of Asia's fiery hair. "Do your hair. Put on some makeup." Her plumped eyelashes batted against her porcelain cheeks. "After all, the prince is back on the market."

Chapter 7

"Please tell me you were raised by wolves," I said, shaking my head as we exited the library. After meeting Lady Maledetto, matricide made sense in a survival-of-the-fittest sort of way, because that woman wouldn't hesitate to eat her young.

Or someone else's.

Just in case, I checked my fingers and toes. Ten. Well, twenty if you're nitpicky. All still intact. Whew.

On the bright side, what Asia's mother lacked in parenting skills she more than made up for with her subtle, single-minded desire for Asia to marry the freshly unengaged Prince Charming.

No wonder Asia had left the kingdom.

Asia stopped outside the library door and grabbed the collar of my T-shirt, dragging me toward her lips. She kissed me, thoroughly and completely. No half-assed brotherly peck for her. Nope, she gave me a full-on I-want-to-suck-your-brains-through-your-lips kind of kiss. Our tongues met in the middle, playing a quick game of tag. She tasted like warm brandy and evil deeds. Her mouth taunted mine, teasing and tempting me until I nearly lost control and took her right there in the hallway. Her knee slid up the inside of my thigh. I groaned in response, pulling her closer in anticipation of her naughty parts melding with mine.

We came up for air a few seconds later, and she pushed me away. Unsteady, I stumbled, grabbing the wall for support. I stammered something like: "Ohgodwannaget-marriedandhavemybabies?"

Asia answered by smacking me in the back of the head. Once I regained my manly composure, she said, "Sorry about attacking you like that. But my mother makes me so crazy I lose all control."

"No problem." I wiped a string of drool from my lips, not sure if it was hers or mine. "Happy to help. Really. Feel free to lose control anytime you want. I'm here for you. Day or night..."

I continued rambling for a few more minutes, but Asia had already disappeared down the hallway, the damp outline of my handprint visible on the leather of her skirt.

For the next two hours Asia guided me through the kingdom of Maledetto. We stopped at the Butcher's, the Baker's, and the Sex Toy Maker's, not staying long enough to interrogate anyone, let alone sample any of their wares. A shame, really, since I was both hungry and curious about a certain vibrating item no bigger than Thumbelina. Asia smiled at each shopkeeper, but the Sex Toy Maker seemed to be the only one happy to see her. The Butcher and the Baker both sighed with resignation when we entered their shops.

The rest of the kingdom looked like any other kingdom with shops, markets, and wind-tattered straw, stick, and brick houses circling Main Street. Asia guided me through the back alleys, diving deeper and deeper as we trekked through Cinderella's former home. Was her killer lurking somewhere? I smiled at the thought, remembering the joy of lurking. Ah, the good old villainous days.

Eventually our trip ended at the crown jewel of Maledetto. The Three Blind Mice Tavern. According to Asia, the tavern served the finest mead in all the land, as well as cheesy doodles. "Just don't order the Mice-a-roni," she warned, her face wrinkling with disgust even as her tummy grumbled.

I prayed the food tasted better than the tavern looked. With a sigh, I decided it couldn't taste worse. Peeling pink paint covered the exterior walls, only interrupted by broken, greying shutters and streaks of vomit stains. The inside was slightly better, in that peanut shells covered the puke stains on the pink shag carpet.

Asia and I strode into the bar like something from an Old Western fairytale. All heads swiveled our way. I would've laughed if most of their lecherous looks weren't aimed at the lady standing next to me.

My hand shot to the small of Asia's back. Mine, I branded, my eyes staring down each of the degenerate characters inside the smoke-filled room. One guy with a hook on the end of his hand gazed at Asia much too long. I tilted my head in warning, and he quickly backed down.

Asia didn't appear to notice our exchange. Instead, she pushed her way through the crowd, pausing in front of a scarred booth. Four burly henchmen sat in the booth, their muscles bulging with evil intent. I recognized one of them as the dude with a foot fetish on the last season of *New Never City's Most Wanted Bachelors*.

"This is my booth." My slim-hipped companion stabbed her finger at the table. Much to my surprise, the four minions jumped from the booth as if it was on fire. They stumbled out of Asia's way, whispering apologies as they ran.

I should've realized right then that there was more here than met the eye. But in my defense, Asia looked so hot, standing there with her arms crossed and her foot tapping, that I probably wouldn't have noticed a midget drag queen in pink chiffon.

A midget drag queen in pink chiffon appeared at our newly acquired booth. He squinted at Asia and then asked for our order. Asia pointed at me. "He'll have the cheesy doodles and the finest mead. I'll have," she sighed, "water."

I raised an eyebrow, but didn't comment on her high-handedness or her order. I would have, but my mind was elsewhere, about four booths elsewhere.

Sitting as pretty as a picture in a booth much like ours was the reason for my current plague of niceness.

Natasha.

Hate rose within me, bitter and burning.

My ex-wife Natasha swirled her dirty vodka martini and laughed at the much-too-pretty man sitting across from her. She looked amazing, dressed all in black. The only burst of color was her blood-red lips. I shivered when she bit said bottom lip, drawing it through her teeth as if savoring every inch.

My, what sharp teeth you have. . . .

The better to ruin your life with. Damn her.

I hadn't seen Natasha in a while. Not since the day she walked out on me and our villainous future. This wouldn't have been bad, except she took off with the Frog Prince, leaving me with a bad case of warts.

After her departure, a couple of painful applications of liquid nitrogen to my affected areas, and a brief nervous breakdown, the union had deemed me unfit for duty. I blamed Natasha for it all. We'd been the perfect villainous couple, then she left, and my life went to shit.

From that day on, I vowed I would never fall in love again. It wasn't worth the nice.

"Problem?" Asia glanced over her shoulder. Her eyes scanned the bar for whatever held my attention.

"Always. But nothing I wanna discuss. Not when I'm

seated across from you." I cleared my throat and reached for her hand. Her attention returned to me, saving me from an uncomfortable explanation about my soul-sucking ex-wife, not to mention a plausible excuse for my inspector impersonation.

The midget drag queen slammed a plate of cheesy curls in front of me and stalked away as fast as his tiny pink heels could carry him. The scent of cheddar and boiled oil circled us in a heavenly aroma. Gooey, melty strings of cheese dripped from the edge of the plate. Asia's stomach growled loud enough to attract the attention of every patron in the bar, even the three deaf mice, notorious cousins of the three blind ones.

Natasha glanced over.

I ducked my head, nearly landing face-first in the scalding cheese like some kind of villainous fondue. Asia's stomach grumbled again, even louder than the first time. A four on the villainous Richter scale at least. My mead bottle rattled, toppling off the table and onto the floor with a dull thud.

Once the tavern stopped shaking, Natasha rose from her booth, her long, lean legs as long and lean as I remembered.

The faithless bitch.

"What do you say we get out of here?" I asked Asia, not adding, before I killed the one woman I'd sworn to dishonor and disobey until her death did we part. I'd written my own vows.

Call me a hopeless romantic.

"But you didn't touch your food." Asia's eyes locked on my cheesy plate with almost orgasmic intensity. A string of drool dribbled from her lips. Damn. I wanted her to look at me like that. Drool included.

"Um . . . Asia?" I prompted.

Asia finally glanced up, her eyes burned with gluttony and mild confusion. "Am I missing something?"

"Yes," my traitorous mouth answered. I slapped my hand over it before it could say more. Asia raised her eyebrow in a perfect villainous arch. Damn beginner's luck. I'd spent hours in the mirror trying to get my eyebrow to rise like that.

Natasha appeared over Asia's shoulder. "Is that you, Ru—"

I cut her off. "Do I know you?"

Her black eyes narrowed, but she caught on quick enough. The slashing motions I made across my throat probably helped.

"My mistake." Her smile grew as she glanced from me to Asia. "I thought you were a man I used to know, but I guess not."

Asia tilted her head at my former wife. "I haven't seen you in the kingdom before. Are you new to town?"

"Why, yes," Natasha said. "I'm recently divorced and needed to get away from the city for a while. Some men just can't accept it when the relationship's over. They follow you around, from city to kingdom. It's quite pathetic really."

Whore.

"Oh," Asia said. "Well . . ."

"Well, it was nice chatting with you." I stood, smoothing an invisible wrinkle from my T-shirt. "The princess here," I motioned to Asia, "promised to show me the rest of the kingdom, so we must be on our way."

Asia's brow puckered, but she didn't question me. Instead, she rose from the booth and offered her hand to Natasha. "Nice meeting you . . ."

"Natasha." My ex smiled, showing off shark-white teeth and a penchant for fresh blood. "Natasha Stiltskin."

"Stiltskin," Asia said. "That name's familiar. Are you by any chance related to—"

"Stiltskin is a really common name. Kind of like Smith. I've met tons of them in the city. Ray Stiltskin. Boris. Bill. Robert. So many Stiltskins," I babbled like a leprechaun intent on escaping with his pot of gold. "Just last week, I met a dude named Barack—"

"Anyway, it's been a pleasure," Natasha said to Asia, and then she turned to me. "Perhaps we'll meet again. Soon."

Chapter 8

"That was weird," Asia said, crossing her arms over her ample chest. I tried valiantly to ignore the swell of her breasts, but failed. Suffice it to say, Asia had to repeat her statement twice before my mind caught up.

"Weird?" I stuttered. Damn Natasha. She could ruin everything for me. Again. I should've locked her in a tower years ago.

Asia grabbed my hand. "So you saw it too?"

Saw what? My bitch of an ex-wife? Oh yeah, I saw every damn deceitful inch of her. Good thing for Natasha the union had rendered me impotent, at least fiendishly so. Otherwise, my shoelaces would be a necktie for her right about now. I pictured her bulging eyeballs as my shoelace tightened around her throat and felt instantly better. Ah, the power of positive thought.

"I wasn't sure at first," Asia was saying as my mental murder fantasy faded from my mind. "But then he snuck out the back door, and I knew it was him."

I shook my head, clueless. "Who?"

"Cindi's childhood friend Hansel, of course."

Who the fuck was Hansel? "Of course. So what do you think it means?" I gave her my best sincere smile. The one that often made old ladies cry.

"He's hiding something." Asia bit her bottom lip. "Why else would he duck out the back door?"

I nodded sagely and hopefully detectively, and motioned for her to continue.

"I bet he knows why she was killed."

"Could be."

"What do we do now?" Her eyes stared at me with such faith I almost felt guilty for my deception. Almost.

I gestured into the dark forest. "Let's go find this Hansel and ask him some questions." I stepped forward like a man on a mission, consequences be damned. Asia grabbed my arm, pulling me to a stop. I raised a questioning eyebrow.

"He lives that way." She pointed in the opposite direction.

"Of course." I spun on my heel and started forward once again. This time Asia fell into step beside me, the gentle sway of her hips a pleasant distraction after the run-in with my ex.

The forest closed in around us as we ventured down a rocky path to Hansel's place. In the trees above our heads birds chirped to the beat of a familiar ditty, but I couldn't place the song. A cold wind swept across my arms and I shivered. I was a city boy at heart. Enchanted or not, forests freaked me out. Too much nature, not enough graffiti. And what was with the smell? It stank like those pine-scented urinal cakes in the bathroom of Fairy Central Station.

My cell phone rang. "What?" I answered without glancing at the caller ID.

"Not your usual type. Too nice," my ex-wife said, her voice muffled by static. "So how rich is she?"

"What do you want?"

"What makes you think I want anything?" She paused for a beat. "Maybe I just missed you."

I snickered, and Natasha joined me. The bitch. Once my peals of bitter glee ended, I took two steps away from Asia and growled into the phone, "Don't mess with me. I'm not in the mood."

"Oh, but I am."

I closed my eyes and counted to ten. Then I counted to twenty. When I reached four hundred and thirty, I was calm enough to whisper, "Meet me tomorrow. In the alley between the Butcher and the Baker. I'll be the guy wishing you dead."

Natasha laughed again, high and light, just like I remembered from our many nights of debauchery. "Till we meet again," she said and hung up.

"Who was that?" Asia stood next to me, a soft smile on her lips. Sunlight danced in her coppery hair. I stared at her, unable to draw my eyes away. She grew more beautiful with each moment, rounder, softer somehow.

Yep, I was truly fucked.

Her head tilted to the side. "Are you going to tell me?"

I bit my tongue and shook my head no.

Her smile grew wider. "Fair enough." She patted her tummy. "But please stop gnawing on your tongue. I'm hungry enough as it is."

I saw an out and took it. "This morning you slaughtered an innocent egg, and now you're on a crash diet. What gives?"

"I'm thinking of auditioning for *Neverland's Top Model,*" she said. "What's it to you?"

I shrugged. If she didn't want to tell me the truth, I could respect that. I held a secret too. Many of them, in fact. If she wanted to keep one little one for herself, so be it.

Not that it would work.

I was a villain, for fuck sakes. How hard could it be to crack one little princess?

A girlish scream ripped me from my fiendish thoughts. Asia glanced at me, and we both took off running toward the terrified shouts. I broke through the Enchanted Forest first, pulling to a stop at the sight in front of me.

In the middle of the forest, a guy covered in caramel goo flapped like a marionette on a string. His puppet master was a seven-foot-tall chick dressed in a leather catsuit with a bulbous nose, warts, and a suspicious lump in her throat.

"Hansel," she screamed, yanking at Hansel's sticky arms, "how many times have I told you no sweets before dinner!"

Hansel yelped, but the corners of his lips curved into a devious smile. "I'm sorry, mistress. Please, please don't eat me."

"Oh, you are a dirty, naughty boy." The witch smacked Hansel's bottom, much to his delight and my disgust. Sex games had a right time and place. Four o'clock in the afternoon, surrounded by malevolent maple trees, wasn't it.

"Sorry to interrupt," I said.

The witch dropped Hansel, and he landed hard at her feet. A cloud of dust and caramel circled him, nearly obscuring the gingerbread house behind them.

But not enough.

Asia stood transfixed by the decadent sight of white icing and rainbow-colored gumdrops. Her stomach gurgled, and then growled, and drool dripped from her pink lips. It slipped down her chin and onto her sweatshirt, leaving a big, round wet spot on her chest.

I reached for her hand and squeezed. "Probably tastes like cardboard."

"Uh-huh." She nodded, her eyes still locked on the gooey goodness.

The dominatrix in spandex started to speak. "Your Highness, what a pleasure—"

"Are those gummy bears?" Asia pointed to a row of multicolored bears lining the walkway. "I love gummy bears. . . ." With a heartsick sigh, she waved at an outcropping of rocks piled high behind us. "I'll be over there."

Asia slowly walked, shoulders slumped, to the rocks and sat down, her back to the delicious gingerbread house. I returned my attention to Hansel and his mistress. Both looked up at me expectantly. "She's dieting," I said in way of an explanation. The couple nodded as if I'd unveiled the meaning of life. I decided to get to the point. "Hansel," I said.

He nodded, his silver eyes seeming to peer into my very soul, but not in a girly way. I crossed my arms over my chest, flexing my biceps to intimidate the smaller man. "Her Highness," I nodded to Asia, "thinks you might know something about Cinderella's death."

"I—" he began.

A smack to the back of his head delivered by his loving leather-clad "lady" stopped him.

"Ouch," Hansel squealed.

"He don't know nothing," the witch said, flexing her own biceps. Biceps twice the width of mine. "Neither of us do," she added with a sneer.

I winced at the grammatical slight and tried another approach. "Are you sure? There's a pretty big reward for any information leading to Cindi's killer."

"We don't need money," Hansel blurted. "We live off love."

Ew.

"And the wonderful bounty the good forest provides," added the witch. She lifted her hand and waved toward her gingerbread house. My eyes followed her wave, pausing briefly on the boiling cauldron on the porch and the ruby red slippers sticking from its depths.

"So you see," the witch's eyes narrowed, "mister, we don't need your reward money."

"Really?"

"Really."

"Not even for a new roof?" I motioned to her gingerbread house with a six-foot hole where the frosted ceiling used to be.

"What?" The witch spun around. "No!"

But her cries were in vain. Asia sat atop the house, munching away like a gerbil. Her cheeks puffed out and a string of saliva coated the rooftop. She swallowed prettily and then glared down at us. "I skipped lunch!" she said.

While the witch staggered to her half-eaten house, Hansel stood next to me, shrugging as if to say, "Women. What can you do?" I nodded in silent understanding.

"We just had it reshingled," he said. "Cost us a bloody fortune."

I raised an eyebrow. "Where'd you get the money?"

Because, let's face it, love, even the dirty truck-stop kind, wouldn't raise nearly enough to shingle a gingerbread house, not in the current frosted economy.

For a second Hansel looked like a dwarf caught in headlights. His wide mouth formed a perfect circle, which, on a guy as pretty as Hansel, wasn't attractive.

"Come on," I said. "Confession is good for the soul." Or so I'd been told. My own soul consisted of black goop, so a bottle of bleach and lots of elbow grease seemed more appropriate. "Whatever you say stays between us." I made the sign of the cross over my chest, watching the sky for any sign of lightning. When I didn't burst into a fireball of villain parts, I added, "Nobody has to know."

"Gretel did it!" he said, and then quickly slapped his hand over his mouth. Overhead a bird squawked, causing Hansel to jump around like a marionette.

Damn, this was easier than I first thought. Maybe I had a knack for the detective biz after all. "Gretel, huh? Where can I find her?"

"I don't know." He burst into tears. Thick, drippy, wet, man tears. The kind made from puppy-dog tails and snails. Snot slipped from his pointy nose, sprinkling the ground around us. A glob landed on the toe of my boot and slid to the ground with a wet splat.

Feeling uncomfortable, disgusted, and not particularly villainous—damn it—I unwillingly patted Hansel on the back. "There there." I needed to get back into the union, and soon. Either that or beat myself to death with a gummy bear. "When did you see Gretel last?"

Hansel wiped his eyes and glanced at the witch, who was busy trying to stop Asia from eating the snickerdoodle chimney.

She wasn't having much luck.

"Two weeks ago," Hansel said. "We took her to the market. Missy," he nodded to the witch in leather, "told me not to sell her, but . . ."

Any sympathy I'd felt for Hansel dried up instantly. Selling his sister? What the hell was that about? Not even a villain would stoop that low. Okay, one might stoop that low for the right price. "But what?" My fingers dug into his shoulder until he winced.

"He gave me beans!" Hansel started to cry once again. I rolled my eyes. At this rate, the gingerbread house would have a six-foot-deep moat before he finished his damn story.

Enough was enough.

I grabbed his shoulders and tried to shake him. Of course, with my evil impotency, the shake turned into a hug. Stupid union.

Pulling away, I sighed loud enough to stop Asia mid-bite. From the rooftop, she gave me a thumbs-up and continued to shovel sugarcoated shingles into her mouth. I smiled and waved back, watching her until Hansel got a grip.

This took about ten minutes.

Hansel blew his nose, and like a little kid, he used his sleeve as a tissue. I'd known trolls suffering from a cold with better hygiene.

"Beans," I said, reminding him of where our conversation had left off. "Who gave you beans?"

Hansel shrugged. "An old man. Or at least I think he was old. He had white hair and smelled like feet. Oh, he also had a tail and a hump."

Great. My one and only suspect was an old man with a tail. Put out an APB.

Hansel paused to scratch his whiskerless chin. "Of course, Missy has a hump too, and she's only twenty-seven. You wouldn't believe what she can do with that hump. I remember this one time—"

"Forget Missy," I said, ready to strangle Hansel, which was frustrating since I'd probably botch his murder and end up in some kind of man-on-man hugfest. "Why would this old man with a tail and a hump want to buy your sister?" My voice grew louder with each word.

Hansel frowned. "My sister? What does Greta have to do with any of this?"

"What? Who's Greta?"

"My sister."

"Then who the hell is Gretel?"

"My bluebird." Hansel sighed loud enough to rattle the windows of the gingerbread house. "I sold my bluebird, Gretel, to the old man for a bag of magic beans. Not my sister. What kind of dirtbag do you think I am?"

Missy, the witch, interrupted before I could comment.

"He's not the villain here," she said, stabbing the broom in her hand in my direction. What could I say? The witch was right. She was also far from finished. "Cinderella, that little bitch," Missy growled, "deserved exactly what she got. She was the wicked one."

For a supposedly widely adored princess I'd yet to find one person, besides Asia, in mourning for the squashed Cinderella. Hell, the queen had barely acknowledged her existence. "Oh yeah?" I gave Missy my best smile. "Why? What'd Cinderella do to you?"

"She used to—" Missy began.

This time Hansel slapped his hand over her mouth. Not an easy feat since she was at least two feet taller than he was. I smothered a laugh watching as he dangled in the air. His fingers locked on her red-stained lips.

"Nothing," Hansel said. "Missy doesn't know what she's saying. The heat," he waved his other hand in front of Missy's face, which nearly toppled them both, "it gets to her. We loved Cindi like a . . . sister. Everyone did. If you search the entire kingdom, not a soul will say one bad word about Cinderella."

From behind Hansel, Asia gave a small groan and clutched her stomach. Cookie crumbs and frosting stuck to her sweatshirt and her knees were stained cotton-candy pink. "I feel sick." She whimpered again.

As much as I wanted to finish interrogating the odd couple, a peek at Asia's green face changed my mind. The poor princess appeared ready to spew her pretty, pretty guts. I took her arm and led her toward the forest. Pausing, I did my best Peter Falk impression and turned back to Hansel. "One more thing."

"Yes?" He blinked at me.

"Don't leave the kingdom." I waited a beat and nodded toward Missy. "Either of you."

"Are we suspects, then?" Hansel looked excited by the

prospect. His eyes widened, as did his smile. Missy, on the other hand, appeared to shrink under the accusation. She swallowed hard, her Adam's apple bobbing in her throat like . . . well, a transgendered warlock suspected of smashing a princess under a bus.

Chapter 9

"Thanks," I said to Asia a few minutes later. We walked hand in hand through the enchanted darkness, our path lit only by the occasional flutter of brightly lit fairy butts.

"Thanks?" Asia stopped. "For what?"

"The distraction, of course." I grinned. Asia's ploy to distract Missy so I could interrogate Hansel had worked perfectly. "We make a pretty good team."

"You think?" Her head tilted to the side, begging me to stroke the pale flesh of her throat. Helpless to resist, I stepped closer to her and trailed a finger down the curve of her neck. Her skin felt so soft under my fingertips, like the finest of Mary's sheared little lambs.

"I do think," I said, my voice barely a whisper.

"Somehow I doubt that."

"Hey—"

Her index finger pressed against my lips. "Shhh . . ." She followed her command with a kiss. It started out soft and sweet, but quickly twisted into an explosion of lust. I wrapped my hand in her hair and deepened the kiss. Our tongues met in the middle, fighting for control, mine, hers, ours. The intensity of heat burning inside me nearly drove me mad. I wanted Asia, wanted her more than I ever wanted anything else.

Asia must've felt the same. She shifted her body closer

to mine, our naughty parts melding through layers of fabric. One of my hands cupped her backside, digging into the soft flesh like a drowning man. Baby sure did have back. And I didn't mind one little bit.

Groaning, Asia reached for my belt buckle, her nimble fingers working some kind of magic, and before I knew it, my Levi's were around my ankles. A draft tickled the hair on my legs.

"Oh God," Asia said, pulling away.

"You ain't seen nothing yet."

"I think I'm gonna be sick," she said and promptly threw up. Gingerbread-frosted puke splattered over my boots with a splat. She heaved again, and I jumped back. The sound of her retching echoed through the forest.

I hoisted my jeans, wincing at the replica of Hansel's gingerbread house splashed over my shoes. To be honest, Asia wasn't the first chick to vomit at my feet. It actually happened more than I cared to admit.

When her heaves subsided, she wiped her mouth with the back of her hand and straightened. "Sorry." She pointed at my boots. "I must've eaten a bad gummy bear."

Or ten. But who's counting? "Feel better now?"

She nodded. "What did you find out from Hansel? Did he kill Cindi?"

I shook my head at the sad change in topic. Less than two minutes ago, Asia had her hands down my pants, and now, we stood in the middle of a dark forest, me smelling like the Gingerbread Man after a sugar binge, discussing murder. Who said villains don't know how to show a girl a good time?

Rather than answer, I asked my own question. "Why do you care?"

"What?!" Her eyes widened with shock. "She's my sister. Of course I care who murdered her."

"No one else seems to." I tilted my head and examined my ugly princess. Something was definitely rotten in Maledetto, and it wasn't the leftover vomit on my boots. Even though that smelled nearly as bad. "The king and queen certainly weren't devastated by her death. And neither was Hansel, who claimed to love Cinderella like a sister. So why do you?"

Asia pursed her lips, which I found oddly sexy. Images of her wearing nothing but small, round librarian glasses and wielding a black leather whip flashed in my head. I shook the wayward thought away and focused on a speck of leftover gingerbread clinging to her cheek.

"Hansel loved Cinderella like a sister, huh?" She laughed. "In my book that makes him our number one suspect."

"Why?"

"You saw the feet sticking out from Missy's cauldron, right?"

"Yeah," I said, picturing the bright red slippers and fishnet stockings. "So?"

"Meet Greta."

"The killer bluebird?"

"No. Hansel's very own sister. I do believe they planned to make Greta-flavored pie." She licked her lips and patted her tummy. "I do like pie . . ."

I swallowed hard. "You're kidding me."

"Listen . . . Inspector," she said. "Cindi had her faults. She could be selfish," she paused, as if weighing her words, "and more than once I wanted to—"

Gong.

The palace clock rang, cutting off whatever juicy nugget Asia was about to reveal about her stepsister.

"What time is it?" Asia's hand flew to her throat.

The clock gonged again.

I glanced at my watch. "A few seconds to mid—"

Before I finished my sentence, Asia took off, running full speed toward the palace. Her legs ate up the distance to the castle, like her mouth had done to the gingerbread house. I stood frowning after her.

For a gingerbread-sick princess dressed in a leather miniskirt, she was surprisingly fast. She leapt over a fallen log and disappeared from my view. What the hell was that about?

The clock tower gonged yet again.

At a much more sedate pace, I started after Asia. My boot caught the edge of something and I fell face-first into a pile of moss. It smelled faintly of dirt and Earth, two scents I disliked on city-kid principle.

"Ow!" I rubbed the end of my scraped nose and then glanced around for whatever had tripped me. Something shiny and plastic winked out at me from beneath a dead log.

I peered closer. Damn if I hadn't tripped over a glass shoe. Red ribbons circled the shiny surface. I picked up the slipper and rubbed at a crack in the heel for inspiration like one would a magic lamp. (Word of advice to all non-villains: When asked, avoid rubbing Aladdin's lamp. No good will come of it.)

The clock tower gonged again.

I stood, brushing off my jeans, as my eyes examined the fragile slipper. Damn thing was a menace, much like my princess. With a sigh, I chucked it into the night.

Chapter 10

Seven minutes later, I staggered up the palace steps, bruised and confused. On my way I accidentally knocked over a perfectly round pumpkin sitting on the edge of the stoop. What was wrong with this place? Halloween wasn't for weeks yet. Something was definitely rotten in Maledetto, and I doubted it was the cheesy doodles. The sooner I got away from here, the better. That went triple for my meeting with Natasha tomorrow.

I opened the front door of the palace. A cold wind swept in behind me. The candles lighting the entryway flickered and then went dark. "Hello?" I called into the blackness.

No one answered.

"Anyone home?" Slowly my eyes adjusted to the dim light. The palace appeared as ornate and sparkly as it had earlier that afternoon, but that did little to reassure me. The stench of wealth couldn't hide the stink of decay under the surface.

Always the Villain Scout, I lifted a lighter from my pocket, flicked it, and yelped. Winslow, the butler, stood in front of me. I mean directly in front of me, his troll-like breath hot on my cheek.

"Care for a mint?" I offered him a red-and-white tin of

Altoids. Fresh villain flavor. He declined with a slight shake of his overly large head. The tuft of white hair atop his head bounced in agreement.

Somewhere in the palace, a door slammed and a loud grunt followed, sounding much like Asia. Was she in some kind of danger? Was Cinderella's killer here, at this very moment, attacking my princess? I started forward, intent on rescuing Asia from whatever evil lay within the castle walls. Winslow stepped in front of me, blocking my way.

I raised an eyebrow, as if to say, "Do you really want to do this?" Too bad my intimidating glare worked better in the light.

"Sir," Winslow sneered, "Lady Asia requests you sleep in the Pink Room this evening. If you will follow me." His hand motioned toward the long, perhaps a mile or so, winding stairs off to the right. Long pewter rails lined the staircase, twisting upward into the sky.

I debated knocking the troll-like butler out of my way and charging after Asia, but the sound of laughter stopped me. It sounded somewhere between a giggle of pleasure and a cackle. Not the kind of laughter associated with being brutally bludgeoned to death with a bluebird. So much for my playing the hero to Asia's damsel.

"Lead the way." I motioned to the staircase.

Winslow nodded and did as I ordered. Slowly we climbed the winding staircase, floor after floor, until my lungs threatened to explode. If I die I am taking Winslow with me, was my last coherent thought.

By the time we reached the last flight, my total focus was on restoring a sliver of oxygen to my bloodstream. As much as I hate to admit it, three stairs from the top, I collapsed, sucking air like Goldie, the eighth dwarf, the one with gills.

"After your rest," Winslow said, looking down at me from the top step, "if you'll follow me down the hallway, I'll finish showing you to your room." He adjusted his tie and started to whistle. The troll-face bastard.

Three minutes later, I heaved out a reply that sounded like, "Thh...aaa...nnn...kkks." A few minutes after that, I crawled to my knees, begged for death, and when that didn't happen, I followed Winslow down the hall.

Framed photographs and paintings of the Maledetto family tree lined the walls. I paused in front of one picture in particular. A young boy, perhaps nine or ten years old, dressed in a fur coat and hat stood next to the king. The kid looked unsure, his mouth a flat line, while the clueless king beamed into the camera. A part of me felt sorry for the lad, like one feels for a puppy at the pound. I shook my head, ridding myself of my girlish sympathy for the unknown boy, and jogged to catch up to Winslow. Stupid union.

At the end of the corridor, in front of a twelve-foot pink door, Winslow stopped dead. I smacked into the back of him and dropped to my knees. Damn troll-butler was built like Little Pig #3's brick house.

He sniffled.

"You okay?" I asked, stumbling to my feet.

He nodded and swiped at a tear sliding down his cheek. "Allergies," he said.

"Uh-huh," I said but didn't press him. Instead, I opened the pink door and peered into the darkened bedroom. The sugary scent of ginger and something else, something really nice, filled my nostrils. My hand fumbled along the wall searching for the light switch without any luck.

Winslow stepped inside the room, sniffed again, and clapped his hands. A sudden and intense glare of light exploded around us. I glanced his way and he nodded to the hundreds of tiny glass bulbs lining the walls like track lighting. "Fairies," he said. "Damn things love applause."

I looked up and damn if there weren't itty-bitty blondes locked inside each bulb, their tiny fairy butts glowing like floodlights. The aura surrounding each fairy nearly blinded me with its intensity. Sort of like the lights of Cin City without the noise or hookers.

Shielding my eyes from the retina-burning glow, I glanced around the Pink Room. Pink wasn't a strong enough adjective to describe the horror around me. Everywhere I looked, from the neon bedspread to the Pepto-Bismol-colored curtains, the vomit-inducing pinkness surrounded me. I hated pink. As did any villain worth his salt.

"I can't sleep here." I motioned to the pink stuffed teddy bear on the four-poster princess bed. Its black, blank eyes followed me around the room. "It's so . . . ," I paused, "girly." I feared that every second I spent inside would shrink my manhood by a millimeter. A nightmare for any villain not so well endowed. Still, I didn't want to risk an inch.

"This was Lady Cinderella's room," Winslow said, as if reading my mind or more likely the look of horror on my face. "She spent hours decorating it." He wiped at his eyes, apologized again for his "allergies," and started for the door, but I stopped him.

"You loved her," I said, more of a statement than a question.

Winslow's head jerked up. His eyes filled with more than tears. Rage burned within the troll-like butler. The kind of rage any true villain could appreciate. Damn. This detective business wasn't as easy as I thought.

Winslow all but growled, "Love? Ha. I hated that spoiled brat. She got everything she ever wanted. Clothes. Furs. Jewels. The prince. Everything. Why? Because she

was 'beautiful.' She was far from beautiful. Not like her."
He stopped, horror washing over his tear-stained face.

"Her?"

"Lady Dru, of course." His face lit up. "She is the most enchanting princess in all the land." He added, "Any land," in case I missed the point.

If Dru was half as beautiful as Asia, I understood Winslow's preoccupation. Hell, in another day or two, I might be mooning over Asia the same way, spouting poetry and cheesy eighties song lyrics.

"Lady Cinderella treated Lady Dru and Lady Asia like they were . . . ," Winslow halted, "diseased. Now Cinderella's dead, struck by a commoner's bus, which is fitting. Don't you think?"

My villain sense started to tingle. It looked like the butler might've done it after all. What were the odds? 100 to 1? Maybe I should give up detecting and head to Cin City. It probably paid better. So far, the only form of payment I'd received from Asia was puke-splattered footwear and a pair of bluish bollocks. But I hoped for more. Much naked more. I grinned and returned to the job at hand. "You killed her, didn't you?" I stabbed an accusatory finger in Winslow's direction.

Winslow's thick black eyebrows rose. "Certainly not!"

So much for my interrogating technique. "Then who did?"

"Impossible to say. A better question is," the butler pulled at the knot in his tie, "who *didn't* want to see the princess dead?"

Good point.

One day into my investigation and I had more suspects than I could count, not to mention a date with my ex-wife. On the bright side, no one had tried to kill me.

Yet.

*   *   *

After Winslow left I paced around Cinderella's room. I needed a clue. Not in the vague, general sense either. I needed a clue that pointed to Cinderella's killer. A blood-soaked bluebird would be nice. Maybe a matchbook with the killer's name and v-mail address. A part of me feared that name on the matchbook just might be Asia's. Of course, the prospect of a villainous princess excited me much more than it should. Hell, I already knew she looked damn good in black leather. I glanced at the pink bear for help. But the damn thing appeared as clueless as me.

Taking a deep breath, I crossed the bedroom and opened the top dresser drawer. Six pairs of pink panties stared back, all neatly arranged by the day of the week. Princess OCD.

My fingers brushed the first three pairs, pausing on an empty space. I counted again. Monday. Tuesday. Wednesday. All lay freshly laundered and returned to the drawer. Thursday was missing. The same day Cindi ended up smashed under a bus. Yet Friday's pair lay neatly folded, as if awaiting Cindi's return. Which brought up an interesting point.

Cinderella didn't plan to stick around New Never City. According to Asia, if I could in fact believe my demented princess, Cinderella had something to tell Asia, something so important that she traveled four hours to the city without a change of panties.

That meant one of two things. Either Cinderella planned to return to Maledetto that night, or more likely, Cinderella had left the kingdom in a rush. But why? What was so important?

Scanning the rest of the room, my eyes fell on a small pink book with a gold lock on the front. I lifted the book up. A pink piece of paper fluttered to the floor. I picked it up and squinted at the loopy, girlish handwriting. Over and over the word "Charming" was repeated, a little heart dotting each *i*.

Interesting. Apparently Cinderella was a wee bit obsessed with a certain prince. The question was, how had her obsession caused her to become flat as a princess cake?

I smiled at the pink bear. "Elementary, my dear teddy."

I was one hell of a detective.

Chapter 11

In retrospect, my optimism was a bit premature, but that wasn't my first thought upon waking. Nope. My first thoughts incorporated a naked Asia and a vat of cotton candy. Weird, but understandable when one considered the fluffy pink bedspread wound tightly around my thighs.

The heady scent of "this little piggy" frying and coffee tickled my nostrils, forcing my eyes open. It smelled much like heaven. Or how I imagined heaven smelled, since bacon would be as close to heaven as a villain like me could get. Who needed wings and a harp anyway? Not me. Not when I had a redheaded not-so-ugly princess.

Speaking of my princess. I rolled out from under my cotton candy tomb, stood, and stretched the kinks from my back. The damn pink bed was at least a foot too short. I'd spent much of the night in the fetal position, which wasn't one of my top ten favorite positions.

After showering and dressing in my finest villainous uniform of black T-shirt and jeans, I descended the miles of palace stairs. Down and down I went. My legs burned from the trek, but my mind was focused on obtaining two goals.

Coffee and killing my ex-wife.

Not in that order, necessarily.

I wasn't unreasonable, though; I'd settle for tea if I had to.

Twenty minutes later, I accomplished my first goal. I found a cup of coffee. Literally. It sat at the head of a very long table, in what I assumed from the boar's head on the wall was the dining room. I lifted the cup and sniffed the fresh aroma of scalding water infused with roasted beans. My mouth started to water at its rich caffeinated goodness. Heat warmed my chilled fingers. I brought the cup to my lips.

"Don't touch that!" The queen knocked the cup from my hands with the back of hers. It flew into the air and landed on the green plush carpet, unbroken. Unlike my ears, which rang from the queen's squeals of rage. She raced to the fallen cup and bent down to inspect the damage. "Look what you've done."

I glanced down, surprised to see a hole burned in the carpet where the coffee soaked into its fibers. Peering closer, I noticed a thin trail of smoke wafting from the shag. "Sorry," I said. "I'll get you another cup."

"That wasn't for me. It was for the king." She shook her head at the stain. Her sigh was loud enough to rattle the china in the teak cabinet next to us.

"I . . ."

"Just go away," she said, waving a regal hand my way.

Looking down at the still-smoldering carpet and then back at the queen, I was only too happy to oblige. As I quickly walked toward the kitchen, I prayed the old adage that all women eventually turn into their mothers was a twisted joke. If not, when I did finally lock Asia in a tower I'd damn well better learn to make my own coffee.

Or develop a tolerance to poison.

Unfortunately the latter seemed far more likely.

I opened the kitchen door and ran into a large woman holding a meat cleaver. Her white hair was tied back in a bun and blood drenched her apron. I, of course, assumed she was the cook. I was wrong. Very, very wrong, I soon learned when she screeched, "Make your own damn breakfast!" and tried to stab me with the cleaver.

So much for my powers of deduction.

After proper introductions, I bowed deeply to Asia's elderly aunt, Lizzie. "My apologies, my lady," I said. "Have you seen your niece?"

"Which one are you sniffing after?" She looked me over with her filmy grey eyes. "Unibrow or the fat one?"

"The fat one," a voice said from behind me.

I spun around, nearly colliding with the not-so-ugly object under discussion. Asia reached out to steady me. I enjoyed her touch more than a not-so-villainous villain should. Her fingers were warm and she smelled faintly of pumpkin spice.

"Good morning," I said, my eyes drinking in the sight of her. Damn, she was beautiful. Her red hair fell around her shoulders, covering the swell of her breasts under . . . an extra-extra-large grey sweatshirt, and if I wasn't mistaken, what looked to be super-sized maternity pants. Not a great look for most women, but Asia managed to pull it off. In fact, she looked good enough to eat. I smiled, running my tongue over my teeth.

"Good morning?" she all but screamed. "Good morning? Is that all you can say?"

"Not a morning person, huh?" I could live with that. I shot her a half smile and poured her a cup of coffee, adding two sugars and some cream. "This will fix you up right."

Pressing the cup into her hand, I awaited her gratitude, preferably in the form of plenty of spit swapping and inappropriate groping.

It wasn't to be.

Asia smacked the coffee cup from my hand, sending the contents splashing over the tile floor. Her eyes blazed with the fires of a thousand tiny fairy hells. For a second, I pondered screaming like a girl and running for the hills, but only for a second.

"What's wrong with you?" I frowned at the coffee on the floor, and then at her. Of course, her screaming like the wicked witch gave me a small clue. PMS. Or rather the approved clinical term—Princess Madness Syndrome. A monthly occurrence long associated with the cycle of the Home Shopping Network.

Asia's face, a little softer in the morning light, grew red, as if at any moment she would explode into a pulpy mess of annoyed princess parts. "Wrong with me? Wrong with me? What the fuck do you think is wrong with me?"

As suddenly as Asia's rage appeared, it vanished, leaving her in tears. Big, wet ones. She sniffed once and mumbled something. Something that sounded like, "I cursed."

Wanting to comfort her, a relatively new feeling for me, but afraid her madness was the catchy kind, I stood a few feet away, my arms at my sides. "It's okay, sweetheart. I curse all the time." I paused to gather a vile string of swear words. "Fudge, poking, pig, poop," I said. Damn union.

Lips trembling, Asia glanced up at me through red-rimmed eyelids. Her face cleared, and for a few seconds, she returned to the sane princess I fell so deeply in lust with just yesterday. We stared at each other. Time slowed.

"Idiot," she said with a sigh before she twirled around and stomped out of the room.

I glanced at Aunt Lizzie.

She shook her head, lowered her meat cleaver, and walked away.

Women.

Chapter 12

The rest of my day didn't get any better. After a hearty breakfast of oatmeal, eggs, toast, and a half slab of this little sausage, I stalked around the castle questioning any random servant in my path. Most didn't speak English, or so they told me in astonishingly decent English accents.

One servant, a thin-as-a-toothpick boy with an extremely long, pointed nose, gave me a bit of information. "On the day Cinderella died," he said, "the king was on a hunt. The queen was out shopping. And Princess Dru was backpacking through the Enchanted Forest."

Interesting. No one in the royal family had an alibi. Not even the troll-like butler. "What about Prince Charming?" I stroked my chin. "Any word on his whereabouts?"

"How dare you!" The kid gasped as if I'd just called his mother an oak tree. "Prince Charming would never hurt anyone, least of all his intended. Besides, he was here, in the kingdom, the whole time. Ask anyone."

"All right, Pinocchio. I believe you." I tossed the kid a couple of bucks. "Let me know if you remember anything else."

His eyes lit up as he stared at the cash. "Oh, you can count on it."

I smiled and patted the kid on the head. The poor pine-scented bastard. His nose had grown at least an inch in the time we'd talked.

After my chat with the kid, my search for clues went south. Or north. Could've been east. Villains have a terrible sense of direction, and morals, but I digress.

Around noon, exhausted from detecting, I returned to Cinderella's pink bedroom for a long afternoon siesta. As soon as my head hit the pillow, I yelped in pain and jumped from the bed. Rubbing the back of my head, I glanced down between the headboard and mattress. There, stuck in the crack, was a small makeup mirror. The kind women "powder their nose" with, but in actuality use to catch their unsuspecting villainous husbands checking out the waitress at Hooters.

I pulled the compact from the crack and wiped the dust away, revealing a shiny exterior with a large blue stone in the center. Pretty, but more importantly, the gem alone was worth $127 at the pawnshop. A vill-estimate. Of course, the union would take their 15 percent, calling it a "commission," but in reality, it was extortion, which as a villain, I greatly respected.

Pocketing the mirror, I stretched out across the bed and promptly fell asleep. Or maybe I passed out from the head injury. Either way, when I awoke a couple hours later, I was ready to tackle goal number two—ridding the kingdom of an unspeakable evil, also known as Natasha, my ex-wife.

At two-thirty that afternoon, after a brief stop at the pawnshop, I stomped through the Enchanted Forest on my way to meet my ex. Overgrown fir and arrogant oak trees swept across the well-worn path. Dried dead leaves in an array of colors blanketed the dirt, swirling in the sudden brisk wind. I pulled my hooded sweatshirt tighter and grinned. The air smelled of rotting leaves, ozone, and a touch of evil.

I loved the fall.

About a mile from my destination, a small pond filled with lily pads sat under the shade of a copse of pine trees. Toads croaked and flies buzzed around the greenish water. But they didn't capture my attention.

Nope.

A perfectly formed ass caught my eye. Bent over the pond, the woman attached to the butt appeared not to hear me approach. I stopped a few feet away, afraid if I startled her she would fall headfirst into the murky water, which of course would force me to dive in after her. Since I was more of the "make the damsel distressed" type, rescuing her might send the wrong message.

The woman in question bent even closer to the water, scooped out a toad, and kissed it. Yuck. As perfect as her butt was, the woman had obviously lost her mind. I started to turn away, intent on escaping from yet another crazed chick from Maledetto. Damn kingdom bred them like blind mice. I took one step before the woman screamed. A loud splash followed.

Using every ounce of evil willpower, I fought my body's do-gooding desire to rescue her. Of course, my treacherous body ultimately won, and I dived in the cold, stagnant pond water. Green sludge oozed through my fingers as I dove deeper, searching the black waters for any sign of the chick with toad breath. My lungs began to burn and a low-pitched whistling reverberated inside my skull. Yet there was still no sign of the woman. I forced my body to continue the search.

There. At the very bottom of the pond sat the toad-kissing lunatic. She wasn't even struggling. Rather she sat on the pond floor, her hair floating like seaweed around her. In fact, she seemed to be waiting for something. Or somebody.

I wrapped my arms around her waist and tugged her toward the surface. Her petticoats, about five layers of them, worked as counterweights, pulling us both to the bottom of the pond again. By this time, my body had lost the will to survive, or at least the will to save a crazy chick from a watery death. Of course, my cursed self failed to see my body's point, and worked that much harder to climb back to the surface.

When we finally broke through the skin of lily pads, the woman screamed and began to thrash around. Her arm smacked me in the nose, and I nearly let her go. "Stop it," I said as her knee collided with my thigh. "If you knee me in the bollocks I swear I'll find a way to drown you."

Villain impotency be damned.

My threat seemed to work, for the woman stopped fighting, and after a few minutes, we emerged from the water covered in pond sludge. I stood shivering at the edge of the pond. My clothes clung to my body, dripping wet with slime and water.

The woman looked in worse shape. Her black hair hung in clumps around her head, obscuring her face. I winced, lifting what appeared to be a squished toad from a tangle of her curls. The woman brushed her hair away from her face, caught sight of the squished toad in my hands, and promptly burst into heaving tears.

My reaction was similar when I caught sight of her face. "Ahhhh!" I yelped and quickly jumped away.

Unfortunately, my recent swim had messed with my equilibrium, and I fell back into the slimy pond. The weight of my boots dragged me down, deeper and deeper into the slimy water. Water sloshed into my throat and down into my lungs. I sputtered, trying to swim and cough at the same time. The result wasn't pretty. Snot bubbled from my nose, mixing with the toady water. Using my last shred of strength, I pushed to the surface, gulping in mouthfuls of fresh, urinal cake–scented air.

Pulling myself to the edge of the pond, I crawled to dry land and collapsed in a heap at the woman's feet. She sat on the ground crying, ranks of horny toads surrounding her.

"Don't cry," I said. "I'm all right."

She sniffed, but didn't raise her head to look at me. Which I was grateful for. It wasn't that she was ugly. No, that was too kind a word to describe the horror plaguing the poor, shapely girl.

I stumbled to my feet and wrung my T-shirt out. I owed the woman an apology. After all, it wasn't her fault she had six inches' worth of pubic hair running across her forehead in the shape of an eyebrow. "Hey, listen," I began. "I'm sorry about . . ."

"Forget it," she said, scratching the nearest toad on its wide head. The toad's leg bounced up and down in ecstasy.

Now I felt ten times worse. Sure, I was a villain, evil to the core, in fact, but I wasn't heartless. Growing up, I had my fair share of bullying and insults. In elementary school, kids called me Tiny, which didn't sound that bad. But when you're ten years old and only three feet tall it leaves a few lasting scars. Thank God for puberty. By the age of fifteen, I sprouted to six feet and came into my villainous own.

I glanced at my watch. Ten minutes until three. Damn. "Ummm . . . have you tried waxing?"

She frowned, her unibrow puckering like a squirrel tail across her forehead. "What're you talking about?"

Oops. "Nothing," I said, reaching out my hand. "My name's RJ."

Her toad-coated fingers wrapped around mine. "Nice to meet you," she said. "I'm Dru."

Shit. Asia's uglier stepsister. I'd now alienated, insulted, or pissed off every member of the royal family. Hell, by nightfall, I could annoy every man, woman, and child in Maledetto. It was good to have goals.

Dru lifted the closest toad to her lips and gave it a smacking kiss. I tried not to cringe, but failed. "Hey, Dru," I said. "What's with . . ." I waved my hand in the direction of her and her new beau.

Dru carefully placed the toad on the ground and wiped her lips. "I'm searching for a prince."

"I see," I said, but really didn't. Hell, I was searching for a princess killer, but I wasn't sexually harassing every pigeon in town.

"No, you don't." She shook her head. "You see, for some reason, men don't find me attractive."

Oh, I could guess why. "I'm sure that's not true," I said instead.

"I can't stand being single anymore." She sighed. "A princess's life is just too short."

Truer words were never spoken. Just ask Cinderella.

"So I've taken matters into my own hands." Her fingers brushed the toad again. His throat bulged and I'd be damned if the green guy didn't smile. Dru sighed. "A legend swears that somewhere in this pond, a frog prince lives, a frog prince who waits for a kiss from a sweet, smart, beautiful princess like me."

"I don't think that's gonna happen," I said. For one thing, Dru wasn't all that smart, and definitely not beautiful in the legendary sense. Secondly, that damn frog prince had run off with my ex-wife, and more importantly . . . "Umm, Dru," I said. "Those are toads."

Her blank eyes met mine.

"All you get from kissing a toad is warts." With true amazement I watched as my words filtered through her pea-sized brain. It started in with a wrinkle in her forehead, and then slowly slipped down until her lips curled and she let out a scream followed by a barrage of spittle. "Ptui... Ptui... Ptui."

When Dru finally stopped spitting, I shot her a small smile. "Listen, I have an appointment right now, but I'll help you snare a real prince later. Okay?"

"Why?"

"Why what?"

"Why would you help me?"

This was where things got tricky. Helping Dru might help me find Cinderella's killer, which might help Asia out of her pants, which would help me immensely.

But I couldn't admit that to Dru.

Moreover, I felt a little sorry for the clueless princess. It must be hard having a baboon eyebrow and an IQ of 75, on a good day. So I decided to lie, or rather, tell Dru the absolute truth. "I'm a villain on leave from the union. I can't do anything fiendish no matter how much I try. Therefore, I have no choice but to aid you in your quest for true love, if you only ask."

She nodded as if my story made complete sense. "Will you help me find my prince?"

My stomach recoiled at the thought, but I nodded. Be careful what you wish for, I wanted to warn to her, but wasn't sure the poor, dim princess would understand. "If a prince is what you want, a prince is what you shall get."

"Thank you. Thank you. Thank you." Dru jumped to her feet and wrapped her toned arms around me, warming my chilled body with hers. Her breasts pressed into my chest, and for a minute, I thought finding her a prince might not be that hard. Then of course she pulled away, and her furry forehead wrinkled.

"Yeah." I stepped back. "Just promise me something."

She nodded.

"Before your first date with Prince Not-so-charming, you'll buy some Compound W."

With those parting words of wisdom, I bid Princess Dru adieu and headed off to save yet another princess from finding out I was not a famed inspector, but instead, the biggest, baddest villain around.

Chapter 13

I walked the rest of the way from the pond to my meeting with Natasha without further incident, my waterlogged Levi's squishing with each step.

The streets of Maledetto were nearly empty, odd for a bustling kingdom in the middle of the day. But I was used to the craziness of New Never City, a city that never slept unless it was fed an apple filled with roofies. I missed the sounds of sirens late at night, of kittens yelling for their mittens, and homeless fairy godmothers wrestling over the last shot of Mad Fairy 20/20 wine.

I passed a group of schoolgirls playing ring-a-round Rosie. They squealed with delight when Rosie fell down and burst into tears. I shook my head, remembering my own childhood games, most of which ended up with a trip to the ER. Suffice it to say, I didn't have many childhood friends, at least none who survived the last round of Red Rover Extreme Slaughterhouse Edition.

Shaking off my vivid and disturbing childhood memories, I glanced at my watch as I entered the alley between the Butcher and the Baker. Three o'clock on the dot. Where was Natasha? I sighed and squatted down to wait. Story of our brief marriage. I was always waiting on Natasha—waiting for our first date, for our first kiss, for the first time she slept with my worst friend.

By three-thirty, with still no sign of my evil ex-wife, I'd worked myself up into a wicked lather. When I got my hands on Natasha I would show her how villainous I could be.

Or not.

Fucking union.

"Hello, lover." Natasha sashayed into the alley like a prom queen. Her short black hair and blood-red lips looked almost out of place in our drab surroundings.

Slowly I straightened, brushing straw and toad slime from my Levi's. "Where's your Frog Prince?" I asked about my former worst friend and Natasha's latest victim.

She shrugged. "He croaked."

I rolled my eyes. "What do you want, Natasha?"

"I want to help you," she said, sounding almost sincere. I didn't buy it for a second. My expression must have said as much because she started to add, "Rum—"

"RJ," I reminded her.

It was her turn to roll her eyes. "RJ, I never meant to hurt you. I love you. I've always loved you." Tears sparkled prettily in her black eyes.

"Enough." I stepped toward her, intent on causing her grievous bodily injury, but my legs froze before I reached her. I took a calming breath. "Let's just get this over with. What do you want in return for your silence? Cash? Jewels?"

"Fine." Her tears instantly dried. "I need your help."

"For what?" I smirked. "Because of you, the union pulled my villain card. I'm impotent."

She shook her head. "It happens to every man at one time or another."

Bitch.

"But don't you worry, sugar." She patted my arm, her fingers dancing along my skin, loverlike, as they had a million times before. A shiver ran through me. A part of me still wanted my treacherous bitch of an ex. But a bigger part of me wanted her dead, so I felt somewhat better.

"I can make it all better," she said, her fingernails scraping across my skin just hard enough to leave a red welt, but not draw blood. Sort of like a fisherman chumming the water to tempt a great white.

"I doubt you can make anything better." I jerked away. "Least of all my impotent state."

Anger flashed in her eyes, turning her pupils even darker, almost obsidian in the sunlight. "It's because of her, isn't it? You're in love with that . . . that . . . princess." She sneered the last word, her beautiful face twisting into an ugly mask.

My blood heated. Damn, she looked good. For a deceitful, cheating bitch bent on destroying me. I shook my head. "With who or if I'm even in love is none of your business." I glowered. "You left me, remember?"

Natasha's lips curled back, showing off her rows of perfectly pointy teeth. *All the better to eat you up with.* "How much do you know about your precious princess?"

"Watch it."

"Struck a nerve, did I?" Natasha's eyes lit with satisfaction. "Poor RJ. Always falling for the wrong woman. Why do you think that is?"

"If you have something to say, say it." I crossed my arms over my chest. The soft, damp fabric of my T-shirt bunched under my fingers.

"Fine." Natasha's lips pulled into a pout. "Your new girlfriend is cursed."

"And?"

"And a week from now, she'll weigh a ton, and I'm not exaggerating. Anytime the poor dear eats or drinks while in the kingdom, she gains ten pounds."

Well, that explained the maternity pants. "You said while inside the kingdom. What about when she's in the city?"

Natasha smirked. "That's the sad part. Inside the kingdom, she can't eat at all, and outside, she can't stop eating. The poor dear can never be satisfied." Her grin suggested Asia's lack of satisfaction extended to other areas as well. "But there is a way to save her."

"And you'll tell me how, right? For a price."

"Oh, sugar, you know me so well," she said with a toss of her jet-black locks. The setting sunlight reflected in every silken strand. "But don't you worry. It's a price you'll be happy to pay."

"What do I have to do?" I agreed without hesitation. Saving Asia mattered more than whatever evilness Natasha had in store. This wasn't the first time my former wife had blackmailed me into some sort of devious deed. In the past, I'd killed, nearly died, and ended up naked in a vat of Jell-O for her. And like the last eight times, I'd survive, a wee bit wiser, and slightly afraid of whipped cream.

"Join me." Again, she stroked my arm with her manicured nails. A month ago, one touch and I would've done anything she asked, but not today. Today, whatever dirty deed I orchestrated for Natasha was solely to save my not-so-ugly-or-skinny princess.

"Join you how?" Again, I peeled her fingers away.

For a second rage filtered across Natasha's normally expressionless face, but it quickly passed, leaving a serene smile on her lips. "In developing a new villainous union. A union for the villain about the villain. That can be our slogan. Or maybe, what have you done for your union today?"

"Are you crazy?"

"Just think about it. No more union dues or forced mental health leave. No more nepotism." Her eyes shined with a demented glow. "How many times were you passed up for a promotion only to watch one of those damned Brothers Grimm get the corner office? If we start our own union, you can have it all. We can have it all."

Oh, it sounded good, all right. But only the stupidest of villains would cross the union. Hell, the union made the dwarf mob look like a bunch of flower-sniffing pansies. The last villain dumb enough to cross the union ended up buried under a house and missing a very valuable pair of ruby red sneakers.

Natasha wasn't finished. "We can rule New Never City. Maybe the world. But first, we need to leave Maledetto."

"Can't." I shrugged. "I vowed to solve Cinderella's murder, and I'm not leaving until I do." Or at least until Asia agreed to play a rousing naked game of doctor.

"Fine." She crossed her arms over her chest, her breasts swelling above the collar of her black tank dress like the snow-capped peaks of the Blue Mountains. "Cinderella was killed by—"

Those were the last words Natasha ever spoke.

An arrow sliced through the alley, and with grim accuracy, found its target in the center of Natasha's chest. She clutched the pink-feathered arrow, her eyes wide, and toppled into my arms.

"Natasha." I grabbed the arrow, trying to stem the flow of blood. With each fading beat of her heart, more blood poured from her chest. So much blood. Almost black in color. "No! Come on. Breathe," I repeated over and over. My lips found hers, forcing air into her deflated lungs. Her chest rose with each breath. Up and down. Her cold mouth against mine. I gagged, tasting the coppery flavor of blood and cherry lip gloss.

"Natasha," I said, my breathing as ragged as the wound in her chest. "Damn you. Don't die."

But she was beyond saving. Blood soaked into the paving stones. A small stream trickled from Natasha's bloodless lips, mixing with the puddle growing larger on the ground beneath us.

Maybe it was the shock of it, but I felt nothing—no sadness, grief, or anger at her death. Even stranger, Natasha looked peaceful, her face softer in death, more so than she had ever looked in life.

I slowly lowered her body to the ground. Her blood stained my hands and seeped into my clothes. The coppery scent of death clogged my throat. The horror of what occurred had yet to fully sink in. Natasha was dead. My ex-wife was murdered, probably by the same person who murdered Cinderella.

While I stood less than a foot away.

My hand hovered above her slack face, and after taking a deep breath, I staggered to my feet. Was the killer lurking at the top of the alley? Lying in wait for his next victim?

I started down the alley, my boots slamming against the hay-strewn pavement, intent on escaping before a second arrow flew my way. Not that I feared death. Nope, I just didn't want to ruin a perfectly good T-shirt. Arrow holes were hell to remove from cotton.

Before I reached the end of the alley, something smashed into my head. Something hard and metal. A shovel came to mind, well, really more like *at* my mind, smacking me full on the side of the noggin. The blow sent me flying backward into a pile of discarded little piggy parts. I landed with a squishy thud, knocking the back of my head against the brick wall. Pain exploded inside my already contused brain. Stars rocketed through my vision.

Shaking my bruised head, I tried to focus on the figure standing in the opening of the alley, but blackness seeped in. The world shifted from blue to grey and finally faded to black.

I closed my aching eyes and let the tiny bluebirds circling my head carry me away.

Chapter 14

Sometime later, I woke to a chorus of "It's Not That Small a World After All" echoing inside my swollen brain. Sadly, when I opened my eyes things only got worse. My body rested on a bed of moldy straw that smelled like rotted meat and pond scum. My stomach rolled. On second sniff, I decided the straw wasn't the problem. I was. Holding back a wave of bile crawling up my throat, I rose from the straw bed and surveyed my new home.

The Maledetto Kingdom Jail.

Steel bars blocked the one and only door as well as a small window toward the back. A stream of dirty moonlight filtered through the bars, causing my head to ache even harder. This was a personal record. Not even two days after arriving in town, I'd wound up in jail, and for once, I was completely innocent of any charge. That was an embarrassment in itself. What kind of villain didn't murder his ex-wife?

"Hey," I yelled to the guard standing outside the jail cell. "I want my one phone call." Not that it would do any good. Who was I going to call? The union? With Asia pissed and Natasha dead, my options for bail were limited at best. "And some clean clothes," I added after getting another whiff of myself.

The guard ignored my demands, so I took matters into

my own hands and stripped off my Levi's and T-shirt. They were stiff with dried blood. Natasha's blood.

Under normal circumstances, standing in the middle of a jail cell, naked, would make one evaluate their life. In my case the opposite occurred. I reviewed the last couple of days, analyzing every statement and seemingly innocent gesture, searching for a clue to the identity of Cinderella's killer.

Apparently whoever it was wasn't finished yet. Natasha's murder was proof of that. I clenched my fists and vowed to find Natasha's murderer. I hadn't loved Natasha, not with the true love forever kind of love. Even so, the villainous code of conduct required swift and immediate malicious revenge, which I was willing to provide. I was done playing around. It was time to catch a killer.

"Rump—" a guard began.

"That's me." I waved my arm to cut him off.

"You made bail."

"Really?" My brow puckered.

"Unless you'd prefer an extended stay." The guard sneered, his gun and teeth gleaming green in the fluorescent lights. "We'd be happy to have the likes of you."

Since this wasn't my first stint in the slammer I kept my mouth shut and waited for the barred door to open. When it did, I stumbled from the cell as if I'd spent years locked inside, rather than a few unconscious hours. Of course, I was still completely naked, but that didn't seem to bother the guard.

"This way," he said, leading me down a long grey corridor. I followed behind, my head aching with each step. I fingered the shovel-shaped bruise on the side of my face. Flakes of dried blood stuck to my fingers.

At the end of the hallway another door opened as if by magic, but really, a female guard stood on the other side, one hand on the door handle and the other on her gun.

When my nakedness passed her, she rolled her eyes, but

like the first guard she didn't say a word. The doorway opened into an atrium filled with angry midgets, swash-buckling cops (eye patches included), and tearful chicks in red carrying baskets of half-eaten goodies. A typical police station, with one small exception.

Prince Fucking Charming.

You might wonder how I knew the douche bag standing in the center of the chaos-filled room was indeed the afore-mentioned prince. Easy. Who else but a prince named Charming would wear a frilly lace pirate shirt opened halfway down his chest? Not to mention, his flowing blond locks of hair appeared windswept even in the stag-nant air.

I hated him on principle, and on sight.

Charming started forward, his manicured hand out-stretched to shake mine. "Inspector, it is a pleasure to meet you," he said as if we'd casually met on the street corner rather than inside a police station, me charged with mur-der and naked to boot. "My name is Prince Charming." He bowed low at the waist. "The beautiful Princess Asia requested my aid in securing your release."

Well, that answered one question. "How did Asia know I was here?"

"A little birdie, perhaps?" Charming shrugged his mas-sive and surprisingly girlish shoulders. He smiled and winked at a man in a paisley uniform standing next to the guard.

My eyes narrowed. Was Charming making a joke or was that a threat? Not that it mattered. Any villain worth his weight could wipe the floor with an effeminate prince. Blindfolded, if need be. "Where is Asia?"

"She awaits your return at the palace." He smiled, showing off perfect rows of teeth only an orthodontist could love. "I will escort you to the princess at once."

I waved to my nakedness. "How about a detour to King-Mart first?"

"As you wish." Once more, he bowed, this time much too low for my heterosexual comfort.

An hour later, dressed in a freshly purchased pair of Levi's and a black T-shirt, I strode to the castle doors. Prince Charming fell in step behind me. I rolled my eyes, tired of his constant and irritating goodness.

Wherever we went, people bowed and scraped to His Annoyingness. Charming, in turn, tossed gold coins at peasants, kissed leprous babies, and called every ugly maiden by name. It was like being stuck with Mother Teresa before she married Father Goose.

By the time we reached the palace steps, I determined two things. If Charming killed Cinderella, it wasn't due to his obsession with her. Sure, the guy was deeply in love, but not with his dead fiancée. Nope, Charming's one true love was, in fact, Charming. The guy couldn't keep his hands off himself.

Secondly, I decided, when the union reinstated me, my first order of business was to strangle His Annoyingness with his lacy pirate shirt. I pictured his bulging eyes and grinned.

"RJ!" Asia threw open the palace door and rushed toward me. All 147 pounds of her. Natasha was right. Poor Asia suffered from a curse, but honestly, I didn't mind. To me, skinny or fat, Asia looked beautiful. In fact, she carried those new pounds in all the right places. What man didn't appreciate D-cups?

"I was so worried when you didn't come back to the palace ... worried about you, that is," she said, her eyes searching my face.

"As you can see," I gestured to each of my appendages, "I am just fine. No need to worry." I almost added "your pretty little head" but I wasn't in the mood to pick up my teeth from the shag carpet.

Asia stepped back, her eyes narrowing. "So what happened?"

"Happened?"

"Yes. Happened." She tapped her foot like a schoolmarm. "This afternoon you left the palace in search," she lowered her voice to a whisper, "of Cinderella's killer, and now you're charged with murder. What the hell happened?" She shouted the last part so loud my eardrums nearly exploded. I grabbed my aching head and frowned.

"According to the police, the inspector shot his ex-wife with an arrow during a domestic altercation," blabbed Prince Big Mouth. "Furthermore, the police suspect he—"

"Thanks for the ride." I shoved the prince out the door and slammed it closed before he could finish his statement. Then I turned back to Asia. "I didn't do it."

She raised her eyebrow.

"I swear."

Again silence greeted my pronouncement. "Fine," I said. "Don't believe me. What do I care?" But I did care. The spot right below my breastbone started to ache as bad as my head. What the fuck was wrong with me? So what if Asia didn't believe me. I knew the truth. Someone, very likely the same someone who killed Cinderella, had murdered my ex-wife and framed me for the whole bloody thing. I had to give the killer a measure of grudging respect. Framing me was a bit of villainous brilliance.

With a harsh sigh, I plopped down on the living room couch and waited for Asia's condemnation.

"I do believe you."

"Really?" I asked. Was she stupid? Sure, I really was innocent, but still, I had means, motive, opportunity, and pretty decent aim. I guess she wasn't the brightest princess in the box after all.

She moaned. "But why didn't you tell me Natasha was your ex-wife? And why would you agree to meet her? Do . . . Did you still love her?"

So many questions with way too many chances for my treacherous tongue to spill the proverbial magic beans. I decided to answer the last question first. "I haven't loved Natasha in a very long time, and sometimes I wonder if I ever did." Which was the truth. What I felt for Natasha resembled love at times, but mostly only when we were both naked and covered in sweat.

"Why did you agree to meet her, then?"

It was my turn to sigh. Not because I didn't have an answer. Oh, I had an answer, something about how I tricked Asia into hiring me, a master villain, to find a wannabe villainous murderer in hopes of getting into said princess's chastity belt, and when my evil ex found out, she tried to blackmail me into joining her in an uprising against the union. Even in my head, it sounded bad, and not something I wanted to share with an already pissed-off princess. "Natasha . . ." I paused. "She . . ."

"She what?" Asia's eyes narrowed.

"Natasha knew who killed Cinderella." Asia gasped as her hand flew to her mouth. I quickly continued, "But before she revealed their identity, someone shot an arrow through her heart."

"That's terribly inconvenient."

"Rude too," I added with a grin, which slowly twisted to a frown. "Natasha knew something else too."

"Oh yeah?"

"Yep." I reached for Asia's hand and pulled her down next to me on the couch. A cloud of dust rose up between us. I sneezed.

"Bless you," Asia whispered, her emerald eyes staring into mine. How I wanted to take Asia into my arms and forget the last few hours. Forget Natasha's bloodless face. Forget the stench of death and little piggy parts. But thanks to the union's curse, my brain failed to comply with my manly parts. Too much was at stake for a little afternoon delight. Stupid brain.

"Um, RJ? What else did Natasha know?" Asia asked, voice trembling.

Her face was pale and so beautiful. I smacked myself in the skull. Take that, brain. I winced, my head pounding at double speed. I needed an aspirin. You know what they say, an aspirin a day keeps the brain damage away. I wrapped my hand around Asia's warm fingers. "She knew about you," I said.

She bit her bottom lip and glanced around. "What are you talking about?"

I raised an eyebrow. It kept inching higher until I thought my brow would break. Higher and higher it rose. But still Asia didn't say a word. When my eyebrow reached my hairline, I gave up. "Natasha said you're cursed!"

"So?"

"So!?" I dropped her hand and stood to pace. "Why didn't you tell me?"

"I tried." She struggled off the couch and faced me, her cheeks growing red. "This morning, if you remember. We were in the kitchen. I said I'm cursed. You replied 'fudge, poking, pig, poop.' I thought we had an understanding."

Oh yeah. "We did. I mean we do."

"So you can accept me." She waved at her rounded thighs hidden underneath sweatpants and a super long T-shirt as tears rose in her eyes. "Accept this."

"Hell no."

The smack that followed wasn't much of a surprise, but I yelped just the same, raising my forearms to defend against another round of blows. "Wait. I didn't mean it like that."

She stopped mid-swing. "What exactly did you mean? And you better be really clear."

In that moment terror and lust filled my heart. I cleared my throat and lowered my arms. "What I meant to say was," I grinned at my not-so-ugly but clearly annoyed princess, "I can't accept the fact that you, such an innocent, sweet maiden, are cursed with such a vile, unfair blight. It is so unjust. I cannot accept that."

"Oh." Asia tugged on her bottom lip with her white teeth. "That makes sense."

"But you know what doesn't make sense?"

She tilted her head to the side. "What?"

"Why?" I stroked my chin, fingering a day's growth of villainous whiskers. "Why would someone curse you? What'd you do? Piss off your fairy godmother or something?"

"Or something." Asia plopped down on the couch with a sigh. "The curse started before I was even born." Then she launched into the curse of the (not-quite-so) ugly stepsister. . . .

Chapter 15

Once upon a time, in a land far, far away, lived a beautiful, vain princess who would one day be queen.

The beautiful princess spent much of her time staring into a bejeweled hand mirror, admiring her beauty and ignoring the rest of the world. So much so that one day, while walking through the kingdom, the princess stepped on an old lady's foot.

The old crone cried out in pain, but the vain princess failed to take notice. Her focus was diverted by her beauty reflected in the flawless mirror.

I shook my head and Asia stopped her story. "The princess didn't see the old woman?" I asked. "I find that kind of hard to believe. No one's that vain."

Asia's eyebrow rose. "That you don't buy? And yet, you're okay with the whole 'I'm cursed' thing?"

I shrugged. "Fine. Finish your story."

So she did. . . .

Once the princess removed her overly dainty foot from atop the old woman's crushed appendage, the old woman yelped and cursed. Unfortunately for Asia, the curse the woman uttered wasn't of the "fudge, poke" variety, but instead, a curse born of a thousand years of wizardry and warts.

"May you only bear daughters to your king," the old witch said.

The princess, startled from her vanity by the pronouncement, finally glanced up at the old witch. "Sorry. Did you say something?" And then she promptly stepped on the old woman's other foot.

"Ahhhhhh!!!!!" the witch screamed.

The princess brushed a lock of red hair from her shoulder and returned to smiling into the looking glass, again oblivious to the old witch. That only served to enrage the crone more. She snatched the mirror from the princess and smashed it on the ground. There it shattered into a million tiny pieces, each reflecting the old crone's anger.

"Oh, look what you've done." The princess dropped to her knees next to the crushed bits of mirror. "This was my favorite looking glass, and now it's broken."

But that wasn't the only thing broken.

The old crone's foot, crushed by the vain princess, lay smashed upon the pavement too. The princess glanced from the mirror to the witch's foot and then at the old woman. Tears filled the princess's eyes. She sniffed, still delicate and beautiful. The old witch's rage receded under the princess's obvious guilt.

But before the old witch could erase the curse, the princess straightened and gestured to her guards. "Lock her in the dungeon."

"What's the charge, my lady?" one guard asked.

The princess shook her head as if it was apparent to all. "For being ugly, of course."

"As you wish," the guard said.

As the old witch was led away by a contingent of guards, she added the final damning words to her curse.

"Vain. Vain. Vain. May no man, woman, or child bear to look upon your firstborn daughter without feeling pain."

"So your mom locked the witch in the dungeon, huh?" I nodded to Asia, bringing her back to the present. "Rookie mistake."

"Tell me about it."

"What's the catch?"

"What?"

"Come on," I said. "Every curse has a loophole."

"Does not."

"Yeah, it does." My head wobbled to emphasize my point. "Think about it."

Asia stroked her chin, and my mind flashed to her smooth hands stroking my own skin. Heat rose in my gut, lust pooling with sick desire. After a few minutes, she cleared her throat. "You're right."

"About what?" As hard as I tried, I couldn't recall a single word of our conversation. My only thoughts were on Asia's body. The swells of her breasts underneath the soft folds of her T-shirt. My blood slipped south, leaving my brain empty. Not a new occurrence.

"I said, you're right." She bit her lip. "All curses have a way out. Remember the daughter of the miller? The one who was locked in the tower by that crazed midget..."

"Just 'cuz someone's a little on the short side, it doesn't make 'em a midget!" I jumped from the couch and started to pace, my arms windmilling in anger. Asia ducked out of my way as I muttered to myself.

Six feet tall wasn't short, damn it!

I blamed the metric system. It warped people's minds. Not to mention turned an impressive eight inches into 20.32 centimeters. Centimeters, for fuck sakes. That word made anything sound small.

Asia recoiled, her mouth tightening as I continued to pace. I closed my eyes and swallowed. "Sorry," I said. "I've had a rough day." My lips curved into a trembling smile. "So what's the loophole? Did the witch forget to do the Hokey Pokey and spin herself around and around?"

"I don't know." She scratched her head. "But I know someone who might."

Chapter 16

A couple of hours later, I sat in the Three Blind Mice Tavern next to an insanely beautiful, albeit slightly overweight princess and a grumpy bag of wind named Rip. The name suited the grey-bearded man quite well. In fact, as soon as we sat down, Rip let one rip. The stench was so bad that even the drunkest of the patrons staggered from their bar stools and out the tavern door.

Rip shrugged his shoulders. "I had burritos for lunch."

Like twenty years ago, by the smell of it. Rather than comment on his stench, I jammed my hand over my nose and tried to control the tears leaking from my eyes. Asia's fingers brushed mine, sending a shiver along my skin. I swallowed hard and did my best to grin and avoid throwing up.

Things could've been worse.

"What'd you want," Rip said, burping another cloud of toxins into the air. His eyes narrowed and he leaned forward. "Don't I know you from somewhere?" he asked me. "You look familiar."

"I have that kind of face," I said. Which was partially true. God had blessed me with villainous good looks, chiseled features, and lips meant for kissing demented princesses.

Or was it princi?

"Never mind that." Asia waved her hand. "I need your help, Rip."

"For you, my sweet maiden, I'd sleep for a thousand years."

I smothered a groan.

"What can you tell me about my curse? Is there a way to break it?" Asia tilted her head, her eyes locked on the older man's filmy grey ones. Skinny or fat, no one would be able to resist my princess for long. Rip proved to be no exception. I hoped like hell when the time came I was made of stronger stuff. None of that puppy-dog-tail crap. Forget the snails too. I'd need steel bollocks to walk away from a princess like Asia.

"Only one way to break such a dangerous and powerful curse." After a brief pause to exhale a fetid breath, Rip rubbed his whiskered chin. "Truth be told, even I, one of the wisest and bravest men in the kingdom, wouldn't dare to break a curse so vile. How can such a sweet young lady have the courage?"

I nearly sprained my eye sockets with my eye roll. Bravest? Really? The dude took a nap. What was so freaking hard about that? "Yeah, you're a prince among men. Anyway..."

Asia covered her smile with the back of her hand. "I'm sure you're right, Rip, but I'd like to give it a try. Can you help us?"

He nodded, farted once, twice, and then a third time. A stench so foul even the three little pigs would've gagged drifted in the air around us. "To break the curse, the cursed must possess the Devil's Eye." He shivered as if the very words chilled his old ass. Either that or he finally got a whiff of himself. Valiantly, he continued, pausing long enough to add, "Do you smell that?" before finishing his tale. "And in the Eye, the cursed will see the past, present, and future. Good and evil. She will see beauty and death, a lover and a liar."

Not good. If Asia possessed the Devil's Eye she would learn the truth about me, about my villainous past, about my even more dastardly plot to relieve her of her virginity.

But without it, she would never be free.

Rip let out another loud belch. "In the end, she who possesses the Eye will either accept what is reflected back or else..."

"Or else what?" I asked after a few seconds.

"How should I know?" He shrugged. "I'm old, not a fucking rocket scientist."

Some help he was. I started to say just that, but Asia interrupted. Oh well, not like I could've told the old bastard off anyway.

"Rip," Asia said. "What is the Devil's Eye?"

"Evil." Rip stroked his chin. "The Devil's Eye is pure evil born of an unholy alliance."

Britney and K-Fed?

Rip continued, "It is said to possess all the knowledge in the Universe."

That left those two out.

"Those who gaze into the Eye are doomed."

"Have you ever seen it?" Asia asked in a whisper.

Rip shook his gnarled head. "Do I look doomed? Weren't you listening? What is it with you young people today? Why, back in my day..."

Just tell me what the damn thing looks like and where to find it, I wanted to tell him, but the old goat rambled on and on for twenty more minutes, spouting dire warnings, boring stories from his past, and toxic fumes. Finally, he got to the point. "From what I've been told, the Eye looks like a handheld compact. Sort of oval shaped with a blue jewel covering the top."

Shit.

"Worth a pretty penny too."

Shit, shit, shit.

I pictured the shiny blue-jeweled looking glass that, up

until a day or so ago, had resided in the pocket of my Levi's. The very same looking glass I discovered in Cinderella's bedroom and subsequently pawned it.

Just my villainous luck.

"I'd pay anything to end this curse," Asia said, her voice soft, warm, and pure like my princess herself. She was far too good for the villainous likes of me; yet I couldn't walk away. Not yet. Not until I solved her sister's murder, found my ex-wife's killer, and freed my pretty, pretty princess from her curse. As to-do lists went, mine sounded nearly impossible, almost as bad as Snow White's daily chore of scrubbing out seven pairs of stained dwarf boxers.

But I vowed to find a way to break the curse for Asia, even if it cost me my life. I ran my fingers across Asia's expanding skin. "Don't worry, sweetheart. I'll find the Eye for you."

"Thank you," she whispered.

I nodded and swallowed hard. In order to save my distressed damsel I would have to become the one thing I hated. A hero. The very word sent sickness pooling in my gut, sort of like eating bad sushi in the hot sun. My face must have betrayed my emotions because Asia shot me a sweet, endearing smile. My stomach started to ache even more.

I rose from my bar stool, leaned over, and gave Asia a smacking kiss on the lips. Her eyes widened, but she didn't pull away. Instead, she deepened the kiss, drawing my mouth into hers. Our tongues met, greeting each other like long-lost lovers after years apart. Her hands fisted in my hair, tugging my mouth harder against hers. I pulled Asia closer, inhaling her scent. She smelled like the best of holidays. Thanksgiving, Christmas, and Rosh Hashanah rolled into one.

For what seemed like an eternity of bliss, but in reality was merely seconds, the world around us vanished. No more stench of rotted beer and decayed old man. No more thoughts of curses or murder. Just us. The two of us.

Happily ever after be damned.

Asia broke the kiss and stared into my eyes as if she could see into the very depths of my blackened soul. Served with a side of collard greens and rice. For a moment I felt completely naked. My villainous armor stripped away to reveal the short, insecure kid underneath.

Rather than scare me, her naked appraisal sent a surge of power through my battered body. I was Rumple Fucking Stiltskin. A badass villain. I could accomplish any feat, big or small. Reacquiring one little bejeweled hand mirror would be easier than getting Georgie Porgie laid. And I'd managed to accomplish that in a matter of a few hours.

I grabbed my princess, kissed her quickly on her pliant lips, and stumbled out of the tavern without a word. It was time to show the kingdom of Maledetto exactly who was the biggest, baddest villain around.

Chapter 17

Or not.

After leaving the tavern, I immediately went to the Pretty, Pretty Pawn & Bait Shop to retrieve the Devil's Eye. The shop was located on the west end of the kingdom, sandwiched between Geppetto's Gyros and a fairy strip club named Wings.

I opened the door and stepped inside the greenish-lit pawnshop. The place was nice enough, clean, and reminded me of the Candlestick Maker's, but without the waxy smell or freaky statues of dead movie villains. Rows of pilfered and pawned electronics, stolen jewels, and magic wands lined dust-free shelves. The recession had hit everyone hard, but it was especially hard on fairy godmothers. Hell, poor Glinda the Good Witch, new mayor of Munchkin County, had to start hooking to pay for yellow brick road repairs while that bitch Dorothy ran off with a priceless pair of slippers and a flying monkey named Bob.

Sometimes fairytales weren't fair.

I strolled up to the counter searching the glass case for any sign of the Devil's Eye. Finding none, I smashed my hand on the service buzzer and waited for the shopkeeper, Baba Yaga, to appear.

When she did, I stifled a scream. Baba Yaga looked ten

times worse than she did the last time I saw her. At that time she looked ugly enough to give trolls nightmares. Baba Yaga's nose had grown two extra warts and her skin turned from pale green to full-on chartreuse. Her shoulders hunched even more, nearly toppling her scrawny body over.

"You!" She stabbed her finger in my direction. I jumped back, afraid her ugly was the catchy kind. Instead of stopping her, my ninjalike move only increased her anger. She flew (literally, broomstick and all) over the counter and leapt on me. We crashed to the floor, bits of ugly witch and villain everywhere.

Baba's fist smashed into my jaw. Pain radiated up my face and into my brain. And yet, I couldn't do a damn thing to end her assault. Stupid union. When she started biting, my survival instinct overpowered my impotency. I lashed out with a stern "Owwwwww! Owwww! Quit biting me."

From a bystander's point of view, it might have sounded more like me begging and squealing like a pretty, pretty princess, but I digress.

"I want my money back. Right now!" Her fist nicked my chin again, opening up a wide cut. Blood welled from the wound, dripping onto my new T-shirt. She punched me again, screaming, "You little sawed-off—"

That did it.

I shoved the old witch off me. "No need for name calling, you old hag. Give me back my mirror and I'll give you your money."

She sucked in a putrid breath. "I don't have it."

"What?"

"The sheriff. He took it." She swallowed. "Threatened to arrest me for receiving stolen goods too."

That didn't make any sense since I didn't steal anything, not really. Okay, that might not be true in a strict legal sense, but still . . .

"When'd he confiscate it?"

"This morning," she said.

Damn. I'd only found the Eye wedged between Cinderella's bed a day ago, and from the look of it, it had been there a while, and now it was missing. Taken by the sheriff of Maledetto. But why? What could the sheriff possibly want with the cursed object? And more so, why would the sheriff retrieve the Eye himself? Why not send his legion of boys in paisley to retrieve the relic? Unless retrieving the Eye wasn't a criminal matter, but a personal one.

I ran my hand through my hair. So much happened in the last day. Natasha was dead. My sweet Asia was cursed by the Eye of the Devil. And if I wasn't mistaken, Baba Yaga was currently picking bits of my skin from her greenish teeth.

She glanced my way and winked. "So where's my dough, pretty boy?"

I pulled out my wallet and tossed her some cash. It wasn't nearly enough, but it would have to do. Her frown warned me of an impending ass-kicking, but I held her off. "I'll have the rest of your money by tomorrow." My middle finger curved into a Villain Scouts salute. "I promise."

Her good eye narrowed, but she didn't attack, so I gathered up my tattered, dirt-stained self and headed into the night on a quest for a mythological makeup mirror.

As far as villainy went, I'd had better days.

Around midnight, I crept into the sheriff of Maledetto's backyard and slipped over a row of hedges shaped like the seven dwarfs. A dog barked in the distance, but nothing else stirred. Lights twinkled from inside the house, giving me a good view of the layout. Not that it would do me, an impotent villain, any good. Damn it. The house looked like many of the single-family brick homes in the area. Three bedrooms, a living room, and a kitchen. The bluish light of a television flickered in the living area, as did the soft glow of candles in the bedroom.

According to *Peasant Magazine*'s Sexiest Sheriffs Alive Edition, the sheriff of Maledetto (#24) was a bachelor, and yet, it appeared as if the unattached sheriff had company. My mind flashed through a list of possible companions. One name kept repeating itself.

Asia.

What if the sheriff reclaimed the Devil's Eye in order to gain my lady's favor? Thereby beating me to her chastity belt? It made sense. Asia was beautiful beyond compare. What man wouldn't risk a life sentence or even the death penalty for a little something something from such a perfect princess? Hell, I'd walk through a pit of Prince Charmings for just one kiss from my princess. My princess who was probably swapping saliva with the sheriff at this very moment.

Rage tickled at the back of my throat. I'd kill him. Sure, it might take a while, me being cursed and all, but eventually I'd find a way. Maybe I'd start by replacing the fat-free mayonnaise in his refrigerator with regular.

The bastard.

Yet my murderous plan had one small problem. Unless the sheriff left his house unlocked, I couldn't replace anything, let alone snatch the Devil's Eye as I originally intended.

Being cursed sucked.

In my heyday, I could pick a lock faster than Jack could climb a beanstalk, but not anymore. Now every time I picked up a lock pick my fingers started to tremble like one of the three bears at a NRA meeting.

What I needed was a henchman.

A dumb one at that.

Across the road, a car alarm screeched and I jumped. A totally uncool move for any villain, especially one hiding in the backyard of a man who I assumed might have numerous automatic weapons.

The sheriff rushed from his home, an AK-47 in his bulging arms. He wore a pair of skinny jeans and a tight white T-shirt. The outline of his nipples popped through the fabric in the cool night air. A shadow obscured his face, as well as the person standing directly behind him, but I could make out the outline of a chiseled jaw. A familiar jaw. One I'd recognized from the Maledetto Kingdom Jail. He was the same man Charming had smiled and winked at. What the hell was going on?

I squinted into the dim light, debating whether Asia was the other person standing behind him. The one draped in shadows. Would she really betray me with this idiot? I hoped not, but the more I squinted into the darkness, the less sure I became. Please no, I thought, crossing my fingers, toes, and any other appendage willing to be tied into a knot.

The outline looked about right in terms of weight, but shadows were by nature deceiving, much like transgendered chicks named Raypunzel.

"Who's out there?" the sheriff yelled into the darkness.

I stepped deeper into the shadows, avoiding his gun's steely stare and a high-velocity bullet. Somewhere on my left, a mouse ran up the hedge, checked his tiny watch, shook his head, and then ran down. The sheriff took a step into the light followed by his companion dressed in a long, flowing, lace shirt.

Prince Fucking Charming.

What the hell was he doing here?

More importantly, it wasn't Asia. My princess hadn't betrayed me. Not yet, at least. Relief filled me, sort of like Little Boy Blue when his STD test results came back clean. But more questions surfaced, like was Asia a top or a bottom kind of princess? And would I have to buy her dinner first?

Guess I'd have to wait to find out the answer to either question. Or I could take a peek into the future with a certain looking glass.

Speak of the Devil . . .'s Eye.

The sheriff pulled the looking glass from his pocket. It swung back and forth like a pendulum, sparkling with evil in the muted moonlight. My eyes followed. That tiny piece of metal could save Asia's life while it destroyed our future. Was it worth the price?

The villain in me said no, to forget the pretty blue jewels, steal Asia away, and lock her in a tower somewhere. But the new semi-heroic part of me had vowed to save my distressed damsel. I hated that part.

"Here." The sheriff held the Devil's Eye out to the bastard Charming. "I hope it's worth the price."

"No doubt." The prince smiled, his eyes reflected a thousand times in the large sapphire nestled on top of the compact. "This is the only way. You and I both know it."

Way to what? I was missing a part of the puzzle, a big part, from the sound of it. What was Charming up to? And why did he have me arrested? Because I was pretty damn sure he did. His "friendship" with the sheriff all but confirmed it. The rat bastard. Was my arrest and subsequent incarceration an attempt to keep me from finding the truth about Cinderella's murder? Or did he have designs on my princess?

Trading up in the sister department. One dead blonde for a slightly round redhead with jade eyes and a damn fine left hook. Who could blame him? My pretty, pretty plump princess overshadowed his pancake-flat fiancée any day.

I smiled, picturing Asia's welcoming arms as I returned victoriously from my quest. Shit. The quest! I needed that Devil's Eye. If I was in full-on villainy mode, I might've launched myself at the idiot prince, snatched the compact from his hands, and run off like the roadrunner after a crack binge.

Alas, the union once again ruined my best-laid plans. Instead of holding my thankful and warm princess in my arms, I watched helplessly as Prince Rotten's fingers curled around the object of my villainous desire. The Eye of the Devil.

Chapter 18

"Son of a biiiiii..." Closing my eyes, I tried to swear once again, but without any luck. That rat bastard prince. He'd just stolen Asia's only chance at freedom and my best chance at seeing my princess naked.

What the hell was I going to do? I couldn't return to Asia empty-handed. I'd yet to solve Cinderella's murder, and now I'd failed to free her from her dreaded curse. Eventually, even a princess as dim as Dru would discover I wasn't the famed detective she'd hoped for, but rather a villain with impotency issues and credit card debt. Again, thanks to my former, bloodless wife. Who purchased an ice sculpture on credit? In summertime? During a heat wave?

I sat on the sheriff's dew-soaked lawn contemplating my options. Murdering Charming held a certain appeal. But how to do it? I could use the union's curse to my advantage and "nice" him to death. Start with listening to his every word, no matter how inane, and then move onto baking lessons and poetry. Finish strong with a manly pedicure and umbrella drinks. I shivered at the thought. On to plan B, or was it C? Math was never my villainous strong suit.

When the sun rose, touching the grey sky with swirls of pink and orange, I finally stood. A man with a promise to keep and a fairly good plan. Okay, a moderately reachable plan. As long as it didn't rain. And the union decided to lift its curse.

But a plan nonetheless.

I strolled down the street flipping through my mobile phone's contact list for my boss's number. She was the only person able to reinstate me to villainhood, and therefore, end my curse, so I could in turn kill Charming and end Asia's curse by stealing the Eye from his bloated corpse.

Lots of cursing going on, and yet, I still felt fucked.

I dialed the phone number and waited as it rang. Once, twice, three times, and then it went to voicemail. "Leave your number at the eek," the computerized voice intoned. A loud eek followed.

"Hey," I began, "it's RJ. Call me back as soon as you get this. It's a matter of—"

Eek. My vPhone call dropped, leaving me listening to dead air. Damn it! Foiled again by Villizon.

I ran my hand over my bloodshot eyes and considered my next move, sans reinstatement. My original plan was to bust into Charming's house and steal the mirror while Charming was otherwise occupied going about his princely duties, like listening to Liza Minnelli CDs.

The more I thought about it, the more worried I became of Charming's motives. Just what was he up to? Was it more than designs on my princess?

"Charming!" I pumped my fist.

"Not from my angle," a woman's voice called from behind me.

I spun around, nearly slamming into the once slim-hipped redhead stalking me. Her pudgy thighs strained against the cotton of her black pants.

Asia smiled, reaching out to steady me. "Hi."

"Hi."

"Rough night?" Her eyes swept over me, narrowing a

bit at my rumpled clothes and the grass stains on my knees. In fact, if I didn't know better, I suspected my sweet princess was a wee bit jealous, which, sick bastard that I was, made my day. A smile cracked through my lips. Asia frowned even more.

"Well?" Her foot began to tap. "Who is she? I bet she's skinny. Blond too. What is it with men? They see a skinny blond princess and it's 'forget poor, fat Asia.' Well, I've had it!" With each statement her foot tapped faster until it became a blur of glass slipper and pink toenail polish.

I held up a hand to still her mounting fury. "No princess in the entire kingdom . . . no, the entire world can hold a tiara to you."

Her foot slowed, but her eyes remained narrow. "So where were you last night, then? I waited. . . ."

I smiled, oddly pleased by the dark circles under her puffy eyes. "Something came up." Before she could ask what, I pointed across the street to Wendy's Darling Café. "Let's go grab a coffee and I'll tell you about it."

With a frown, Asia seemed to consider my offer, finally acquiescing when I promised to let her sniff my vanilla scone. Which wasn't nearly as exciting or sexy as it sounded.

"I'm so hungry," she whispered, patting her bulging tummy, which grumbled like one of Bo Peep's rabid black sheep.

My heart plunged. That damn curse. Asia deserved a scone if she so desired. Hell, she deserved a baker's dozen.

Hand in hand we strolled across the street and into the café. The place was the stuff of nightmares. Creepy dudes in their fifties strode around in tights sipping chocolate milkshakes at ten in the morning as if they'd never grown up. The tights took the Lost Boys' mantra a little too far.

A grey-bearded guy in skintight tights stood behind the counter. His nametag read: Pete.

Pete bowed low and then sprang up to face us from behind the cash register. "Come with me, where dreams are born, and time is never planned. Just think of happy things . . ."

"Forget the happy things." I frowned at the guy who probably still lived in the basement of his elderly mother Wendy's house. "How about you just take our order?"

He sighed. "Fine. What'll it be?"

My eyes scanned the chalkboard menu, settling on a coffee, black, and two scones. As I ordered Asia let out a whine. I smiled and squeezed her hand.

"Make that three scones," I told Pete.

He nodded, and Asia and I went to find a quiet place to chat. We sat down at a table in the back. Deep red and blue crayon drawings of alligators, fairies, and pictures of lost boys marred the tabletop. I set my napkin down on one particularly disturbing image of a pointy-eared Pete engaged in a song-and-dance number with a group of "boys" old enough to know better.

"Wanna tell me about it?" Asia asked when I sat down with a sigh. I quickly glanced down at the table and blushed. She shook her head. "No. Not that. Tell me about last night."

I took a sip of coffee, enjoying the bitter burn as it slid down my throat. The acid bite reminded me of the smug expression on Charming's much-too-pretty face as the sheriff handed him the Devil's Eye.

I broke the first scone in half and placed it in front of Asia. A trail of saliva slid down her chin. She shoved the scone away. I grinned and pushed it back.

"How much do you know about Charming?" I asked.

Asia's forehead furrowed, but her eyes never left the vanilla-coated pastry. "Why?"

"I don't trust him."

She gave a small laugh. "You're joking, right? I've known Charming all my life. He's a good prince."

"No. I'm dead serious." I frowned. "Charming's the devil in a lace shirt."

"Are you insane?"

Until three days ago, I would've answered straight away, but now I wasn't so sure. After all, I'd followed a demented stepsister to an anything but normal kingdom in hopes of solving a homicide, but instead I found myself charged with killing my own ex-wife. My decision-making ability was questionable at best.

"Hear me out." I raised my hand for quiet. "Charming isn't the perfect prince that everyone would like to think he is. For one thing, he had me arrested for Natasha's murder."

Asia grinned. "Why would he do that?"

"Who knows? I'm not a freaking mind reader." I took a sip of my coffee. "Maybe he's jealous?"

"Of what?"

I scowled. "Me. Of course."

"Of course," she said, hiding a smile.

"I'm serious. Who knows why." I sighed. "There's something going on between Charming and the sheriff. Something sinister."

Asia didn't try to hide her smile this time. Instead, she laughed so hard she grabbed my arm to steady herself. Which, let's face it, fifty pounds ago wouldn't have meant a thing. Together, we toppled to the floor, coffee and scones covering us in a hot mess.

I staggered to my feet, slipping on a bit of soggy scone, and landed flat on my back next to my pretty princess. Asia knelt on the floor next to me, tears streaming down her jiggling cheeks as peals of laughter burst from her lips. I grinned in spite of my messy self.

Again, I stood, this time without catastrophe, and reached down to help my caffeine-drenched princess to her feet. A dribble of icing stuck to Asia's pert nose. I grinned and lifted it from her skin with the tip of my finger. It felt warm and sticky against my fingertip. Asia's eyes grew hungry. I moved my finger and the glob of sugary confection toward her plump lips.

Her tongue flicked out.

I smiled, knowingly.

"I—"

"Shh," I said, moving my finger closer.

Asia's lips parted, accepting and ready. I swallowed, the blood in my head heading far south. The tip of my icing-whitened finger brushed her bottom lip. Soft. Gently. I leaned down, our mouths inches apart.

"Ow!" I yelped and jumped back. Blood dripped from my wounded finger. "You bit me!"

Asia shrugged, not an ounce of guilt on her cherub-round face. In fact, her smile lit up the café. "Sorry?" she said with a decided lack of sincerity.

Wrapping my finger in the bottom of my shirt to squelch the flowing river of plasma, I grimaced and shook my head at my princess. God, she was perfect, with just enough of an overbite to make all my fairytale fantasies come true. "Let's get you cleaned up, and me a rabies shot."

Asia flushed, the sugar-rush haze lifting from her gaze. "I am sorry."

"Uh-huh."

She batted her eyelashes. "Really. What can I do to make it up to you?" Her voice turned husky and hot, much like the coffee dripping between the fabric of my Levi's and my skin.

My blood flow changed direction once again. My heartbeat accelerated, flipping around wildly in my chest. My breath came in short, heated gasps until I thought I might die.

"Well, there is one thing." I licked my lips.

"Oh yeah?"

"Oh yeah." I leaned in, my breath against her neck. She smelled like pumpkin pie and vanilla. Two of my favorite things. "Come with me." I held out my hand, and she took it into hers. Her skin was warm, soft, like the rest of my pretty, ugly princess. Our fingers locked, mine rough against her soft ones.

Would I ever be good enough for her? Maybe, but it depended on my solving Cinderella's murder. A task I was having a hard enough time completing without the added distraction of a sharp-toothed princess with a cursed complex.

"Where are we going?"

"To break into Charming's house."

Asia jerked away. A wrinkle formed on her forehead. "What?! Are you crazy?"

Didn't we just have this conversation? Apparently, the curse was affecting more than my princess's waistline. "Just come with me. I promise it will be worth your time."

"Fine." Her hands moved to her abundant hips. "But if we get caught . . ."

"We won't." My bloodied middle finger rose in the Villain Scouts oath. "Villain's honor."

Asia's eyes narrowed, but she followed me from the café just the same, my aching finger pointing the way.

Chapter 19

We stood outside Prince Charming's bungalow at a little past noon. The house looked quiet. Too quiet. A tuffet sat on the front porch, a web dangling from the corner. Along came a spider, spinning its way down the web. I shivered, not a superstitions villain by nature. Add a chick, a tuffet, and a spider, and terror all too often filled my black heart.

I swallowed hard and studied Charming's house. With the exception of the tuffet, the bungalow looked like many others on the block, white with pink trim. A sturdy oak front door stood between us and the end to Asia's curse.

Not for long.

I grinned, my eyes sliding to my pretty, pretty princess standing so sweetly beside me. She looked amazing in a kimono a few sizes too tight. Her breasts heaved against the silk material outlining the imprint of her braless nipples.

Earlier when we dropped by the palace to change our coffee- and scone-coated clothes, I raised an eyebrow in villainous appreciation. She said, "Nothing else fits," and then stormed from the castle. I had to jog down the yellow brick sidewalk to catch up. Suffice it to say when we arrived at Charming's that Asia was far from pleased.

"Door's locked," she said, rattling the doorknob of Charming's bungalow.

Damn.

I peeked in the window. The bungalow appeared empty. No sign of Charming. "Wait here," I told my princess as I strode around to the back. Flowerpots lined the walkway in an array of colors that reminded me of Saturday nights in Easter Village.

Peering into the kitchen window, I noticed a sink full of dirty dishes and empty wine bottles lining the countertops. Either Charming had recently thrown a party and forgot to invite me, or he was one lousy housekeeper. Interesting.

What could a recently almost-widowed prince have to celebrate? The recent acquisition of a Devil's Eye, perchance? Maybe the sudden and tragic murder of Mrs. Nearly Charming, a.k.a. Cindi-flat-as-a-pancake-rella? Just how devastated by Cinderella's murder was His Annoyingness?

One way or another I needed to get inside his bungalow to, at the very least, locate the Devil's Eye before Asia nipped off a far more important appendage from my body. I jangled the kitchen door, but it was locked too. Damn. What kind of prince locked his doors? It wasn't like Maledetto was a hotbed of villainous activity. Hell, before Natasha's killing, the worst crime in Maledetto was a boy who cried wolf in the middle of a crowded movie theater.

I stroked my chin for inspiration. The window over the kitchen sink appeared sturdy and large enough for one tall, currently impotent villain to squeeze through.

Stepping on the nearest flowerpot, I stuck my hand through the opening of the kitchen window. Of course the union's curse quickly kicked in. My other, free hand closed the window above me, nearly ripping my arm in two. I screamed and fell from my flower box perch, landing in a patch of rosebushes that would make a porcupine insecure.

"Pig, poke, peanuts!" I jumped around yanking thorns from my ass. Pain, like a thousand bee stings, burned my backside. "Ow! Ow! Ow!" I screamed, pulling at a particularly large thorn in my inner thigh. An inch to the left and the thorn would've ended my quest to get into Asia's panties, and my will to live.

Asia stuck her head around the corner. "Are you all right?"

"I'm just peachy," I said, yanking the thorn free and tossing it to the ground.

"You don't have to be a jerk about it."

Guilt rose inside me. I'd asked Asia to come along, after all. It wasn't her fault I was now legally considered a villain / rose hybrid. "Sorry," I said, gesturing to my now-holey jeans. My princess gawked at the torn fabric so long that I considered forgetting about Charming, tossing Asia over my shoulder, and making her scream my name. My real name.

Asia suddenly snapped from her staring contest with my crotch. She blushed a pink color at odds with her coppery hair and quickly ran back to the front door.

I watched the sway of her hips until she disappeared from view, and then got back to work. I needed to get inside Charming's place, if only to prove he wasn't the prince Asia believed him to be. In my impotent state, breaking in was impossible. But what if the door was already open? My lips curved into villainous grin.

"Ummm . . . Asia, honey," I said. "Do you smell that?"

"Smell what?"

"Smells like," I sniffed my sleeve to keep my treacherous tongue from blurting the truth, "vanilla. I think Charming's baking cookies."

"Cookies? I love cookies!"

Two seconds later, Asia burst into Charming's kitchen via the now-destroyed front door, hope and hunger burning in her eyes. She glanced around, her nose sniffing the air like a bloodhound. "There's no cookies." Her tone was both accusing and sad.

I winced, but assured myself the end justified the means, especially if at the end, Asia and I lay naked in a vat of cookie batter. I tapped on the kitchen door. "My bad. Can you open the door?"

Her eyes narrowed, but she did as I requested. Once inside, I took stock of Charming's abode. The place wasn't palace size, but it wasn't a size-eight shoe either. The kitchen, living room, and library took up most of the first floor.

I searched each room quickly while Asia helped herself to a box of pink-coconut-covered snowballs. I checked under the couch, in the entertainment center, and even through a stack of CDs. Plenty of adult contemporary bullshit, but not a Devil's Eye in sight. Damn.

I did find a picture of a much younger Charming, his arm wrapped around a little fat girl, her cheeks puffed out like a balloon. They looked happy. Like kids enjoying the last days of freedom before Charming School started. The round girl looked familiar. I peered closer. My beloved stared back. I smiled and ran my finger along the edge of the photograph.

The second floor looked like a replica of the first except it housed a bathroom large enough to fit the Jolly Green Guy. On the countertop sat soaps that smelled of exotic lands and enough hair products to coif an army of gay rats. Of course, the Eye was nowhere to be found.

My next stop chilled my blood.

Like Alice in the porn version of Wonderland, I found myself in a place I never wanted to be. Charming's bedroom. All decorated in gold. Not the color but actual gold. My better, villainous half itched to relieve Charming of his lighter and easier-to-carry golden knickknacks. I shook my head. His pillow was even gold-plated. What kind of douche slept on a golden pillow? Guess that ruled out greed as motive for his murdering Cinderella.

I scanned the room for secret hiding places. A wall painting of a wolf in a tiara that looked suspiciously like the wolf corpse in King Maledetto's library caught my attention. A wall safe maybe? My fingers slipped along the edges of the painting, but I found nothing but an annoyed dust bunny.

With teeth.

I jumped back and grabbed my dust bunny–chewed fingers. "Bugger it," I said.

"Problem?" Asia stood in the doorway behind me, pink marshmallow clinging to her fingertips. She stuck her index finger into her mouth and sucked the goo from it.

I nearly swallowed my tongue, but managed a manly "Ummmmammmmammaaaa."

"What?"

I cleared my throat. "I can't find Charming's safe." He had to have one. It was like a princely rule or something. That and unnaturally white teeth.

"Oh." Asia strolled into the bedroom, yanked the bedspread from the bed, and tapped a few buttons on a console under the frame. A metal door popped open from a hidden panel. Without glancing inside the now-open safe, Asia walked back out of the room and down the hall. I stared after her, a sick feeling in my stomach. Just how well did my princess know the effeminate prince?

A minute later, the Devil's Eye safely in my pocket, I headed down the staircase and into the kitchen. Asia sat at the table, a glass of wine, a bag of cheese doodles, a bowl of porridge, and a half-eaten cake in front of her. I snatched a cheese doodle from the bag and popped it into my mouth.

Asia growled.

"Let's go." I pulled my ten-pound heavier princess from her seat. The chair whined and started to crack. I caught Asia before her bottom hit the floor. "We're done here."

"But I haven't finished my cake."

Before I could comment, a high-pitched, girly shout came from the front of the house. The prince had returned.

Asia glanced at me and then ran for the door, surprisingly fast for a chick wearing slippers made out of glass.

I ran out the door after her, tripped over one of said slippers, and landed face-first on the cement. Blood poured from my nose. I wiped it away with the back of my hand. Shakily I stumbled to my feet, grabbed the slipper, and limped up the block. My ankle ached like Dopey after a binge.

Over the thundering of my heart, I heard Prince Rotten exclaim, "Someone's been eating my porridge!"

I winced.

"Someone's been sitting in my chair!"

I limped a little faster.

A minute later, Charming yelped with fury. "Someone's been messing with my bed!"

Sprained ankle be damned. I took off running at full steam, not even slowing as I passed Asia, who stood on the side of the road, puking her pretty, pretty princess guts up.

Chapter 20

Outside the palace, I fingered the Devil's Eye in my pocket and contemplated the future. The one Asia would see once she gazed into the jeweled looking glass. Sure, her curse would be broken. But I feared my head would be as well. Asia didn't strike me as the kind of girl to ignore a tiny thing like my total and complete villainy.

Even if, by some godmother's magic, she accepted my occupational choice, what did I have to offer her? I was impotent, for fuck sakes. I had no money, a pilfered apartment, and one dead ex-wife. A real catch if you happened to be a wicked witch, but Asia was far from wicked.

Oh, why couldn't she be a little more wicked? Not Natasha evil. No, been there. Done that. But maybe a nice "poison Snow White's apple" sort of depraved. Someone I could spend the rest of my villainous days living in fear of. Just like dear old Mum and Dad.

"You . . . could . . . have . . . waited . . . for . . ." Asia stumbled to my side and paused to catch her breath. ". . . fuck . . . it."

She grabbed my arm and hustled me inside the palace, not even stopping to offer Winslow a friendly hello. I gave the butler a small wave, nearly tripping on the rug as Asia ushered me up the stairs.

By the time we reached Cinderella's pink room, I was as out of breath as she was. That didn't stop Asia from kicking the bedroom door open, clapping fairy sconces to life, and tossing me on the bed like a Frisbee.

"Wha—" was all I got out before Asia's tongue buried itself in my mouth. Interesting. It seemed my princess was a little more wicked than I first suspected. I wrapped one hand around the back of her neck and deepened an already tonsil-cleansing kiss.

My other hand found its way into the folds of Asia's kimono. I stroked her soft flesh, my heart racing like a hormonal teen on prom night. I wanted her like I never wanted another princess.

Asia pulled away and stared down at me. "I'm a bad, bad girl."

"Do you need a spanking?"

She laughed and threw her legs over mine. The warmth of her against my jeans drove me over the edge. Her hands fisted in my T-shirt, nearly ripping it from my body. My fingers gripped her waist, kneading her yielding flesh. I wasn't sure how long I could last. My body felt as hard as steel, and just as red hot. If I didn't have Asia soon I'd go insane.

Or maybe I already was.

With the way Asia's fingers roamed the button fly of my jeans, that line wasn't all that clear. I ran my hand across the plane of her stomach, enjoying the nooks and crannies like one does with an English muffin. My mouth went dry at the feel of her velvety skin against my calloused palm. I paused to regain a shred of control—not a smart move when dealing with a half-naked, self-conscious princess.

"You do want me?" She bit her lip, tears welling in her jade eyes. "I'm not wrong about that."

I bit out a harsh laugh. "What gave it away?"

She shifted her weight, pushing her lacy panties against

my rigid erection. I groaned, my breath coming in gasps. My fingers groped for the strap of her kimono. I had to have her. Now.

She raised her hand. "Wait."

"I don't think I can."

Her index finger ran up my naked chest and she leaned over me. Her breasts pressed against me, silk and skin. I nearly came right then. Asia clapped her hands. The fairy lamps winked out.

I clapped my hands.

The fairies sprang to life and again the room lit up.

Asia raised an eyebrow.

"I wanna see you." My hands once again pulled at her clothes. She shook her head. I nodded. For once in my life, I'd be the victor or die trying, which wouldn't be a bad way to go.

Tears sprang into Asia's eyes. "I'm fat."

"You're perfect." I lifted her butt in my hands, enjoying the weight of each fleshy mound of princess. "Thin, fat, wicked or not, you are perfect. Don't ever think you're not."

For a second Asia said nothing. She simply stared at me, her bottom lip quivering. Finally, she glanced at the palms of her hands and then at the brightly lit fairies overhead. "If any of you laugh," she said to the tiny blondes locked in their lightbulb cages, "I swear to God I'll barbecue the lot of you."

I grabbed her face and kissed her like a princess deserved, all tongue and teeth. One taste of the princess in my arms would not be enough. Never enough. I blinked away that girlish thought to focus on the woman now licking my navel. Our clothes disappeared, and we made love to the horrified gasps of the prudest fairies in all the land.

The next morning, I yawned, stretched, and cracked an eye open. Then I screamed like a little girl.

Dru lay on the bed next to me, her unibrow looking even furrier in the bright morning light. I scrambled from the bed, suddenly aware of the crispy air on my balls. I dove back under the covers.

"Do you wax?" Dru asked.

"What?" I lifted the covers and glanced down at my boys. Still there. Still hairy.

Dru shook her head and tapped the space between my eyebrows.

"Oh," I said. "Nope. I'm all natural."

"Charming uses wax." Dru rubbed her unibrow. "He said he'd show me how."

"Figures," I said under my breath. "Listen, Dru. Your prince will come, and he'll love you no matter what." The poor bastard. "Don't settle for less."

She nodded.

I waited.

She just continued to stare at me.

I motioned to the door. "Did you need something else?"

"No."

"So do you mind?" I again gestured to the door. "I'd like to shower before Asia gets back."

Dru bit her lip. Tears welled in her eyes, traveling down her pale cheeks like raindrops against a Ford Pumpkin. Dread filled me. I wanted to run, run from the words pouring from Dru's tongue. "Asia's not coming back," she said.

"What!?!" I threw the covers back, searching the floor for my jeans. I found them half hidden under the bed. Pulling them on, I hopped toward the door. "Asia!" No answer. I tried again. "Asia?"

"I'm sorry, Rum," Dru said.

"But why?" It took a moment for her words to settle in. "What did you call me?"

"Rum." She paused as if unsure. "Rumple Stiltskin, right? That is your name."

"Who told her?" I pictured Prince Rotten tattling on me, and Asia's face as the ramifications of fucking a villain like me settled in. The horror and shame my poor princess must feel. Not only had I lied to her, but I'd probably ruined her only chance at finding her sister's killer. Or ending her curse.

"No one told Asia." Dru folded her hands together. "She saw it."

Oh shit! I dug into my pocket. Sure enough, just like my future, the Devil's Eye had vanished. I ran out of the door and down the stairs. Winslow opened the front door, and without stopping, I burst through it.

"Wait," I yelled to Asia's Ford Pumpkin as it bounced down the cobblestone driveway. "Let me explain."

I wasn't sure if Asia could hear me, but I had to try. I couldn't lose her. I ran faster. My ankle, weakened from yesterday's adventure, threatened to crack in two. "I didn't mean to deceive you," I cried.

Halfway down the driveway my ankle snapped and I fell to the dirt. "Please."

The Pumpkin vanished around the bend.

My head drooped and my shoulders followed. I'd lost her. I'm not sure how long I sat grief-stricken in the morning sun. Maybe minutes, maybe an hour. Time no longer mattered. I'd lost my princess.

"What the hell are you doing?" a woman screeched.

I lifted my head to glare at whoever dared to intrude upon my heartache.

Asia.

She stood a few feet away, her hands on her newly slim hips. "Well?" She motioned to my sprawled form. "What have you got to say for yourself?"

"I—"

Her fist smashed into my nose.

Blood exploded from my flattened nostrils. I didn't bother to wipe it away. Instead, I jumped to my feet and gobbled Asia up in a hug. She continued to punch me, but her blows felt like kisses in comparison to the pain in my heart when I thought I'd lost her.

"Let me go!" She went limp in my arms. "Please."

I released her and stood back to examine my ladylove. She had changed overnight. Literally. Gone were the extra rolls of fat and her double D-cup breasts, her chubby arms and swollen feet, the cleft in her backside where I'd spent plenty of time last night. Apparently, three hours of adventurous sex burned trillions of calories. Either that or my pretty, ugly princess had broken her curse.

Damn.

"Why, Rum—?"

"RJ," I corrected. "My name is RJ."

She nodded, her eyes growing wet with tears. "Why'd you lie?"

I hadn't, but now wasn't the time to bring up my own curse, as "nice" as it was. "I'm sorry. I never meant to hurt you." For a second, she looked uncertain. My heart beat faster. Maybe there was still a chance, a chance to solve Cinderella's murder, thereby restoring Asia's faith, and ultimately her love, for me. I could make things right. I just needed her to listen. To understand. I cleared my throat. "When I saw you drive off this morning . . . My—"

"What?!" Her head spun to the empty parking space where her Ford Pumpkin once sat. A dark oil stain was all that was left of her vehicle. "Son of a bitch. Call the sheriff. Someone stole my car."

Chapter 21

Two hours later, Bruce, the pointy-eared sheriff of Male-detto, waved good-bye as his patrol pumpkin disappeared from view. I stood next to Asia on the palace lawn. My princess turned around and glared at me.

"What?" I asked.

Asia pulled the Devil's Eye from the pocket of her jeans. It shone in the sunlight like the Hope Diamond, beautiful and just as cursed. "You had it all along?"

I held up my hand. "No."

Her eyes narrowed.

"Okay, so I found it two days ago." Shut up, shut up, my brain screamed to my treacherous tongue. "But that was before I knew what it was." I slapped my hand over my mouth, but my lips kept moving, spewing mumbled secrets until Asia looked ready to scream.

"Charming had it?" Asia yelled. "That's why we broke into his place?"

I nodded.

"It's all been a lie," she said. I wasn't sure if her comment was rhetorical, but I decided, in my best villainous interest, to remain silent. "Did you even mean it?"

"Mean what?"

"That you wanted me. Or was that part of your devious

plan too?" She shoved me, and I stumbled back a step. "Is that how you get your jollies? Making cursed girls fall in love with you?"

"Heck no," I said. It took a moment for her words to fully register. "Wait. Do you love me? That's what you said. You can't take it back." Happiness swelled inside me, which made me a bit queasy.

"Love you? A villain? Never!" She glanced over her shoulder to the front door of the palace. The king, queen, and Dru stood in the archway, their faces pinched and judgmental. A look every villain this side of New Never City was familiar with.

Happiness turned into pain, a pain so intense my entire body ached. Sure, I had my fair share of bitter breakups. I married Natasha, after all. But I never experienced a pain so deep. So cutting. I wanted to curl up and cry like that kid with Tourette's who kept saying "wolf" at the most inopportune times.

"Tell me what to do." I grabbed Asia's shoulders, digging my fingers into her flesh. "How to make this right. And I'll do it. Just don't give up on me."

"You've done enough." She peeled my fingers away and spun on her glass slipper. Over her shoulder, she tossed the very words that damned me. "Just go. Forget me. Forget us."

As soon as the words left her lips, my memories of our time together started to fade. My cursed mind did as she requested, erasing Asia from my memory bank. A part of me wanted her to disappear, to ease the pain of losing my . . .

What did I lose again?

For the life of me I couldn't remember.

The annoyed yet beautiful red-haired woman standing in front of me shouted something. Then she rammed her fist into my nose. Pain shot through my head. I grabbed the crazy chick's fist before she planted another punch. As soon as our hands touched, my fading memories stormed back. The ache in my heart returned, but I was thankful for it.

"Asia," I whispered.

Her rigid body relaxed and she slumped against me. "You promised me," she whispered.

"I'm sorry." I sounded like a broken country-western record, but what else could I say?

"Sorry doesn't find Cindi's killer," she said.

"But I will."

"I'm supposed to buy that?" She let out a bitter laugh that sounded much like bluebird talons on a chalk outline. "You're a villain, why would you bother? Hell, for all I know you killed her yourself."

Anger, like a flash fire, swept through me. I'd be damned if a demented princess would question my word. I was a villain, after all. We kept our promises, when we felt like it. "I had the same thought about you," I said.

Asia gasped. "Are you accusing me?"

I hadn't been. Not really, but suspicion niggled in the back of my mind. Asia would've done anything to rid herself of her curse, and yet Cinderella, Asia's very own stepsister, had the power to do so, but didn't. Why? Did Asia murder Cinderella to get the Eye? Was her decision to hire me nothing more than an elaborate smoke screen?

"Why was Cinderella really in New Never City?" I asked. "Did she come to rub the Devil's Eye in your face? Did she laugh at you? Call you names?"

"You're wrong," Asia said. "I loved my sister."

"Stepsister," the king, queen, and Dru shouted in unison.

I shot them a frown.

Asia grabbed my chin, yanking my eyes to meet hers. "I had no idea Cindi possessed the Eye, or that there even was an Eye until a few days ago. Why would I kill her for it?"

She had a point. That or my princess was an Oscar-winning actress. For some reason, I suspected the latter. "So why was Cinderella there?"

Dru answered for Asia. "To apologize. Cindi went to New Never City to apologize to Asia."

"Apologize for what?" I asked. Before she even said the words, I knew I wasn't going to like it.

"For stealing Asia's fiancée."

Chapter 22

"Tell me it's not true. That you weren't engaged to Charming before Cinderella was," I said. My eyes bored into Asia's. The thought of her in the arms of Prince Rotten made me want to strangle a golden goose. "Why? What did you see in him? He's gay, for fudge sakes."

Dru gasped as if I slapped her, but Asia's face remained expressionless. "He is not," Dru said. "He's in love with me."

Asia and I both swung to face the poor, deluded, uni-browed princess. I hated to disillusion her, but even Prince Charming wasn't that hard up.

"Don't be ridiculous," I said.

Dru and Asia stared at me as if I'd grown two heads. I patted the top of my head. Nope, still only the one. But it never hurt to double-check. I cleared my throat and tried again. "What I meant to say is," I smiled my most charming smile, "now that Asia has the Devil's Eye, she can break your curse, Dru, and you'll find your very own prince. Not a used piece of prince doodie like Charming."

"Ummm . . . RJ," Asia said.

I waved her off. "Underneath all that," I gestured to Dru's furry brow, "is a beautiful princess. Once you are free, you'll have to beat the princes off with a fiddle stick."

"RJ!" Asia smacked me in the arm.

"Ow." I rubbed my injured appendage. "What'd you do that for?"

Asia's teeth clenched. "She's not cursed."

"What?"

"I'm not cursed." Dru sniffed. "I'm just ugly."

After that bold statement, Dru ran into the palace, sobbing. Winslow glared at me and took off after her.

I closed my eyes. "I didn't know. I'm sorry."

Asia shook her head. "Whatever."

"No, I mean it." Which oddly enough was true. In my own way, I empathized with Dru and her furry forehead. "I wasn't always this fine sample of manliness, you know." I paused, waiting for Asia to gasp and shout her denial for all the kingdom to hear, but she didn't. "When I was a kid they called me Stunted Stiltskin."

"Kids can be cruel."

"My parents."

"What?"

I took a ragged breath. "My parents called me that. My schoolmates were much meaner. But the point is," I motioned to the palace, "she needs to open her eyes and see what's right in front of her. She has a man who will do anything for her. A man who will kill or die for a kind word or a simple kiss." Asia's eyes grew misty. But I wasn't finished yet. "A love like that doesn't happen often."

"She's a lucky princess." Asia batted her eyelashes at me.

"I guess."

"A man willing to die for his ladylove can't be all bad." Her finger brushed my nose. "In fact, a man like that would make a terrible villain."

"Good thing Winslow's a butler, then."

"Why do I even try!" Asia screamed and stormed toward the palace. "Idiot . . . moron . . . can't villain his way out of a paper bag . . ."

"Hey," I called after her. "What'd I do?"

My answer came in the form of a glass slipper aimed at my head. I ducked, but forgot about slipper number two, which beaned me in the chest, in the space right above my heart. Sadly, this was the highlight of the rest of my day.

"Thanks for letting me stay over," I said, my voice straining over the words. I hated being beholden to anyone, especially Prince Rotten. But there I was sacking out on his plush leather sofa. I had no choice, really, after Asia tossed all my clothes into the palace moat, that is.

According to King Maledetto, I was no longer welcome at the palace. Of course, I'm paraphrasing, since his actual comments contained words like "off with your head" and "boiled in bollocks stew." Unappetizing, to say the least.

So I found myself at Prince Charming's bungalow in a borrowed pair of pink (seriously) boxers. Charming was gracious through it all, his having me incarcerated and maybe murdering Cinderella aside.

My investigation could wait, at least until morning. First, I needed a place to stay, and Charming offered without hesitation when I arrived on his doorstep, my duffel bag dripping moat water on his porch step. He merely smiled and motioned for me to enter.

"Would you like an extra pillow?" Charming asked.

"Nope. I'm good."

"Very well." Charming stopped outside the living room door. "Good night, then."

"Night," I said.

Charming gave me another vague smile and disappeared up the stairs. I settled into the plush cushions and considered my next move. Every villainous fiber in me wanted to say fuck it, grab my wet bag, and leave this twisted kingdom.

But I couldn't do it.

Not yet.

From Charming's bedroom overhead, an off-key falsetto

version of "Luck Be a Lady" sounded. Followed by what I can only imagine from the loud thumping over my head was a ball-change dance step.

I closed my eyes and tried to count villainous deeds, but the pounding above me kept me awake. Finally, two maddening hours later during a rendition of "When You're a Jet," I staggered to Charming's kitchen, stuffed my ears full of whey (don't knock it until you've tried it), and fell into a fitful sleep. Much to my annoyance, I dreamed of redheaded princesses wearing amazing Technicolor dreamcoats.

I awoke the next morning, jumped from the couch, and headed to the shower. Cold water beat down on my body until the taste of Asia faded from my mind. I turned off the shower, toweled off, and glanced in the mirror. Maledetto was taking its toll. My nose was a bit flatter thanks to Asia's left hook, but most of all, my eyes had lost their villainous glow. I shook my head. Nothing I could do about that right now.

I wrapped the towel around my waist and walked seminaked through the bungalow. "Mind if I borrow a pair of jeans?" I asked Charming, who was whipping up a batch of something in the kitchen. A pink apron with the words "Kiss the Chef" across the chest hung over his head.

"Help yourself." Charming grinned, motioning to the staircase with a pink-handled spatula. *"Mi casa . . ."*

"Thanks." I jogged upstairs and into Charming's golden bedroom. It was funny how no matter what I did, I ended up in Charming's bedroom. Yesterday to steal the Devil's Eye. Today to borrow a pair of jeans. How far the villainous had fallen. I stuffed my legs into a pair of peg-legged jeans, all the rave with the hero crowd, and headed back to the kitchen, still shirtless.

When I returned to the kitchen, Charming stood at the stove, a metal skillet in his hand. A gooey yellow substance bubbled in the pan, reminding me of the first meal that Asia and I shared. I closed my eyes, took a few deep breaths, and let the pain of losing my princess slowly fade. Not that it worked, but a villain had to try, right?

"You miss her," Charming said.

I nodded and sat down at the kitchen table. If anyone understood, it was Prince Rotten. He'd lost Asia once upon a time too. Yet he'd managed to survive. I would too.

One villainous day at a time.

Charming poured me a cup of coffee and patted my shoulder. I took a sip of the sweet, milky brew. Figures, I thought, but drank the rest without comment. When I finished wiping the milky mustache from my upper lip I nodded to Charming. "Asia told me you and she were engaged."

Charming shrugged. "It's true. Asia and I were engaged before Cinderella and myself. But Asia wasn't really my type. So we broke up. No hard feelings."

"And then you got engaged to Cinderella the very next day." I frowned. "And Asia was okay with that?"

"I thought so."

"But you're not sure?"

Charming scratched his chin. "No. Cindi called me a few minutes before she died. . . . She was upset. Said Asia threatened her."

"Why didn't you tell the police?"

"Because I know Asia," he said. "She's just not that kind of princess."

His words made me want to strangle him with my impotent hands. I knew Asia. Not him. She was my princess, damn it!

"She would never hurt anyone."

I pictured poor sunny side up Humpty Dumpty. He never stood a chance. Had Cinderella?

Charming continued, "Of course, Asia has a jealous streak. In Princess School, she shaved Rapunzel bald after Quasimodo asked her to the prom instead of Asia."

I smiled. That certainly sounded like my princess. She wasn't the kind of girl to let what she wanted slip away. So why did she let Charming get away? Or did she? "How long have you known the Maledetto family?"

"All my life, it seems. You see, I lost my father," he crossed himself like a good altar boy, "God rest his soul, when I was a wee lad. The king stepped in. Showed me what it meant to be Charming."

Really? I'd met the king, and he wasn't what I called charismatic, let alone altruistic. Maybe Charming had him confused with someone else. "The king? Guy about," I held my hand up, "this tall. Potbelly. Looks like Jack Sprat's wife, but with a beard."

Charming laughed, high-pitched and girly. "That's the one. But don't let his appearance fool you. The king is no pup. He's ruthless. Before Cinderella . . ." He swallowed heavily. "Well, the day before she died, the king cut her off without a cent. It broke Cindi's heart, but that's the king. No one thwarts him and lives to—" Charming's hand flew to his mouth. "I didn't mean it like that."

Interesting. It seemed my list of suspects grew every second, and all with the last name of Maledetto. "Did you kill Cinderella?"

Charming choked on his egg, sending bits flying my direction. I ducked, but a glob landed on my shoulder. Charming quickly jumped up and wiped it away. His hand lingered a bit too long for my comfort. I pushed my coffee cup away and stood.

"Sorry," he said. Was he referring to groping me, spitting egg at me, or murdering his fiancée? Or maybe all three?

"Well? Did you do it?" I motioned to a photograph of Cinderella on his counter. She smiled at the camera, all big eyes and teeth. In a way, she reminded me of Natasha. Not in appearance, since Cinderella was blond and blue eyed, whereas Natasha sported black hair and eyes like a wicked bitch.

I couldn't put my finger on it, but something bothered me about the dead women. Was I just paranoid, or did the women share some common trait that led to their murder? Was a serial killer who'd tired of Fairy Flakes lurking in the Enchanted Forest?

"Of course I didn't kill Cinderella! I loved her." Charming glanced at the photo, and then at my bare chest. "You know, like a sister. A very special sister."

"Uh-huh." I crossed my arms over my naked nipples and frowned. I needed to find new accommodations, and fast. "So if you didn't kill her, who did?"

"I don't know. I've tried everything to bring her murderer to justice. Rewards. Threats . . . other stuff . . . But nothing's worked."

"That's why you wanted the Devil's Eye, isn't it?"

"How did you know about that?"

"A little blue birdie told me."

His eyes widened. Fear filled his gaze as if at any second I might attack. It was laughable, really, given my current state. Still, it felt wonderful. It had been so long since anyone looked at me with terror. I sat at the table, my eyes staring into his. He leaned in, our faces inches apart. His lips parted, and his hand stroked the knee of my Levi's.

Shit! I'd misread the look in his eyes. It definitely wasn't fear. I jumped up and started to pace the pastel-tiled kitchen. "Tell me about the Eye," I said in a rush.

"Stupid thing's broken." His lips curled into a snarl. "Every time I opened the damn thing, it said 'Try Again Later.' No matter how much I shook it. Same thing. Do you know how frustrating that was?"

"I can imagine."

"I was glad when someone stole it from my safe." His eyes bore into mine. I swallowed, but for once, my treacherous tongue stayed quiet. Maybe my curse was finally lifting. God, I hoped so. This nice shit was for the bluebirds.

"If Cindi knew she could break Asia's curse, why did she keep the Eye in the first place?" I asked.

Charming shook his head. "It was a wedding gift."

"From who?"

"The queen, of course."

Chapter 23

"Asia." I pounded on the front door of the palace. "Open the gosh darn door. Come on, we need to talk."

"Language, son," King Maledetto said from behind me. "This is a G-rated kingdom."

I swung around, surprised by both the king's appearance and the king's *appearance*. The daft old man wore purple boots and a top hat. Nothing else, except for a thong and an assault rifle three times his size.

"Can I help you with that?" I asked as he bobbled the firearm. The barrel nicked the ground and then twirled toward the palace.

Boom!

The living room window exploded, showering the air with tiny particles of glass. I ducked out of harm's way as another round of gunfire spurted from the weapon.

"Damn it, Marty!" The queen barreled through the front door, a trickle of blood seeping down the side of her gown. "I told you. No guns near the house. You remember what happened the last time!"

The king didn't look a bit sorry, but said, "Sorry, my pet. I was on my way to the forest when," he waved toward me, "Stiltskin over here stopped me."

The queen's glare turned on me. I stumbled back a few steps. "I really need to talk to Asia."

"Too bad." The queen spun on her glass slipper and disappeared back inside the relative safety of the palace. I stared at her retreating form, and then glanced at the king.

"Women. Can't live with them . . . ," he gazed at his assault rifle with a lustful gleam in his eye, "can't shoot 'em. The sheriff frowns on that kind of thing."

"Sir," I began. "I really do need to speak with your daughter. It's—"

"Stepdaughter," the king interrupted.

I lost it. A burning started in my ears, and before I knew it, my forearm wrapped around the king's neck. Of course, being cursed and all, my headlock quickly turned into a manly, backslapping hug.

"She's your daughter. Say it!" I screamed over and over again. Asia deserved a real father, one who loved and cared for her. Since the king was the closest thing she had, I'd be damned if I'd let him treat her like the redheaded stepchild she was.

The king started to cough, his face growing the same shade of purple as his boots. "Fine," he choked out. "It's no wonder the union gave you the boot." The king broke away, his hat askew. "Asia's my daughter. Always has been. Are you happy now?"

I nodded, regaining some of my composure, but the desire to beat the idiot king to death still tickled my blood. His words finally penetrated my brain. "How the heck do you know about my . . . leave from the union?"

The king grimaced as if he had just repeated a state secret. "Asia must've said something."

"How could she?" I shook my head. "Asia knows nothing about my curse." Because if she had, my semi-sweet princess would've used it against me. Of that, I had no doubt.

"Maybe the wife mentioned it," the king said with a shrug. "I'm the king. People tell me things all the time. Am I supposed to keep track of every one of them?"

Pretty much. Since this line of questioning wasn't getting me anywhere, I let the matter drop. It wasn't like my difficulties with the union were a secret.

Hell, on the day the union relieved me from duties, they placed a two-page (color) ad in the *New Never News*. The headline read: STUBBY VILLAIN CURSED. CAN YOU GUESS HIS NAME? The newspaper soon retracted the "stubby" adjective. I'm pretty sure it had something to do with my threat to blow up the editorial department. Not that I could. But the point was still the same.

"Never mind that," I said with a wave at the king. "Is Asia here or not?"

"Not."

Shit. "Where'd she go?"

"Can't say, son." He paused to heft the assault rifle farther up his shoulder. "But if I was you, I'd leave Maledetto before someone else gets hurt."

"Is that a threat?" A grin curved on my lips. Up until a few weeks ago, I was one of the best villains around, and now, a bloke wearing a G-string threatened to kill me. It put the villainous meaning of life into perspective.

The king shook his head, his beard bobbing like a terrier. "No threat. It's just that since you came to town three people have died. Don't think it's a coincidence. And the sheriff don't either."

"Three?" I swallowed heavily.

"Three," he repeated.

Damn.

At a little after five in the afternoon, I arrived at what used to be Hansel and Missy's candy-coated house, but now served as exhibit A.

The front door stood open. Pink-uniformed cops lined the gumdrop walkway, flashlights in their manicured hands. Dusk fell around the kingdom. I headed up the sidewalk, unmolested, as long as you didn't count my earlier encounter with Prince Annoying and his grabby hands. Which I didn't. In fact, I was doing my best to forget my entire morning, and even some of last night, namely Asia's hatred and Prince Charming's rendition of "A Boy Like That" from *West Side Story*.

I shook my head and focused on the matter at hand. Murder.

In the doorway of the gingerbread house, two florescent lights illuminated the bloodless corpses of Hansel and Missy. Millions of tiny holes dotted their flesh like road rash. But they weren't killed in an automobile accident.

Nope, they weren't that lucky.

Something had pecked the poor bastards to death. Blue feathers littered the scene. I sneezed. Death by bluebird. What a way to go.

"You can't be here," Bruce, the pointy-eared sheriff, called. He waddled his way over to me, his hands planted on his gun belt.

I acknowledged his statement with a nod, but didn't make a move to leave. "Any suspects?"

"Suspects?" He laughed. "A whole forest full, but they ain't talking." His hand motioned to the huge hole in the roof of the house. My eyes followed his finger. A heavily laden tree branch, littered with birds, perched above the hole. The bluish birds squawked, occasionally dive-bombing the deputies below.

"The bluebirds didn't act alone," I said. "Someone put them up to this." I gestured to the bloodless body of Hansel. Even in death, the bloke looked happy. A smile circled his dirt-crusted lips. I leaned closer. Not dirt. Chocolate. Hansel's killer used cocoa to lure the bluebirds. A trick fit for a villain.

"He's right," said a much-too-perky woman in a pink cheerleading outfit, the words "Maledetto" and "Coroner" emblazoned across her chest. "This is a . . . give me an *M*."

The surrounding deputies shouted *M*.

"Give me a *U*."

Again they shouted.

"Give me an *R*."

"Murder. I get it," the sheriff yelled. "But how?"

I gazed at the hole in the ceiling and at the two dead bodies. Poor bastards. They never had a chance.

Ms. Cheerleading Coroner bounced over to us, her little blond pigtails bobbing up and down. "We won't know for sure until the toxicology report comes back, but my guess is the victims," she scissor-kicked in the direction of the bodies, "were drugged, and then coated in chocolate."

The sheriff scratched his whiskerless chin. "Drugged? Chocolate? None of this makes sense. Missy would never invite someone in, let alone someone carrying a half-pound of cocoa." He turned to me. "She's been leery of strangers ever since the night a couple of Snow White's dwarfs got drunk and tried to burn her at the stake."

"A stranger didn't do this," I whispered to myself.

My eyes raked over the crime scene, settling on the wineglasses on the coffee table. The lip print on one of the wineglasses matched Missy's pale pink lips.

A greasy red smear marred the second glass.

A familiar red smear.

My pretty, pretty princess had some explaining to do.

Chapter 24

"Clear the scene," the sheriff said, motioning to the corpses sprawled on the floor. He pointed to the pigtailed coroner. "Bag 'em and tag 'em."

Pigtails bounced up and down in agreement.

I held up my hand. "Wait."

The sheriff and pigtails glanced my way.

"I . . . ahh . . ." Shit. I needed that wineglass. The thought of Asia behind candy bars terrified me. What if she started batting for the other team? Think, I demanded of my brain. It, of course, refused to comply.

"Sheriff," I began, my voice breaking mid-sentence, "can you give me a minute?" I motioned to Hansel's and Missy's bloated, beak-riddled bodies. Tears welled in my eyes, mostly because I was bending my index finger backward. Farther and farther. When it snapped, I yelped. "Fudge."

The sheriff's eyes widened.

"Sorry." I sniffed and wiped my eyes. "I'm in pain here."

"I didn't realize you were close." The sheriff smiled, slimy enough to make me uncomfortable. My creepiness level increased when he stroked my arm. "There there." He patted my hand, his fingers lingering a bit too long.

I quickly stepped away, moving closer to the bodies and

the damning lipstick-coated wineglass. "I loved him like a brother. B-R-O-T-H-E-R," I repeated in case the sheriff didn't get the point.

The sheriff nodded.

"Why!?" I dropped to my knees, my back to the sheriff. "Why did this happen! He was so young! So very young! And ... um ..." I had nothing. Alive, I wasn't that fond of the guy. Dead, he was even a bigger pain in my ass.

"I know it's hard," the sheriff said. "Try to remember the happy times."

Happy times? I snorted with laughter, which thankfully sounded much like grief. Hansel's body lay sprawled in front of me, bloodless, sugarcoated, and bloated. His blank eyes stared into mine, as if accusing.

I'd seen that look before. Many times, in fact. Longing filled me. Ah, the good old days. I missed sugarcoating do-gooders and murdering them with a flock of diabetic blue-birds.

I missed being a villain, damn it.

I sighed. Oh well, I had more important princesses to fry.

With a wail, I pounded on the coffee table where the wineglasses sat, evidence of Asia's crime. Cocoa and dust sputtered to life around me, but the damn wineglass refused to move. I pounded harder. Still nothing.

Fuck it.

I picked up the wineglass stained with red lipstick and threw it across the room. It shattered against the bricks of the fireplace with a loud crash. I instantly felt better.

The sheriff didn't share my relief, though. Instead, the bastard tackled me, sending us both sprawling across the dead bodies. Just my luck I landed on top of Missy, my face in her overly lumpy crotch, which smelled faintly of cheese. I gasped for fresh air, but the sadistic sheriff pressed my face deeper into Missy's lace-covered junk.

This was both fortunate and unfortunate.

The unfortunate part was fairly obvious. The fortunate part surprised me, though. While getting better acquainted with Missy, my hand brushed her thigh and a tiny scrap of paper stuck to it. I carefully peeled the paper from her hairy thigh and grinned. A clue at last. In the form of a receipt for one bluebird.

Son of a transvestite bitch.

Hansel had known all along who'd purchased Gretel and used her to kill Cinderella. And this receipt proved it.

I squinted at the tiny black signature scrawled on the bottom of the receipt. It looked familiar, loopy and girlish, but the name wasn't one I recognized. Nigel de Wolfe. A pseudonym for sure or a really bad dwarf porn name. Had Hansel tried to blackmail Cinderella's killer with this receipt? Was that why he was dead? If so, how was Asia involved? After all, it was her lipstick on the wineglass. At the very least that placed her at the scene.

The sheriff pulled me to my feet and quickly handcuffed my hands behind my back for the second time in as many days. "You are under arrest for obstruction, tampering with evidence, and . . . whatever the hell else I can think of." He shoved me toward the door.

"Wait." Prince Charming poked his head through the open window. "Bruce," he said to the sheriff. "RJ didn't mean any harm. Just let him go." When Bruce shook his head, Charming added, "Please."

The sheriff sighed hot and wet against the back of my neck. "All right." He unhooked the handcuffs and spun me around to face him. "If I catch you interfering with one of my investigations again, I will toss you in a cell for the rest of your villainous days."

As threats went, it was a pretty good one. Locked up, I'd never solve Cinderella's murder, or keep Asia from the slammer, let alone see my princess naked for a second time. I doubted the sheriff would allow us adjoining cells. Not that the idea of Asia in handcuffs was a bad one.

The sheriff's finger stabbed me in the chest, drawing me from my fantasy. "And if I find out you're behind these killings, I will personally rip out your black heart. With a spork," he added. Overkill, really, but how often can you slip the word "spork" into a conversation? "Do you understand me?"

I nodded, more to avoid a brutal beating than in agreement. As long as a birding serial killer roamed free, I would damn well interfere. I owed it to my dead ex-wife, the poor clueless Hansel, and the unknown number of victims still to come. Asia's face flashed through my mind. I wouldn't let anything happen to her. Victim or killer, she was still my princess. Nothing could change that.

An hour later something did happen to change my mind. It came in the form of a bullet whistling through the air aimed at my heart. I dived to the ground, smashing my face into the dirt. Charming, who stood behind me, landed a few feet away.

"Owwwww!" he said. "I'm dying."

I glanced over. Hope filled my heart. But my luck hadn't changed. Charming would live unless a prince could succumb to a hangnail. Admittedly, the fleshy string of skin hanging from his index finger looked painful.

"Awwwwww . . . ," he moaned. "Will this pain never end?"

I grabbed the offending hangnail and smiled.

"Noooooo!!!" Charming pushed at my hands. "Don't do it."

I ripped the skin free. It tore away, leaving Charming weeping and curled in the fetal position. Damn, I enjoyed that. My smile increased until I glanced down.

A pool of blood seeped around us.

A lot of blood.

Too much blood for a simple hangnail.

I scanned Charming for additional injuries. Nothing.

Damn.

I peered down at my own body. Blood oozed from a wound in my side, soaking through my last clean T-shirt. The pain started then, burning, stinging, throbbing pain that reminded me much of my wedding night.

As much as I wanted to curl into the fetal position and weep like Prince Idiot, I couldn't. The reason was hiding a couple of yards away behind a downed pine tree, waiting to kill me. No way was I going out like this, cursed to be nice and lying next to a flaming prince.

I started crawling my way behind an outcropping of pet rocks. Their googlie eyes stared at me with mock judgment. Another shot kicked up the dirt at my feet.

Charming yelped, jumped to his feet, and ran into the forest. I followed, stumbling my way through the trees like a blind mouse. A quick succession of rounds pierced the air around us, but none of the bullets struck true. Surprising if one considered the sheer amount of girlish screeches coming from Prince Idiot. It was much like running for your life with an out-of-tune Pied Piper playing the bagpipes.

I ducked behind a tree and scanned the forest, my breath coming in sharp, painful gasps. The pain in my side increased with each breath. Closing my eyes, I lifted my shirt to assess the damage. A small round hole bubbled up about six inches from my belly button. Relief washed over me. The wound wasn't deep enough or close enough to any major organs to do much damage. Yeah, it hurt like a wicked witch, but I'd live to play the villain again. If the shooter didn't get his way, that was.

The enchanted trees swayed in the wind like marionettes on a string. The air smelled of blood and gunpowder, not unpleasant. In fact, it reminded me of my childhood without the embarrassing uncontrolled erections whenever I saw my best mate's wicked stepmother. In my defense, she was hot, sort of a cross between Snow White and the devil.

If I wanted to get out of the forest alive I needed to act, and soon. Bluebirds were starting to circle. "We can work this out," I said to the nameless, faceless killer. "You don't really want to kill me."

About fifty feet in front of me a branch snapped. I jumped at the sound. Somewhere behind me Charming whimpered. The pump of a shotgun echoed in the air. I cleared my dry throat. "Okay, so maybe you do. But think about it. This is too easy. You need more of a challenge."

The killer answered with a load of buckshot. The pellets slammed into the trees behind me. Charming screamed. It was now or never. I leapt from my hiding space and ran at full villainous speed toward the would-be assassin. My lungs burned, my side ached, and my eyelids watered from gun smoke, but still I ran. Or rather I limped at a good clip.

I reached the killer's hiding place expecting to take a round or two. A fitting villainous end, as long as the shooter wasn't a hero, or twelve. But no bullets punctured my spleen.

For some reason, the shooter held his fire. In a perfect villainous world, I'd chalk it up to my intimidating manner and scary "please, please don't shoot me" face. Since the kingdom of Maledetto was far from perfect or particularly villainous, I had no clue why I wasn't lying splattered all over the Enchanted Forest. Honestly, how hard was it to shoot a charging moron, even one as good-looking and witty as myself?

With one last prayer, I dove over a fallen log and into the shooter's lair. "Aha!" I screamed, ready to tackle the would-be killer. Unfortunately, the only thing I caught was the heel of a glass slipper, right in the forehead.

Chapter 25

I've died and gone to hell, I thought upon waking from my footwear-induced nap a few minutes later. Nope. This was worse than hell. I was in hellish hell with a hell-grown cherry on top. I shoved Prince Charming off me and wiped a string of princely drool from my lips. "What the fudge do you think you're doing?"

"Giving you the kiss of life," Charming said, frowning. "I took a CPR class with Asia at the annex. They showed us how."

I spat out a glop of saliva, trying to wash the nasty taste of prince from my mouth. "Don't ever. Ever. Kiss me again. Even if I'm dead. Got it?"

Charming's bottom lip quivered. "I was only trying to help."

I didn't bother to respond. Instead, I pulled the size-eight glass slipper from my forehead and held it up to the dim light.

Overhead a bluebird tweeted.

An hour later, still bleeding from the wound in my side as well as the dent in my head, I dizzily shoved the palace doors open and stomped inside. "Darn it, Asia. I said I was sorry. No need to shoot me."

A ton of brick rained down on my head, sounding much like an avalanche of . . . well, bricks against pink shag palace carpeting.

I ducked, avoiding the falling bricks like a true villain. When the brick dust settled, I glanced up, not that surprised to see a woman with red hair standing on a ladder, her face a mask of rage.

The queen frowned down at me, a brick in her lace-gloved hand. "Look at what you've done," she said, tossing the brick at my head. It missed my noggin but smashed into my toe.

"Hey." I hopped on one foot. "What'd you do that for?"

"Do you know how long it took me to arrange those bricks?" She didn't give me a chance to answer. "Two hours. The king will be here any minute. And you ruined my . . . surprise."

"Sorry."

"I'll say you are," she said. Her eyes scanned my bloody forehead, clothes, and now-swollen foot. "Do you have any clue what it takes to make a marriage work?"

"Attempted murder?" I took a stab at answering.

"No. To have a good marriage you must sacrifice. That's why you'll never win Asia's favor."

"Since when is beaning your spouse with a brick a sacrifice?" I laughed.

"Go ahead and laugh," she huffed, "but one day you'll regret not heeding my advice."

I doubted it. Dear Abby the queen wasn't. So why did she bother to advise me at all? Especially since her sights were set on Prince Rotten as an in-law. Or were they? She did give Cinderella the Devil's Eye; yet she didn't bat an eye at her murder. Just whose side was the queen on?

Before I could question her, the front door flew open and the king strolled inside. He stepped over the pile of bricks, nodded at me, and headed toward the living room, pausing long enough to kick the bottom rung of the ladder.

The queen shrieked as the ladder toppled. I debated catching her, weighing the pros and cons. In the end, I caught her seconds before impact. I had to. I had no choice.

Fucking union.

As alike as Asia and her mother were in looks, holding the queen in my arms failed to rouse anything inside me. She was a bitter replica of my pretty princess. Sourness, jealousy, and disappointment replaced Asia's stubborn determination and pride, not to mention her stunning left hook and ability to make a grown villain beg for mercy with one little finger. Ah, what my pretty princess could do with that finger.

The queen put her slender fingers on my arm and kneaded the skin beneath. I shuddered and quickly dropped the offending monarch. The queen fell on her butt, her legs hanging in the air. Blue cotton granny panties peeked out from between her birdlike thighs. From her red-lipped mouth came threats of beheading and revenge.

I smiled politely, reached into my pocket, and measured her majesty's foot against the glass slipper from the forest.

Two sizes too small. Damn.

"My lady." I tipped my invisible hat and took off in search of more princessly feet. One suspect down, a palace full to go. I wandered the palace, searching for suspects in general, and Asia in particular. As much as I hated the thought of Asia attempting my murder, could I blame her?

Damn right!

And I would too as soon as I found her.

"Asia," I yelled.

No one answered.

I tried again, louder. So loud, in fact, the chandelier over my head shook. Dust rained down on me, mixing with the drying blood on my forehead to form a pinkish paste. "Darn it, Asia. Get your skinny butt out here."

A door at the end of the hallway sprang open. Thousands of tiny Tinker Bell asses blinded me, backlighting the outline of a slim princess in the doorway. I squinted against the onslaught. Those damn fairies twinkled all the more. "I don't believe in fairies," I yelled in hopes of dimming the blinding light.

A tiny blonde screamed and her fairy butt winked out. I smiled. How very villainous of me. Maybe my luck was finally changing. The fairy jumped up and laughed, her fairy butt working at double speed. Stupid union.

Farther down the hallway, the princess shadowed in darkness limped toward me, her right slipper missing from what looked like a size-eight foot.

Damn Asia. I'd teach her to shoot at impotent villains.

Or not.

My fingers stroked the reflective surface of the slipper in my hand, waiting. Dark thoughts swirled through my head as villainous rage filled me. A princess would pay for shooting me, even if I had to wait an eternity. A vision of Asia locked in a tower, serving my every need, brought a smile to my lips.

"Does this look familiar, perchance?" I held the slipper toward the princess. Fairy butts glinted off the glass.

The princess took another step into the fairy light.

I stepped back, but not in time.

The corridor filled with high-pitched girlish screams. I covered my mouth, but the screams bubbling through my lips didn't stop.

Chapter 26

"Sorry about that," I said to Dru. "You startled me." Which wasn't exactly true. When Dru had stepped into the light, my bollocks traveled north and my stomach south.

Not for the reason one might expect, either.

In fact, I doubted anyone could've expected the monstrosity in front of me. Imagine a baboon's butt amplified by a thousand; now give it a harelip, and bingo, you had the poor princess in front of me. The poor princess with one fucking shoe.

Whatever sympathy I felt for the unsightly girl vanished under the burning in my side. That ugly bitch tried to kill me. I stepped forward, the slipper in my hand raised like a weapon, not that I could actually hit her, but a screech of terror would be nice. Hers, not mine.

"Where'd you find my slipper?" Winslow asked from behind me.

I spun to face him. "What?"

"My slipper." He pointed to the glass slipper in my hand and then to the matching slipper on his left foot. I squinted down at the slipper with a red ribbon and scowled. My eyes crawled to Dru's slipperless foot. Even though her foot appeared too small to fit the slipper in my hand, I wanted it to be hers. Wanted it more than I'd wanted anything in my life—okay, wanted anything in the last hour. Damn.

"You're telling me this is *your* slipper?" I jabbed my finger into Winslow's chest with force. Instead of flinching and apologizing like I expected, he giggled like a little princess. I glared down at my finger, which was currently tickling the troll-like butler.

"Stop." Winslow laughed. "Please stop. I give. I give."

I stopped tickling him and took in the scene in front of me. Winslow stood perched on one high-heel slipper, his meaty toes squished like Vienna sausages in the tip. A bead of sweat dripped down his pale forehead, running down his cheek and splashing against his stark black tuxedo jacket. He glanced at Dru, who stared back at him, her eyes wide.

"What the fudge is going on?" I asked, ending their staring contest.

"I tried this hair-removing cream, and now I look like a baboon's ass!" Dru yelled with enough force to rattle the fairy bulbs overhead. "And it's all your fault." She pointed at me, tears streaming down her bright red cheeks.

"How do you figure?"

She ignored my question, and instead screeched, "How can I marry Prince Charming now? He'll take one look at me and run for Mexicanada."

For those who failed geography in Charming School, Mexicanada bordered New Never City on the southernmost side. A nice place to visit, but I wouldn't want to villain there. They frowned on that sort of thing, eh.

I held up a hand to halt the wailing princess. "That wasn't quite what I meant when I asked what was going on. What I do want to know is, which one of you took a shot at me?"

"What?!" Both Winslow's and Dru's eyes flew to mine.

"Someone shot at you?"

I lifted my shirt, revealing the neat bullet wound in my side. They each examined the wound at length, equal expressions of confusion on their dim faces. If any couple belonged together, it was these two morons.

After staring at my side for an eternity, Dru raised her head and frowned. "You're bleeding."

"Yes. Yes, I am. And do you know why?"

Winslow fielded this one. " 'Cuz someone shot you?"

"Exactly. And that someone lost this very slipper." I shoved the offending shoe at Winslow. "Do you have something to tell me?"

Winslow glanced down at the slipper and then at his ladymoron Dru. She gave a barely perceptible shrug of her thin shoulders. "Not really," Winslow said.

"Why not give it a try anyway?" I poked the slipper into his stomach, causing him to giggle once again. "From what I've been told, confession's good for the soul. So I suggest you start talking before you find your soul seeping out of your body through a size-eight hole."

A rush of power flickered through me. Damn, but it felt good to threaten him. Too good, in fact. My body started to tremble. Electrical sparks shot along my nerve endings.

Shit.

I spun to stop Dru, but it was too late. She pressed the Taser against my skin again. Zap! Fifty thousand volts of electricity shocked my battered body. I dropped to the ground. The tinkle of tiny fairy laughter, like static, echoed in my ears before my world went black for a second time in a matter of hours.

"Asia," I whispered, pulling her toward me. She pressed her fingertip to my lips. Her skin tasted like cinnamon, her lips like fine wine. I kissed her shoulder, tasting the salt of her flesh. Her legs straddled mine. The weight of her hips pressed into my thighs, stirring my blood to a near boil. I wanted her. Needed her.

"Don't leave me," I said against her hot mouth. She lifted her head and stared into my eyes.

Then she was gone.

Jolted from the fantasy, my eyes snapped wide, my breath came in sharp gasps. Sweat dripped from my naked body, pooling on the pink satin sheets underneath me. I glanced around, unsure of my surroundings, much less my mental health. The dream had seemed so real. I could still taste Asia on my lips, but the pink-covered bedroom was empty. Longing filled me, the kind only a villain could know.

Swallowing hard, I tried to erase the dream from my mind and hoped my heated body would get the message. The last thing I needed was another four-hour erection. I wasn't some horny teenage villain anymore.

"Come on," I whispered to my little Stiltskin ("little" being relative). "Work with me here." I lifted the sheet covering my nakedness and sighed. I tried picturing Baba Yaga naked, warts and all, but that merely gave me a headache. Damn it.

"I see you're feeling better," a voice called from the shadows. Little RJ instantly recoiled, for which I was grateful, mostly.

"What are you doing here?" I asked Prince Charming. The last time I saw him, he was going wee wee wee all the way home. He still smelled faintly of urine.

Charming slithered from the darkness, his lacy shirt billowing in the still air. "Dru called me. She said you were here, crazed, threatening people with an invisible shoe."

"Glass. Not invisible. And I'm not crazy." I frowned and rubbed my aching head. Thankfully the Taser had few lasting effects. Of course, my side still burned like Little Boy Blue when he peed, but it was a distant pain. Manageable. Also, a good reminder of the dangers of falling for a certain redheaded princess. "I'm not," I repeated when he remained silent.

"Uh-huh." Charming patted my arm.

I slapped his hand away. "Don't patronize me. The evidence is right here." I reached for my clothes neatly piled on the bed next to me. No slipper, though. "I mean, it was here. Dru must've taken it." The bitch. First, her sister tried to kill me, and then Dru sent fifty thousand volts of electricity through me. To top it off, she pilfered the one bit of proof that I wasn't some drooling, insane villain. I wiped away a string of saliva running down my chin and faced Charming.

"Why would Dru steal your invisible shoe?" Charming tapped one long whisker on his otherwise hairless chin. "She has plenty of her own. I mean, have you seen her closet? It puts my invisible slipper collection to shame."

For the briefest of seconds I considered how to choke the life out of Charming in my impotent state. Accidental choking came to mind. What if I slipped and to save myself from a nasty bruise, my hands wrapped around his neck? Surely, the union would understand.

"Have you seen the latest Kenneth Cole Invisibles?" Charming grinned. "Of course you haven't."

"Don't. Push. Me." I held up a hand. "Do me a favor, go find Dru. I need that slipper."

Charming shook his head. "I'd rather not."

"Please?"

"No."

"Pretty please?"

He rolled his eyes. "Fine. But you owe me."

"She's your fiancée, remember?"

"How could I forget?" He grimaced. "Every time I see a caterpillar I'm reminded of my upcoming nuptials."

My eyes narrowed. If Charming didn't want to marry Dru, why did he ask her in the first place? Why had he proposed to any of the Maledetto daughters? First Asia. That I could understand. After all, she was beautiful, smart, sexy, and bent. The perfect princess. Cinderella, his second choice, wasn't a bad option either. The chick had a devious streak and smelled like spiced rum. Last and definitely least, Dru, a chick who could barely utter a logical thought and looked like a cross between ugly and her uglier sister.

"So why are you—" I began.

Charming waved me off. "Ours is not to question."

"What?"

"The Lord works in mysterious ways," he said with a nod, as if that explained everything. Which it didn't, and never had. My mom used to say that whenever I asked where babies came from. I hadn't believed it then, and I'd be damned if I'd accept it now.

"Well, it starts with a bee...," Charming said.

"Huh?"

Charming frowned, scanning my head for injuries. "How babies are made. You asked. I was merely explaining."

I ran my hand across my face. I must've taken more volts than I thought because everything seemed surreal, as if I was still dreaming, but instead of being naked with my lovely princess, I was being tortured by a dim-witted prince.

Clearing my throat, I pointed to the door. "Go. Find. Dru." Of course, much to my dismay, my cursed tongue added, "Please."

Again, the prince shuddered at the mention of his intended. I filed my suspicions away and waited until he left the room. Then I quickly dressed and ran down the palace steps.

My mind already felt like mush, and another round of Q&Idiot with Dru would send me over the edge. I had no choice but to leave the palace before something even worse happened, like Asia's aim improving. Or Charming realizing I'd escaped and coming to find me. Besides, I had a murder to solve. Well, four of them if you counted Hansel and Missy.

When I hit the bottom landing, Winslow opened the front door. "Good day, sir," he said.

I stopped in the doorway, my eyes boring into his. Slowly my gaze lowered until it reached the tops of his black polished butler boots. His eyes followed mine and he smiled.

"Something wrong, sir?"

I shook my head, muttered something about "finding good help in a kingdom of crazy people," and headed out the door, my feet sinking into the shag carpet with every step along the way.

Winslow called, "Don't forget your shoe."

I spun around expecting to see Asia's slipper. Instead, Winslow stood in the doorway, a pair of combat boots in his hands. I glanced down at my sock-encased feet. Oops.

A black boot nearly clobbered me in the forehead, but I ducked out of the way and laughed. "Nice throw," I taunted Winslow.

A second boot followed the first. This one connected with my bollocks. I grabbed my man jewels, puked on my socks, and dropped to the ground with a groan. The cold earth felt wonderful against my aching nutsack. I closed my eyes and took a shallow breath, praying the pain would recede. It didn't. Damn butler.

I had to give Winslow credit, though. Like a true manservant, seconds later, he arrived with a mop and bucket, a smile on his thin, troll-like face.

Chapter 27

I recovered quickly enough from the affront to my testicles, laced my combat boots up, and struggled to my feet before heading for the kingdom's one and only market, a place where, for a price, one could purchase anything, including a killer bluebird or two. Not that I wanted or even needed a killer bluebird. I preferred to take my revenge on my princess in a much more personal and naked way. However, my only clue to Cinderella's murder was the fancy scrawled signature on the receipt I found at Hansel's.

Missy had died protecting the cocoa-covered receipt, and it was time to find out why. I pulled the receipt from my pocket and checked the signature again. Nigel de Wolfe. The killer had added a smiley face to the *O* and dotted the *I* with a heart.

Where had I seen this handwriting before?

I frowned, trying to picture Asia's handwriting, but nothing came to me.

She didn't do it.

She couldn't have.

Or maybe she did.

Asia was certainly capable of murder. But she didn't strike me as the bluebird type. It was too detached. Too cold-blooded. If Asia wanted someone dead, she'd do it herself. I prodded the bandage covering the bullet wound in my side. Case in point.

So I was back at square one in my search for Cinderella's killer, with one exception. Someone, probably the woman I loved, wanted me dead. I took it in stride, though. After all, I was a villain. If people didn't want me dead within a few days of making my acquaintance, I wasn't doing my job.

I shoved the receipt back into my pocket and hiked a mile and a half to the market. The trek took longer than I expected since I had to pass Old MacDonald's Pot Farm on the way.

E-I-E-I-O.

By the time I arrived at the market it was a little after five. I was starving and most of the shops had closed for the night. Yet a few remained open, mostly those catering to a more jaded and naked kind of clientele. I walked by a red-lit window where a dark-haired maiden danced behind the glass. She winked and motioned for me to join her inside.

"No dough," I mouthed.

She shook her head, moving on to the next victim, a giant with a golden harp under his arm.

The harp glared at the harpy in the window, and the giant blushed. "Her beauty cannot compare to yours, my dear," he said to the harp as they strolled by the window.

Ah, the age-old tale of boy meets musical instrument.

The tall, slim maiden in the window sighed, glanced around for another victim, and finding none, she finally motioned again for me to enter the establishment.

I lifted my pockets of my Levi's inside out to show that I was indeed a broke loser. The girl rolled her eyes, paused, and then waved me inside again.

As much as I'd like to think my villainous good looks changed her mind, I suspected boredom played a larger role. The streets were deserted with the exception of me and a couple of Snow White's dwarfs on a bender. Everyone knew those guys had no cash, not since Snow White bought a poison-apple-red Lexus.

The girl behind the glass tapped on the window again to gain my attention. She put her hands together as if begging and motioned for me to enter the establishment. I considered her offer and her legs for a moment. She couldn't compare to my pretty princess. She also hadn't shot at me.

Yet.

I opened the front door to Bob's Bordello.

Smack!

A tiny fist smashed into my nose. Blood dribbled from my nostril and my right eye started to tear. As far as injuries went, I had worse. In the last hour. But it still hurt.

I wiped a tear from my cheek and raised my other arm to protect my face from another barrage of fists. "Stop," I yelped, ducking and covering like a drunken Muhammad Ali.

My tone had the intended effect. My assailant stopped her pummeling, handed the woman from the window a twenty, and smiled down at me, her slight chest heaving with exhaustion. The chick from the window snatched the money and disappeared behind a large wooden door. My assailant and I watched as she sauntered away.

"Been a while, Miss Muffet." I nodded to my assailant, the small, fragile-looking woman wearing saddle shoes and a bonnet. "How's tricks?"

"Don't 'how's tricks' me, RJ," she screeched in an annoying tone. No mortal, villain or not, could stand to converse with Miss Muffet for long. She sounded like an angry elf after a hit of helium.

Muffet frowned, raising her fists. "What have you done?"

"Nothing."

"That's not what I heard." She shook her head. Golden

threads of bleached hair danced around, nearly blinding me in the dim light of the brothel. "The union's not happy, and neither am I."

"Too bad," I said. "I'm on leave, remember? I don't have to answer to you, or anyone." It felt good to say, but as soon as the words left my mouth I wanted to gobble them back. Miss Muffet wasn't the kind of villainous boss to be messed with. Termination, to her, usually included painful and permanent scarring.

Her dark eyes narrowed.

I swallowed hard but refused to back down. After all, my impotent state was her fault, and following that logic, whatever happened after was her problem as well.

Finally, she shook her head and sighed. She strolled across the room and sat on a tuffet. "I always liked you, RJ. You do good work, usually without any problems."

"Thanks. I—"

She cut me off. "But when you screw up, you screw up big."

"I—"

"Remember the three bears incident a couple of days after Natasha left?" Her finger wagged back and forth. "We never did find that porridge."

"I—"

"With the way things are right now, we can't afford a loose cannon. Too much is at stake."

Loose cannon? Who talked like that? If anyone was loose, it was the chick sitting on the tuffet. She was a legend among villains, but not for the reasons one might suspect. In her day, Miss Muffet lured many a hero to his death while innocently eating her curds and whey.

"How'd you find me?" I finally asked when I could get a word in. Then I remembered my desperate phone call to her mere days ago. Had she tracked my vPhone?

"Like it was hard." She snorted. "I know you. I know how you think. What you think. It was simple logic." The edges of her lips lifted, flashing whey-stained teeth. "Impotent or not, a Stiltskin cannot resist boobs. I knew that eventually you'd find your way here. It was only a matter of time."

For the record, the boobs thing wasn't completely true. Man-boobs did nothing for me. But that wasn't the point. If Miss Muffet was here, in Maledetto, I was in deep trouble. She rarely left union headquarters, not since Flaming Friday, which I still insist wasn't my fault.

Who knew lemon juice was flammable?

"What do you want?" I crossed my arms over my chest and waited. It wasn't long in coming. Miss Muffet jumped from her tuffet as if a spider sat down beside her. I grinned, which in hindsight was a mistake. Her fist connected with my stomach, and I dropped to my knees. Stomach bile along with my liver crawled into my esophagus.

"I came here to offer my condolences on Natasha's untimely demise, you twit." Her foot connected with my thigh.

"And?" I wheezed. After all, we both knew why she was really in Maledetto. The union wanted me, either a) back on villainous duty or b) dead. While the first option held some appeal I suspected the latter to be true. The chokehold Miss Muffet currently held me in was a pretty good clue.

Her forearm tightened. "We'd like you to return to active duty. Now. Today."

"No," I choked out.

"Wrong answer." She jabbed her index finger into my eye socket and dug around. As much as that hurt, I wasn't giving in, not without a raise at the very least. They ruined the past three weeks of my life, and I wanted payback.

When Miss Muffet loosened her grip, I yanked free. "If you want me back so bad, what's with the butt-kicking?"

"Suck it up, you big baby." Miss Muffet chuckled. "That

was a love tap. Besides, you liked it." She winked at me, which scared me more than her tiny flying fists had.

I shivered, but still held firm. "Listen, it's not that I don't appreciate your coming all the way out here. I do. It's just . . ."

"All right." She tapped her foot. "How much?"

"Fifteen percent."

Smack. Her right fist caught me off guard, but I stayed on my feet. Once the blinding pain faded from my head, I said, "Fine. Twelve percent."

She raised her fist.

"Ten. Ten percent," I said. "And full medical."

Her hand jutted toward me again. I jumped back, and she grinned. "Nice doing business with you," Miss Muffet said, shaking my hand. "Now, go grab your stuff and meet me back here in an hour. The bus to New Never City leaves at midnight."

That was too easy.

I was missing something, but I wasn't sure what. Miss Muffet and the union must've needed my expertise pretty bad. But there was one problem. A red-haired problem.

"I can't leave," I said with a sigh. Don't get me wrong, I really, really wanted to. It wasn't like I had much going on for me in Maledetto. Asia wanted me dead. Dru wanted me to find her a prince. And Charming, well, he just wanted me, which in itself was enough reason to hightail it out of the kingdom. But I couldn't leave. Not yet.

"What?" Her eyes flashed.

I swallowed, hard. "I can't leave right now."

"That's all right."

"Really?"

She nodded. "Yeah. Like I said a few seconds ago, the bus leaves in an hour. Not right now."

"That's not what I meant."

"But it is what you said." Her eyes filled with disappointment. "That's your problem, RJ. You're never clear.

Communication is very important. Without it, mistakes are made. Remember that time—"

"I have to stay in Maledetto," I said, cutting off her lecture. "At least for a few more days."

"Why?"

"I promised to find a killer."

She glowered. "So? I promised to love, honor, and cherish my last three husbands. Instead, I bludgeoned, beat, and crushed each. Grow up. Promises are made to be murdered."

While Muffet had a point, I couldn't stop picturing Asia's face as she stared down at the chalk outline of her pancaked stepsister. Besides, if I left now, I would never avenge Natasha. More importantly, I would never see my princess naked again.

I cupped my testicles to protect them. "Be that as it may, I can't leave. Not yet."

Miss Muffet took a step forward. "Don't mess with me, RJ. I'm not in the mood. The union needs you. I need you."

Had any other cute blonde in distress said those words I might've reconsidered. But not her, and not today. The union had fucked up my life too much already for bygones to be bygones. They'd robbed me of my villainy, forced me to be "nice." and now wanted me to hop on a bus to New Never City, leaving behind my princess? Wasn't going to happen. I'd made a vow to Asia, and I would keep it.

Just this once.

I told Miss Muffet as much. She reacted as expected, lots of threats, sucker punches, and shots to the bollocks. I'm proud to say I took it like a man, by which I mean I whimpered and tried to hide under a tuffet.

After a while, Miss Muffet either tired of smacking me around or proudly accepted my stubborn determination. She stopped pummeling me and yawned. "All right, RJ. You win, but don't say I didn't warn you."

"I—"

"The union frowns on any employee with a will of his own. That and Sundays off." She strolled to the door and opened it. A cold breeze, like a bad omen, blew in. "Find your killer, and find him quick, and then return to active duty. Otherwise, the next time we see each other," she grinned, "you won't like it."

I can't say I was too pleased with this visit. My head, side, and balls ached in parts I didn't know existed. Plus, due to our dalliance, I was no closer to solving the rash of murders than I was a couple of hours ago. I doubted the next few hours would hold the final clue either. On the bright side, the union was off my back for now and I still had the bluebird receipt.

I patted my pocket, smiled, and then frowned.

"No." I shoved my hand into my empty pocket. "Arachnophobic witch!" I shouted to no one. Little Miss Muffet was gone, as was her tuffet, and my one chance at catching a killer.

Chapter 28

I wandered the streets of the marketplace replaying the last hour in my head. Why would Miss Muffet steal the bluebird receipt? It didn't make sense. Was the union in on Cinderella's murder? I doubted it. For one thing, what was their motive? The union gained nothing from her death. That's not to say villains didn't kill on a whim. In fact, most of our dastardly deeds lacked any planning at all.

And that was the problem.

Whoever killed Cinderella did so with absolute calculation and cunning, which meant the killer must've gained something from her death. Money? Fame? Revenge? Who knew, but one thing was certain. I was clueless.

A gaggle of Snow White's drunken dwarfs staggered by me. The tallest one, his face red from booze, pointed at me. "Hi hoe," he said with a slur. His shorter friends laughed, slapping him on the back. I rolled my eyes.

"RJ, son, is that you?" the king's voice boomed from behind me. "Just the man I need."

That didn't bode well for either of us, but I turned around anyway. "Sir?"

"Help me with these bags." The king tossed two paper sacks with wide green lettering on the front at me. I caught them, grunting under the weight. Each sack weighed at least fifty pounds and smelled like old shoes. Unless the king had started collecting feet, I deduced the bags contained fifty-pound blocks of cheese. That, honestly, didn't make much more sense. Who eats that much cheese?

"Rats," the king said as if I'd voiced my question aloud. "The castle is full of them."

Didn't I know it.

"I've devised a trap." He pulled a jumbo-sized mousetrap from another sack. A lighter sack, I had no doubt. "I load a piece of cheese here. The quee—I mean the rat steps here." The king's finger pressed the lever. "And snap. Off goes her head."

I glanced from the trap to the deluded king and shook my head. This would not end well. No sooner had that thought crossed my mind than a loud snap rang from the trap.

The trap had sprung, crushing the king's porky finger beneath hundreds of pounds of pressure. His scream of pain nearly burst my eardrums.

"Ow. Ow. Ow." He danced around, trap and finger mercifully intact. I stepped back to avoid his flailing arms, a smile hovering on my lips.

When the king paused in his litany of acrobatic tricks, I reached for the trap and yanked his hand free. The villainous part of me enjoyed it more than a man should. As did the other less desirable part, the same stupid part who agreed to find Cindi's killer and break my damsel's curse.

"Thank you, son," the king said, rubbing his mangled fingers.

"You're welcome, sir." I paused. "But in the future, you might wanna rethink your 'rat' traps."

"It wasn't rats I was after."

"Really? I would've never guessed."

"Let me tell you a story, son." His bruised and bloody hand reached around my shoulder, leaving streaks of red on my shirt, and pulled me close. "When I was a wee lad, my father pulled me onto his lap and offered me a bit of advice. And this advice I will give to you."

"How nice," I said with a smirk.

"He said, 'son, nobody likes a smart-ass.' " The king's unmangled hand smacked the back of my head. "Now, do you want to win back Asia or not?"

"I do."

"Good." The king smiled, showing off stained teeth and swollen gums. Apparently, the king of all the land never heard of dental floss. The king added, "Go back to Charming's and wait for my signal."

"Signal? What kind of signal?"

"You'll know it when you see it. Have faith."

I snorted. Villains believed in faith as much as we believed in truth, justice, and the Neverlandian way. The king frowned. When I didn't respond, the old guy frowned even harder, so hard I worried his bottom lip would disappear forever.

Finally, I rolled my eyes and nodded. "All right. I'll wait for your 'signal.' " I added finger quotes for effect. "But tell me this, why the sudden change of heart? Yesterday you threatened to boil my bollocks in oil."

"People change, son."

That was it? Somehow I doubted the king's sudden epiphany on the merits of villainy. More likely, he found a way to use my villainous skills against the missus. The joke was on him, though. Until Miss Muffet reinstated me to full villainy, I couldn't use my villainous skills to boil an egg.

I followed the daft king to a bright blue moped with training wheels. He climbed aboard, strapping on a matching blue helmet. His beard tangled in the strap, causing his face to resemble a troll doll. "Listen, son," he said. "One day you will look back on this moment."

"And?"

He kick-started the moped's engine. It buzzed to life like an angry fairy. "How should I know? I'm the king, not psychic."

I shook my head. If anything, I hoped that one day this damn conversation would make a lick of sense. The king revved his engine. "Hey," I said. "Did your father really sit you on his lap like that?" If so, it might explain a few things, especially if the child-king had fallen off and landed on his noggin.

A frown creased the king's mouth. "I don't think so. My biological father died when I was a wee lad. But I was lucky, son."

"How so?"

"The king took me in." The current king smiled. "Raised me as his own son."

"That was nice," I said, nearly choking on the most hated word in the villainous language. That and "G-spot."

The king nodded. "King de Wolfe was a good man." With that, the king hit the gas and took off into the late-night traffic at a top speed of fifteen miles per hour.

For the next six hours of my life, I sat in the most dreaded institution in all the land. A place whose very name caused lesser villains to beg for mercy. A place that catered to the most depraved of degenerates.

The Maledetto Public Library.

The library was open twenty-four hours a day. Unlike 7-Eleven, it served a greater purpose, enlightenment rather than just overcooked hot dogs. Of course, like 7-Eleven, it did offer a fine selection of beers and slushies. Unfortunately, the enlightenment as well as the beer was watered down.

I walked into the library at a little after one in the morning. A cold wind swept inside after me. I shivered, glancing around the dark wood-paneled room that smelled like dust and decaying bookworms.

My face ached from Miss Muffet's tiny fists, but not nearly as bad as my side hurt. Getting shot sucked. But getting shot by the woman you . . . lusted after really blew. Not only did my side burn, but the spot just left of the center of my chest did as well. I let out a loud burp that my cursed self quickly apologized for, even though the library appeared empty.

A muskrat-faced librarian wearing hair rollers and granny glasses shot me a dirty look and raised her hairy finger to her hairy lips. "Shhhh!" she shouted in an ear-splitting screech.

I looked around the room and laughed. Who was I disturbing? The book fairy? Not a soul stood inside the library, or near the library, or even in a mile radius of said library.

"Quiet!" The librarian pounded her fists on the countertop until my chuckles subsided.

"Sorry," I whispered, which seemed to mollify her, or at least it stopped her from chewing on my limbs. "Can you help me find a book?" I asked with my most charming smile. A smile I'd stolen from the dim-witted prince himself.

"No." Muskrat-face pointed her finger at her chest. "Do I look like the reference librarian to you?"

"Ummm . . . no?"

She nodded. "Reference section's in the back, past the self-help section. If you get to the self-mutilation section, you've gone too far."

Tell me about it.

I nodded my thanks and walked through racks of books, all neatly arranged by Dewey himself. I passed the non-fiction section, pausing for a second in front of *Grimms' Fairytales*. I picked up the weighty tome. The cover showed the dark (incredibly handsome) outline of a terrifying villain towering over a distressed damsel.

Those damn Brothers Grimm. For years, I did the dirty

deeds and they reaped the rewards. Maidens swooned at their overly large feet. Size fifteen in socks! What kind of abomination wore boots that big? It just wasn't natural.

I glanced down at my own size twelves and smiled.

With a shake of my head, I returned the book to the shelf and continued on my quest for information about the Maledetto lineage. The name de Wolfe kept repeating in my brain, sort of like the soundtrack of a bad three little pig-on-pig porno.

Someone had used the name Nigel de Wolfe to purchase Gretel, the killer bluebird. It was time to find out who and why.

My journey took me through the cookbooks and into the fiction section. Rows and rows of books offered far-away adventures, romance, and the occasional STD. I lifted a book titled *My Life As a Slipper Addict* from the shelf at random. Cinderella's face stared back at me, her eyes and teeth as sharp as I remembered from the picture in Charming's living room. Was it censure or warning in her pale gaze? Was I finally on the right path? A path led me to a killer and eventually back into Asia's panties.

After a sojourn through the gay and lesbian ogre section, I arrived at my destination. The reference section. Thick books, maybe three feet in size, sat on a bowing bookcase. The titles ranged from *Maledetto: The Early Years* to *The End of an Earl*. Damn. Without knowing where to look, my search would take an era.

I rang the bell sitting on top of a desk with the word REFERENCE on it. The bell chimed, sounding more like a scream than a ding.

From behind a stack of towering dictionaries stepped the muskrat-faced librarian. But this time instead of granny glasses, she wore green tinted contacts and a pink wig.

"May I help you?" she asked in the same sour voice.

"Ummm," I motioned to the front of the library, "weren't

you..." I shook my head. "Never mind. I need some help."

"Self-help is two stacks up. I recommend *The Joy of the Female Orgasm*." She looked down her nose at me. "Or in your case, *Are You There, G-Spot? It's Me, Man*."

"No. Not that kind of help." Not today at least. "I'm looking for some information on Nigel de Wolfe."

"Should I know that name?"

"I'm not sure." I scratched my chin, my fingers coming away rust-colored from dried blood. No wonder the librarian didn't want to help me. I must look like an escaped little piggy from the crazy hospital. "I believe he might be related to the former king, de Wolfe."

Her eyes widened, causing her tinted contacts to slip. The dark brown of her iris bubbled from underneath the greenish tinting. She blinked them back in place. "This is the reference section, not information. If you're looking for Nigel de Wolfe, try four-one-one. The library can't help you." She twisted on her heel and vanished behind a row of yellow pages.

"Wait," I called, but to no avail. "Darn it."

I slapped the desk. The stack of reference books next to me started to topple. An avalanche of fonts crashed to the floor, choking me in a whirlwind of book dust. The noise was loud enough to wake the Book of the Dead, but the weasel-faced librarian didn't return to admonish me. Must be her crazy break.

Swiping my hand in front of my face, I cleared the air, only to discover a book as old as time itself. Or at least it looked that old. Smelled that old too. Sort of like that elderly lady with all those kids who resided in size-eight housing.

I picked up the book, examining the cover. The text had no title, only the imprint of a paw and the name de Wolfe etched in the worn leather.

Cracking open the book, I choked on years of dust

mites and papyrus. Tiny lettering greeted my bruised eyes in an Old English font with lots of Thous, Thees, and Yeas. Oh Yea!

I skipped the foreword (does anyone really read them?), past the early years of Maledetto history (yawn), and into the last century. The de Wolfe name appeared prominently. In fact, it appeared every fifth word or so, sort of like Old MacDonald's manifesto, but without the racial slurs. Then, about fifty pages and years later, the name Nigel de Wolfe finally graced the yellowed pages of the book in my hand.

With the final clue to solving Cinderella's murder hidden inside the book, I plopped down on the reference desk, popped open a beer, and began to read a story as old as time itself, filled with revenge, love, lies, and the occasional reference to lusting after one's mother.

What was wrong with royalty?

Chapter 29

The following morning, bleary eyed and stinking of hops, dust, and knowledge, I stumbled through the front door of Prince Charming's bungalow. My brain swirled with clues, some of which made no sense. Okay, most of which made no sense. Like the fact the current king wasn't the original heir to the throne. His older brother, Prince Nigel de Wolfe, was, until one fateful day when Nigel and his little brother went into the woods to fetch, as near as I could tell, a pail of water. Nigel apparently fell down and broke his crown, after being shot in the chest. The king came tumbling after, scooped up the broken crown, duct-taped it together, and presto, long live the new king.

There were whispered suspicions and accusations of foul play, but no one came forward. They must've been chicken. For the most part, though, the kingdom rejoiced at Nigel's passing. Dear old Nigel wasn't well liked by friend and foe alike. The old tome suggested Nigel was actually madder than the Hatter and smelled worse than the Cheshire Cat, not to mention his proclivity toward siring offspring like a Catholic school rabbit.

But what did it all mean?

I wasn't sure, but one thing was clear.

The rabbit hole went deeper than I first imagined.

The book provided a big clue, however, in the form of an artist's rendering of Nigel de Wolfe. The image captured de Wolfe's arrogance perfectly. Nigel looked like royalty, his face tilted toward the heavens as his white-blond hair flowed around his broad shoulders, his tail wagging in the wind.

Nigel looked familiar, as if I'd recently seen him.

Inside the palace.

Nigel de Wolfe, former prince of Maledetto, currently graced the tiled floor of the palace library, his white blond hair wrapped around a set of rollers, his broad shoulders and shaggy tail hidden inside a flowered housecoat.

The Big Bad one himself, the king said.

I guess it was true.

I had two theories as to why Nigel de Wolfe's signature was on the bluebird receipt. Either Nigel de Wolfe had mastered the art of reincarnation, or someone had used his identity and his fur . . . coat to commit murder.

And that someone had easy access to the palace, which left me with about a couple thousand suspects, including my sweet, murderous princess. Damn.

With the exception of my unscheduled and brain-damaging . . . naps, I hadn't slept in twenty-four hours. I was exhausted, burned out, and ready to call it quits. This detecting shit was for the bluebirds. I was no closer, was in fact further from solving Cinderella's murder than I had been yesterday. Damn Miss Muffet and her nimble fingers. Without the bluebird receipt, even if I unmasked the killer, I couldn't prove it.

Like lack of evidence had ever stopped a villain before. Remember that trial with the ill-fitting mitten? Those kittens got away with murder according to their recently released biography, *BTW, I Did It!*

Yawning, I staggered inside Charming's bungalow. The soft sound of snoring filtered through the house. Prince Rotten dreamed the dreams of the moronic while I spent hours searching for his fiancée's killer. Which one of us was the idiot?

As I closed the front door, a tiny slippered foot with a bell on top wedged itself between the door and frame. The door flew back open, smacking me in the head with a dull thud.

"Ow!" I rubbed at the newly formed bump that matched perfectly with the four or so other dents I'd recently acquired. With all the new lumps and bruises, I was starting to resemble the ugly duckling before all the plastic surgery.

"What the heck?" I said to the dwarf standing in the doorway. He wore green tights and a green and red jester collar. The outfit should've looked cute, but instead, he looked down on his Rice Krispied luck.

Snapped, as I'd nicknamed him, shoved a clipboard full of papers at me. "Sign here," he said in a high-pitched squeak.

I glanced down at the paper, my eyes too blurry to read the first line. "Fine, but if you're the devil bargaining for my soul, I don't come cheap."

Snapped pointed to a patch on his shirt. "Fey-Ex. Rain, sleet, snow, the dark of night, I'll get your package there in thirty years or less."

"A point of pride, I see."

Snapped pressed the clipboard toward me once again. "Just sign by the X."

I did so with a flourish reserved for parking tickets and autographs at the airport. Snapped barely glanced at my signature when I handed the clipboard back. "So where's this package?" I asked.

"It's on the truck," he said.

"Okay."

He frowned. "It's pretty big."

"Uh-huh."

He rolled his tiny eyes. "Heavy too."

"Oh," I said. "You better lift with your legs, then."

"Stupid . . . villain . . . ," Snapped muttered as he turned on his heel and headed to a white truck barely big enough to fit a unicorn. The words "Fey-Ex" covered the side in large red lettering.

Rather than wait for his return, I strolled into the kitchen to make a cup of coffee. If I was to survive the day, I needed caffeine, and lots of it. As the smell of boiling coffee beans filled the air, Snapped returned with a cardboard box half his size. The dramatic dwarf grunted under the weight as he hefted it onto the kitchen table.

"Well, here it is. Came all the way from the Orient," he said, reading the delivery slip affixed to the top of the box.

The Orient, huh? I'd always wanted to visit, but never found the time. A villain's work was never done.

"It sure was heavy," he said, his tiny pink Vienna sausage–like fingers wiggling expectantly.

I slapped him a high five. "Thanks."

He frowned and then frowned some more. Finally, he turned for the door, his belled feet jingling all the way.

"Hey, wait a second," I called.

"Yeah?" He quickly turned around, his hand extended for a tip.

"Close the door on your way out," I said, pouring a cup of coffee into Charming's World's Greatest Prince mug. What a tool. Like anyone would give him an award. Try to kill him in his sleep, yes, an award, not so much.

Hell, I bet the jerk bought the mug for himself.

The front door slammed shut, reminding me of the mysterious cardboard box. I assumed the delivery was for Charming, but what if it wasn't? What if the package was the king's "signal," or better yet, my subscription to *Sprites Illustrated,* the Nymph Issue? I set my coffee down and picked up the box. The damn thing wasn't that heavy, maybe two stone. Attached to the box was an envelope.

I opened it and read the words aloud: "To a villain among princes." I glanced toward the staircase where Prince Rotten slept. Yep, that was me, a villain smothered by a flaming prince.

Grabbing a knife from the kitchen drawer, I peeled back the edge of the packing tape. The sticky residue clung to the edge of the knife. The faint sound of ticking reached my ears.

A bad sign on the best of days.

Snapped was right. The package was from Asia, just not the continent. Damn it! I chucked the box toward the door. The room exploded into a wall of blue flames, licking at everything in its path, including me. My Levi's quickly ignited, aided by my chicken dance around the room.

"Hot . . . hot . . . hot . . . ," I muttered, flapping my arms, which only enraged the flames. My skin bubbled underneath my smoldering clothes, smelling faintly of roasted villain and marshmallows. Overhead, a fire alarm blared the chorus to "It's Raining Men."

Get out of the house, my mind screamed.

Through the thickening black smoke, I found the front door, half my body consumed in a fireball. Like a ballerina after one too many drinks, I did a jerky pirouette off the front porch and onto the dew-soaked lawn. I dropped and rolled, but forgot the most important part. I failed to stop. Instead, I rolled onto the middle of the street. A Fey-Ex truck bore down on me as Prince Rotten chased me around, beating me with a wooden spoon.

". . . twit . . . house . . . fire . . . idiot," Charming yelled, emphasizing each word with a paddle to my skull.

In the distance, a siren screamed, moving closer and closer. But it was too late. Charming's bungalow was now a towering inferno. I, on the other hand, had stopped smoking like a kielbasa. Thanks in part to my new best friend, Snapped, and his Fey-Ex truck. When the truck struck me the first time, it smothered the flames with its tiny tires, but not completely.

Blue flames flickered up my boots, threatening to ignite the unblackened patches of skin left on my thighs. Being a pal, Snapped shoved the truck into reverse and backed over my flaming body once again.

Disaster adverted.

Or so I thought until Snapped's Fey-Ex truck engine again revved in my ear. That was my last coherent thought before, like the sky, my world turned black.

Chapter 30

I awoke sometime later wearing nothing but a pair of boxer shorts. I wasn't sure where I was, or how I got there. The last thing I remembered was the grinning face of a determined yet demented dwarf bearing down on me.

However, one thing was sure. Wherever I was, I wasn't alone. Asia's body lay curled behind me, her silken hair tickling my bare back. For some reason, she smelled different, as if she'd recently started smoking. A nasty habit, but one I could accept. It beat her constantly trying to murder me.

I yawned and rubbed a hand over my face. The fire had singed my facial hair, leaving patches of five o'clock shadow. But all in all, I survived the fire fairly unscathed. Too bad I couldn't say the same about being run down or my princely smackdown. Adding to my list of previous complaints, my ribs now ached and my nose curved to the right. Too bad the fake detective business, like the union, didn't offer medical insurance.

Holding my breath, I pinched my nostrils and snapped the cartilage in my nose back in place. The pain brought tears to my eyes, but I held my screams in check, afraid to wake my sleeping princess hidden beneath the covers.

Mostly for fear she'd try to smother me with a pillow.

The bedroom was dark, but it didn't take me long to recognize it as Cinderella's much-too-pink room. I slowly sat up, checking each body part. Everything seemed to be in working order. Some parts more so than others. I turned to Asia, running my hand down her downy-covered leg. She let out a loud snort.

"Sweetheart," I began, slowly pulling down the comforter. I stopped mid-much-too-broad-shoulder and screamed. "Ah-hhhh!"

"Ahhhhh!" Prince Charming echoed.

"What the hell are you doing?" I dropped the blanket as if it was infected with princely cooties. Which it was.

Like a true Southern belle, Charming shielded his body with the sheet in one hand and fanned his face with the other. "I was sleeping," he said. "What's got your panties in a bunch?"

"My panties?" I yelled. "Men don't wear panties.... Oh, never mind.... What are you doing here?" My fist waved to the bed, where up until two minutes ago, I'd innocently slept while Charming spooned me. Bile rose up my throat. It wasn't like I was homophobic, but damn it, if I was gay I could do a hell of a lot better than Charming.

"After you burned my house down," he said with a frown and released the blanket in his hand, flashing me his hairless, gym-sculpted chest. It reminded me of a rat without fur. What had Asia seen in this doofus? He continued, unaware of my assessment, "The king and queen graciously took us in."

"Be that as it may," I stalked to the opposite side of the darkened room, "it fails to explain why, out of the two hundred or so bedrooms in the palace, you ended up in *this* bed. And not, say, in bed with Dru, the woman you're about to marry?"

He shivered. "Ew."

"If you find Princess Dru so repulsive," which I really couldn't blame the guy for, "then why marry her?"

He rolled his eyes. "It's what a prince does. We marry princesses. Duh."

As much as I wanted to shake the idiot prince, my need to pee outweighed our ridiculous conversation. First, I needed to set him straight. Well, as straight as a musical-spouting, lacy pirate shirt–wearing prince could get. "Listen," I started. "I appreciate your hospitality. And I'm sorry about your house, but the next time I find you within ten feet of my bed, I'll break you into tiny prince pieces and feed you to a bluebird. Got it?"

I didn't wait for his response. Instead, I yanked open the bedroom door, nearly colliding with Winslow, who was eavesdropping at the door. The troll-like butler's hair stood on end in contrast to his perfectly starched tuxedo.

"Sir," Winslow said, straightening from his spying crouch. "I was just . . ."

I held up my hand. "Whatever. I need a shower." I motioned to the Charming-filled bed. "Maybe two. Do you think you could rustle me up some clothes?"

"Of course, sir." Winslow bowed. "Right away."

"I wouldn't mind a cup of hot cocoa. And some whipped cream. Cherries if you have them," Charming called out from the bedroom.

Winslow glared at the prince, spun on his heel, and headed down the corridor, his boots echoing against the hard wood floor.

"Don't forget the marshmallows," Charming yelled to the retreating butler, who muttered something akin to "I hope you choke on it, you selfish twit."

Charming turned to me. "What'd I do?"

I shook my head and limped to the bathroom at the end of the gold-lined hallway, passing photograph after photograph of the Maledetto family. The king's smiling face caught my eye. He sat on his throne, his arm around Asia's sour-faced mother. The happy couple looked anything but. What had possessed the king to marry Asia's mother?

In the next photograph, a teenaged Cinderella stood on the king's right, looking angelic in a white dress. Dru knelt at the king's feet, her eyebrow covering most of her face. Asia stood behind the throne, beautiful as always, if slightly overweight. She didn't look happy. In fact, no one in the picture did.

With one disgusting exception.

Prince Fucking Charming.

He stood on the king's left, dressed in military blues, a sword in his hand. The smile on his face matched the king's. The picture was at least ten years old, but Charming looked the same as he did today. Minus the sword, of course. The nameplate under the portrait read: THE MALE-DETTO FAMILY.

If those were my relatives, I'd ask to be disowned. Poor Asia, stuck with this group of clueless morons as family. I smiled at the photograph, vowing to save Asia from her family as well as any other curse she could throw at me.

My fingers brushed Asia's two-dimensional face. I missed my princess, and thankfully, she had missed me too. Three times to date. Either my princess had really bad luck or she didn't truly want me dead. I could live with that.

"Better aim next time, my sweet." I smiled, pressing a two-fingered kiss to the picture. I was one badass villain, able to defy death and my murderous princess in a single bound.

Nothing fazed me.

Except . . . a naked Prince Idiot admiring his butt in front of Cinderella's full-length mirror. I shuddered and limped faster down the hallway.

Chapter 31

The icy water of the shower pounded my bruised body, stinging in places I only dreamed existed. Who knew the skin on your elbow could hurt? The stench of smoke and singed villain faded under the sweet scent of lilac soap. I scrubbed my hair twice, watching a swirl of ash disappear down the drain. When I couldn't take the chill a second longer, I turned off the water and reached for a towel.

"Thanks," I murmured to the towel rack.

"You're welcome," Dru uttered back.

"Ahhhh!" I shouted, admittedly in Dru's ugly face. She recoiled, nearly tripping over her feet as she jumped back. I reached out to steady her, my towel dropping as I did so, showing off an array of freshly singed pubic hair. Not my best look. Didn't anyone in this palace know how to knock?

"Sorry," I said, releasing her and scooping the towel back into place. "You startled me."

"I brought you some clothes." She motioned to a pair of Levi's and a black sweatshirt, freshly pressed and smelling of urinal cakes, sitting on the vanity. A pair of white boxer briefs lay on top next to my empty, charred wallet.

"Ummm . . . thanks," I ventured again. "I'll just be getting dressed, then . . ." Dru stood there, not getting the hint, a clueless smile on her lips. I tried again. "Did you need something?"

She shook her head.

"Go wait in the hall," I ordered, shoving her toward the door with one hand.

"Good idea." She nodded as if I'd solved a great mystery. For the briefest of seconds, I felt sorry for Prince Rotten. He went from fiancée perfection in the form of Asia to the moronic Dru in a matter of six months. One fiancée dead, one a possible murder suspect, and the other quite possibly a moron. Bad odds even in Cin City.

My sympathy for His Annoyingness was short-lived, however, replaced by an all-consuming rage. Was that a hickey on my shoulder blade? I spun around to check and slipped on the puddle of water at my feet. My head smacked the sink and little bluebirds rose in my vision.

It took me a few seconds to realize the bluebirds were real and invading the bathroom via an open window. A window that was closed when I first entered the shower. Did Dru open it? Was this another assassination attempt by Asia?

I scrambled to my feet, yanking the shower curtain from the rod with a whoosh. My fingers slipped on the wet curtain, but I held tight, using it like a matador's cape as I shepherded the annoyed birds to the open window. "Toro! Toro!" I shouted, sweeping the birds outside.

"Did you call me?" Dru poked her head inside the door only to be bombarded with a flock of rampaging bluebirds. Her shrieks reverberated around the bathroom, deafening me. I dropped the shower curtain and stuffed my hands over my ears.

"Stop it," I yelled.

She did, but only when her eyes rolled back into her head and she fainted. I tried to catch her before she hit the ground, but again, I slipped, landing naked and facedown on the tile. The unconscious princess fell on top of me, her lips parted, her face flushed. I grunted under her weight. Of course, Winslow appeared in the doorway at that precise moment. His upper lip started to quiver.

"It's not what it looks like," I said. The understatement of the year. Winslow wasn't paying me any attention, though. His gaze was fixed on his not-so-smart princess.

"What did you do to her?" he asked, his voice thick with tears and accusations. "My poor sweet maiden."

"Nothing." I lifted an unconscious Dru off me, placed her on the floor, and staggered to my feet. "The bluebirds"—I gestured to the now bluebird free bathroom—"they came in . . . Dru . . . she—"

"The king shall hear of your debauchery!" Winslow raised his fist. As far as threats went, it wasn't the best one. What would the king do? The man couldn't even kill his wife.

I held up my own hand. "Relax, Winslow. Nothing happened. Dru is still as pure and stupid as snow." And she'd stay that way if she married Charming. Talk about a waste of a wedding night.

Winslow frowned, as if unsure what to believe, his own eyes on my naked, hickey-riddled body. Dru made the decision for him. She awoke, her eyes fluttering like a fly stuck to a wad of flypaper, or in her case, a huge furry eyebrow.

"What happened?" she asked Winslow.

"Are you all right, my lady?" He knelt down next to her, fanning her face with his hand. "Shall I summon the king's physician?"

"No, no. That's not necessary." She took Winslow's hand and he helped her to her feet. "I must've fainted. Too much excitement. You know, with the wedding and all," she said, sounding forlorn.

My eyes went to hers. Did Dru really want to marry Charming? Third Maledetto sister's a charm, right? Up until a second ago, I was sure Dru wanted to marry the idiot prince, but now...I cleared my throat to gain Winslow's attention. He glanced up in question. I nodded to Dru. "Right. The wedding. How are the wedding plans going?"

Dru sighed. "Charming is handling everything."

Of course he was. He'd probably dreamed of his wedding day since he was a wee lad in lace diapers. He'd probably already picked out the perfect dress. I tilted my head to the side. "Is that what you want, Dru? A man who handles you?"

Dru's lips curved into a frown, causing her furry brow to wrinkle even deeper. "I used to think so."

"But?"

"But," she paused, her face growing red, "I want roses! Red ones. And a chocolate fountain! I want...I want..."

"Yes?" Winslow asked, hope filling his tone for the first time.

"A pony!"

"And you deserve a pony." I nodded encouragingly. "Okay, then. Go out there and tell the prince exactly that. Tell him that unless you get roses, a chocolate fountain, and a pony you won't marry him!"

"Damn straight!" Dru nodded to a shocked Winslow and marched out of the bathroom in search of her Prince Charming.

Winslow looked at me and grinned. "Thank you, sir."

"Don't mention it." I patted his shoulder. "Just remember, though, when you and Dru finally do hook up, you'd better buy a pony-sized litter box."

He agreed and turned on his heel to follow Dru down the hall. Her shouts for the suddenly hard-to-find prince echoed from three floors below.

Served Prince Rotten right. That would show him not to give unexpected/unwanted hickeys to random houseguests. I rubbed at the hickey on my shoulder. A smudge of cocoa flaked away under the pressure of my thumb. Oops.

I laughed, pulling on a pair of pants, and headed down the stairs to restart my investigation into Cinderella's murder.

My investigation took me to the far corners of the Maledetto palace, namely, the library. I opened the double doors, surprised to see that nothing had changed since my last visit. The room still smelled of dog hair and dust. Nigel de Wolfe's pelt still lay on the floor, eyes blank, teeth as sharp as ever.

Stepping inside the library, I crept across the carpet and knelt next to Nigel's pelt. The wolf appeared dead, but I wasn't taking any chances. I jabbed my finger into Nigel's left eye. When nothing happened I proceeded to examine my scene of the crime.

First, I turned the pelt over and opened his striped housecoat. Poor old Nigel had a slit cut from his sternum to pelvis. Talk about being neutered. With my hands, I measured the dimensions of the pelt. A full-grown person might fit inside.

A skinny full-grown person.

I decided to test my theory and shoved my head inside the fur coat. The pelt fit like the kitten's mitten, in that whoever had worn it to buy Gretel the bluebird had gotten away with murder too. But not for long. I would find him, her, or them, and once I did . . . well, I'd cross that troll bridge when I came to it.

I stood staggering under the weight of the pelt before righting myself. The fur smelled faintly of bacon. That reminded me that I hadn't eaten in nearly twenty-four hours. My stomach let out a ferocious growl.

Boom!

A splatter of buckshot slammed into Nigel's pelt, knocking me backward. "Ahhhh!" I yelped. In hindsight, it sounded more like a growl, which explained the next volley of shotgun pellets. My wolf-proof armor stopped most of the shrapnel, but a few bits sliced through, flaying my flesh beneath. The rock salt pellets burned like trying to pee after a one-night stand with Snow White.

"You lecherous bastard. I'll show you," my would-be assassin the king said. The click of another round of salt loaded into a shotgun reverberated around the room.

"Stop," I said. "Winslow lied. I didn't touch Dru. She came into the bathroom while I was naked, and she fainted. That's all that happened. I swear I didn't touch her." When I found the turncoat butler, I'd sure as hell touch him. A lot!

"What?" the king shouted.

I poked my head out. "What, what?"

"Oh, it's you," the king exclaimed, his hand clutching his heart. "You scared me, son. I thought Nigel had risen from the dead to take his revenge against me for shoo—" The king's hand flew to his mouth. "I mean . . . What's this about Dru?"

"Not important now." I waved my hand in dismissal. "What's this about revenge?"

The king let out a loud, drawn-out sigh. "Well, son, since you're almost family, I can tell you a thing or two about the Maledetto history." Son? Family? I had my doubts the old man even remembered my name. Not that I wanted anything to do with the king or the rest of his crazy clan, with the exception of Asia and her murderous, naked ways. I had my own family to deal with; I didn't need to add the Maledetto lunatics to the genetic mix.

The king continued, ignoring the look of absolute horror on my face, "You see, son, I never expected to be king. My parents died when I was a wee lad."

"I'm sorry for your loss."

"Why?" The king frowned and patted his shotgun. "Did you kill them?"

"Of course not."

"Then why did you claim you did? It's rude."

"What?"

"Never mind." The king shook his head. "As I was saying before you interrupted, King de Wolfe took me in and raised me as his own second son. Nigel, my big brother, was to wear this crown." The king pointed to his empty head.

"Um, sir?" I said.

"What now?!"

I considered not saying a word, but my cursed tongue won out. "You're not wearing a crown."

"Blast it," he said, dropping his shotgun onto the couch, and ran from the room in search of his wayward crown. I closed my eyes and shook my head. How did Asia stand her family? Either they were the dumbest group of people in the universe, or somewhere in the tangled roots of this family tree, brother and sister fell in love. I was betting on incest. Stupidity seemed like too much of a coincidence.

I picked up the king's abandoned shotgun, unloaded it, and kicked it under the couch. Didn't these people know guns were dangerous? Hell, in the last week I'd been shot at least twice.

I rubbed at my latest flesh wound on my arm. Blood trickled from the cut. I wiped it away with the edge of Nigel's pelt and sighed. I couldn't wait to leave Maledetto once and for all, with Asia of course, and never look back. Not even around the holidays. If Asia got homesick, I'd simply jam a shotgun in her face and talk like a homeless dude with a tinfoil cap.

The king came flying back into the library, a jewel-encrusted crown on his head. He collapsed onto the couch, panting. "Sorry 'bout that. I thought I'd lost it."

Oh, he certainly had.

I smiled and motioned for the king to continue with his tale about the old king. Once he finally caught his breath, he did. "When I was twelve, King de Wolfe and his queen mysteriously died. Some say it was the plague. Others think the large ax protruding from Lady Maledetto's head killed them."

A reasonable assumption.

"After their deaths, Nigel took control of the crown." The way he said it made me wonder if Nigel controlled more than the kingdom. The king added, "Then three years later, the kingdom in shambles due to Nigel's lecherous deals, I became king."

I tilted my head to the side and sat down on the couch next to the king. "More to it than that, wasn't there?"

"Was there? I don't really remember."

"From what I've heard, you shot Nigel. In the back."

The king shrugged. "Well, that might've happened too. But it was an accident . . . We went for a hunt . . . The gun went off . . . No need for revenge."

"Revenge?" I paused to consider this. Was Cinderella's murder an act of revenge? I suppose that made sense, but by who? Unless I failed Health for Villains 101, Nigel de Wolfe wasn't the culprit. So who was?

"With his dying breath, Nigel swore he'd come back from the grave for revenge." The king shuddered, his grey beard jiggling with fear. "Until my poor Cindi's death, I didn't believe it."

I raised my eyebrow. "And you do now?"

He nodded. "Who else would kill my precious daughter?" His voice lowered to a whisper, "Dru, that I could understand. The girl's just plain stupid. But Cindi? She was an angel. Why, Nigel? Why?"

"Nigel isn't back from the dead, sir."

"How do you know?"

At this point I figured it was fairly obvious. I mean, Nigel's pelt was lying under our feet. I gestured to the floor. The king frowned. I motioned harder to the de Wolfe rug. The king frowned harder. Fuck it. "Never mind," I said, rising from the couch.

"Wait," the king called.

"Yeah?"

"Have you seen my shotgun?" The king glanced around the room. "I seem to have misplaced it."

"Nope," I lied with ease and left the room, whistling the theme song from *Pinocchio*.

Chapter 32

The ramifications of my white lie didn't hit me until ten minutes later when Cook handed me a plate of scrambled eggs and half a loaf of buttered toast. I had to admit it; I told a lie. And it felt damn good. Maybe my curse was finally fading.

"Well, well, if it isn't the infamous RJ," the queen said from the kitchen doorway, her red hair shining like fire in the morning light. "Do me a favor, dear. Sit down."

"Fudge," I muttered, doing as the queen ordered. I guess my luck hadn't changed after all. "Yes, my lady."

The queen swept into the room, her long skirt flapping back and forth against her slim calves. With a much too regal air for ten in the morning, she planted herself next to me at the table. I doubted she'd ever sat at Cook's table, let alone entered the kitchen before. "Isn't this nice," she said, her face contorted with disgust.

At the stove, Cook, a bull-faced woman with a heart of lard, frowned. I raised a fork full of fluffy yellow eggs in salute. "Great breakfast." After eating Humpty Dumpty, a plate full of non-breathing eggs tasted like heaven. I smiled at the memory of Asia and her frying pan. Was it really less than a week since we met? A week since she'd boldly pilfered my curry noodles? A week since she walked into my life and turned it sunny side up?

"I wanted to speak with you about my dear one," the queen said, gaining my attention. Here it comes. The dreaded "don't lock my daughter away in a tower" speech. If I'd heard it once, I'd heard it 651 times. Well, 652 times if you counted Tweedledum and her cuter sister Dee separately.

I held up a hand. "Listen, I know what you're going to say, and yes, I'd like nothing more than to lock Asia away—"

"Asia?" The queen's brow puckered, surprising with all the Botox injected into her unlined face. "What does she have to do with this?"

"Excuse me?" My own forehead creased in confusion, not a good look on a villain, especially one with singed eyebrows and nine dents in his head. "You weren't talking about your daughter?"

"Of course not. I wanted to discuss Charming."

Oh God. I'd rather discuss the boil on Goldilocks's butt. "Sure," my treacherous mouth said. "What's up?"

Smiling, the queen tapped my arm. "Tomorrow's the wedding."

As if I didn't already know. There were white tents, white flowers, and white lace everywhere. So either a wedding or a Klan rally was about to take place. I'm not sure which one I'd enjoy less.

"And I want everything to be perfect," the queen continued. "That means having proper nuptials."

"Winslow lied. I never touched your daughter. At least not Dru," I said, springing from the table. My frothy glass of milk toppled, landing in the queen's lap. We both froze, me in fear, her in rage. Cook scrambled across the kitchen, a roll of paper towels in her hands.

"Oh God." I dabbed at the wetness with my sleeve. "I'm so sorry, my lady."

Rather than clouting me upside the head, the queen sucked in her thin lips and smiled. "Quite all right. Please sit back down." Her face pinched from the sheer will of not exploding into a shrieking rage.

I bit my lip to keep from grinning and sat down again while Cook cleaned up the spilled milk. I wasn't about to cry over it, but the laughter in Cook's eyes suggested she might.

"Let's cut to the chase," the queen said. "I want you to throw the prince a bachelor party. Tonight."

"What?!" I shook my head. I'd rather stab a fork through my eye. "Why? I don't even like the guy."

Her eyes narrowed to slits. "It's the least you can do. After all, you burned down his house."

"Did not. That was Asi—"

"Let's not play the blame game." Again, the queen patted my arm. This time with enough force to leave a bruise. "Charming deserves a bachelor party, and since you're his only friend, I expect you to give him one."

Friend? Ew. I wanted to argue, but my cursed brain refused to let me. The queen had asked me for a favor and now I was stuck. Stupid union.

"It wasn't easy for him growing up in the kingdom." The queen shot me a vague smile. "Kids can be cruel. They called him names. Didn't want to be his friend."

That I could understand. After all, the idiot prince was annoying as that song that never ends, but still I felt sorry for him. I knew, perhaps better than anyone did, how painful loneliness could be to a child.

"Will you do this? For that little lonely prince?"

"But . . . I . . . shoot," I said, feeling sorry for the kid and myself. I did owe the guy, after all. "I'll throw him a party."

The queen nodded, satisfied. I wanted to shoot her and then myself. What did I get myself into? I should've left Maledetto before any of this started. Asia sure as hell didn't want me here.

So why was I hanging around? I didn't even know Cinderella, and I doubt I would've liked her had I met her. So why was I sticking around, throwing His Annoyingness a bachelor party, in order to solve Cinderella's murder? I pictured Asia's face as we stood over the chalk outline of Cinderella's flattened body. She had looked so sad, and so beautiful. My chest started to burn in the space just left of my sternum. Damn eggs.

"You're a good man," the queen said, breaking me from my memories. "Asia could do worse. I mean, with her problems a girl can't be too choosy."

"Ummm . . . thanks," I said. "I think."

The queen was wrong. Asia could do a lot better than me, curse or not. She was perfection on the inside and out, even if she did want me dead. That reminded me of a question I wanted to ask the queen. "Why did you give the Devil's Eye to Cinderella and not to your own cursed daughter?"

For the first time, real emotion, shock most likely, entered the queen's eyes. "How'd you know about that?"

"Charming told me." I paused, watching her unwrinkled face. "He said you gave it to Cinderella as a wedding gift."

"I did."

"But why? Asia was the one with the curse. You knew that. Why would you give it to someone else? Didn't you want Asia to be free?"

A long sigh escaped the queen's lips. "Free?" She gave a harsh laugh. "Do you know what it's like to be married? Do you have any clue what it takes to be a wife? I spend my every waking hour caring for my family. Cooking, cleaning." From behind the queen, Cook let out a loud snort. I grinned, but the queen ignored us.

The queen added, "It's almost too much."

Unfortunately I knew all about marriage. I also knew what it felt like to be handcuffed to a bedpost, dipped in Jell-O, and licked clean by angry nymphs.

We all had our crosses to bear.

"Cinderella wasn't strong like Asia." The queen wiped an affected tear from her eye. "I could only save one of them, so I made a choice . . ." Her voice caught in Oscar-winning fashion.

I rolled my eyes, hating the queen almost as much as I hated Charming. Both thought only of themselves, sort of like Jack B. Nimble in bed. "So you 'saved' Cinderella? From what? Marrying your dear Prince Charming? I find that hard to believe."

"They weren't right for each other." The queen's face hardened, as much as it could. "It was obvious to everyone else. The Devil's Eye merely showed Cinderella the truth."

"You wanted Cinderella to dump the prince?"

The queen shook her head. "Not dump. I want him to be happy, which he could never be with someone like her . . ."

"Like her?" What? Did Cinderella have fleas?

"Unstable," she whispered, glancing around the kitchen as if spilling a kingdom secret. "Like her mother. Cinderella had some mental problems. Did you know that daft woman tried to kill me?"

"Cinderella?"

"No, no. The other one." The queen motioned toward the library where the portrait of Cinderella's mother sat. "The first Lady Maledetto. She was a piece of work. . . ."

Like the second Lady Maledetto was much of a prize. The king could sure pick them. "You knew Cinderella's mother? I thought she died before you and the king . . . hooked up." I shivered at the thought of those two having sex. Bumping uglies was right.

"She did."

"Okay," I said. "So how'd she try to kill you?"

"Using the king, of course."

I rose from the table and began to pace. I wondered if

the Maledetto insanity was the catchy kind. "The king?" I exhaled loudly. "Fine. Cinderella's dead mother tried to kill you with a king. It all makes sense now."

"No need for sarcasm." The queen rose as well. "I fell in love with the king as soon as our eyes met."

Fell in love with his wealth sounded more like it.

"He felt the same, so we married. I gained a daughter and my daughters gained a father. We were so happy at the beginning. He'd buy me anything I wanted. Furs, jewels, henchmen named Tim to cater to my fondest wish."

Tim? What self-respecting henchman went by Tim?

"We lived happily ever after...until..." The queen began to sniff, tears welling in her endless blue eyes like a shimmering pond. I half expected the Frog Prince to make an appearance. "Until the curse."

"Asia's curse?"

The queen shook her head. "No. The other one."

There was another curse? Jesus, what did these people do, piss off every witch, fairy godmother, and troll in the land? Hell, I'd decapitated a witch once and the most I got was a case of Montezuma's revenge. "What other curse?" I asked with a sigh even though I knew I'd regret it.

"On her deathbed, the first Lady Maledetto cursed the king." The queen frowned, her eyes sparkling with pent-up rage. "By her word, he would never find happiness with the next Lady of Maledetto."

"And?"

"So the king tried to smother me with a pillow." She bit her lip. "He claims it was an 'accident,' but I know better."

"Why would he kill you? He's already cursed to live un-happily ever after."

"No, you misunderstand." She grabbed my hand and squeezed. "If he rids himself of me, he rids himself of the curse. Therefore the next woman he marries will be the next-next Lady of Maledetto. And he'll live happily ever after. For real."

I nodded. "That explains the poison and the bricks, I suppose. Instead of waiting around for the king to kill you, you've taken the high road and plan to kill him first."

"Of course, dear." The queen smiled. "That's what marriage is all about."

I couldn't have said it better myself.

Chapter 33

I watched Lady Maledetto walk out of the kitchen door as Dru ran down the staircase, her black eyebrow flapping in the breeze. She paused at the bottom step, her eyes met mine, and she let out a shriek.

"Dru?" I ran to the hallway. "Are you all right?"

"I'm getting married tomorrow."

"Congratulations?"

"Is Winslow here?" She glanced down the corridor and frowned. "I need to talk to him . . . about the wedding."

"I haven't seen him."

Tears welled in her eyes.

"I'll go find him," I said, and then without pausing to hear her response, I shoved the front door wide and ran down the steps. Last thing I needed was a weepy princess. It was bad enough I had to throw a bachelor party for a whiny prince.

I searched the palace grounds for Winslow without any luck. I did see the king, though. He was in the toolshed building what looked like a rocket. I motioned to the red and white striped weapon. "Rats again?"

The king nodded, looking overly pleased with himself. So pleased that I knew without a doubt this would not end well. I made a mental note to invest in "blown up by an idiot king" insurance.

"Good luck with that," I said and slowly backed out of the shed. My quest for Winslow continued. I jogged down the palace path, careful to avoid a stream of workers preparing for the upcoming nuptials, and into the dense forest.

Overhead an owl hooted, sounding like a warning bell. Time was running out. I was in too deep and no closer to solving Cinderella's murder. Even worse, I had started to care what happened to the crazed Maledetto clan.

"Winslow?" I called into the thick underbrush.

No answer.

I walked farther into the darkness, pausing as I came upon a small wooden bridge, the perfect size for a moping troll-faced butler. I peeked underneath. "Aha!" I shouted.

No Winslow.

Damn. I straightened only to bash my noggin into the railing. I rubbed at the newest dent in my head, and then glared at the offending railing. Tiny letters floated in my vision. I blinked. Something was carved into the wooden bridge in a familiar scrawl. I peered closer. Yep, the same handwriting from the paper in Cinderella's room sat scratched in the wood. It read: *Star light, star bright, how I wish for a prince tonight.*

Ew.

I frowned. Was the handwriting on the bridge also the same as the handwriting on the bluebird receipt? They seemed alike. But why would Cinderella buy a bluebird that eventually killed her? And if Cinderella was in fact my mysterious ornithologist, who was Hansel blackmailing?

Asia's smiling face popped to mind. I quickly wiped it away. I needed more than a couple of scraps of paper and a vandal to believe Asia killed anyone, let alone her sister. She had it in her, no doubt, but it took real balls to stand there and lie to me, a villain trained in the art of deception.

From the direction of the palace, a loud wail erupted. Dru. Damn, I still needed to find Winslow for her. With one last glance at the bridge, I set out on my original quest for the troll-like butler.

An hour later I arrived at the pond where I first encountered the aforementioned ugliest stepsister, Dru. This time, though, the pond was empty. A few toads croaked at me looking lonely, a bit horny, and forlorn.

"Tell me about it," I said.

"I've lost her," a voice croaked from behind a large oak tree. "Dru. My lovely Dru."

"Winslow?" I asked, hoping it was him and not a suicidal toad bemoaning Dru's upcoming nuptials. Taking a chance, I walked around the tree, shocked at the sight that greeted me. The normally well-dressed, perfect butler looked like death. His tailored suit hung in tatters off his body. Drips of snot leaked down his lapel. The Don King patch of hair on his head bent to the left, making him look like a lopsided elf.

Lost in his grief, he didn't hear my approach. "Winslow," I said again, careful not to startle him. "You okay, buddy?"

His bleak eyes met mine. I nodded with an understanding only a man who lost everything knew. Thankfully my grief was affected, since I held out hope Asia eventually would come around. I also had faith in the strength of duct tape if she didn't.

"He said okay," Winslow whispered through a mouthful of snot. "Why would he say okay?"

"Who?"

"Charming. Dru made her ridiculous demands and the bastard prince said yes. I don't understand. He doesn't love her. How could he?"

How could he was right, but now wasn't the time to bring up Dru's list of flaws. Mostly because I didn't have the time and the list was so freaking long. But Winslow had a point.

Again I wondered why marrying a Maledetto princess

was so bloody important to Prince Rotten. Sure, marrying Dru placed Charming a heartbeat from the throne, but so what? When Asia married, the fact was moot anyway. Her husband would be first in line for the throne. There had to be more to it.

"Why?" Winslow shouted to the sky. "My sweet, wonderful lady. I should've told her how I felt, but now it's too late. I've lost her forever."

I smacked Winslow in the forehead, to gain his attention, sure, but mostly because it felt damn good. "Knock it off." I smacked him again. "Don't be such a drama queen."

"Ow!" he cried. So I hit him again.

"You haven't lost yet."

"But Dru's marrying Charming in less than twenty-three hours." Another volley of tears grew in his eyes. "It's over."

Poor Winslow would never make it as a villain. I lost all the time to lesser men, but I never gave up. The word "quit," like the word "G-spot," wasn't in my vocabulary. I grabbed Winslow's snot-covered lapel and shook him, hard. The back of his head smashed into the oak tree behind him again and again. I didn't stop until his cries turned from grief to pain.

"Ouch. Ouch. Ouch," he stammered, keeping the beat. I added a scat, "Booo . . . ahhhh . . . ooohhh . . . aaahhhh . . . ooooo." All and all, we sounded pretty damn good. Sure, we were far from taking our act on the road, but practice made perfect, so I slammed his head into the tree some more.

"Stop," he begged.

My impotent villainous self did just that. I released his lapel, and Winslow slid to the ground, rubbing at the back of his troll-like head.

"Where were we?" I straightened my sweatshirt. "Right. You've lost Dru and she's gone forever."

Winslow glared at me, showing a villainous spark for the first time. I grinned. "She's not married yet," he yelled, staggering to his feet. "Prince Charming hasn't won. Not until the ring is on her finger."

I nodded, satisfied that I'd done my part. As quickly as Winslow's villainy came, it faded away. His shoulders began to shake with the weight of his unrequited love. "But what can I do? I'm merely a butler. An ugly one at that. I have nothing to offer my sweet princess. No money. No fine house. No jewels."

At this point Charming didn't either, since . . . well, I burned his house down. I reached for Winslow's lapel again, but he backed away in time.

"Dru doesn't want or need fancy things." I smiled. "She needs a man who loves her."

"I do love her."

"I know." I paused, taking a deep breath. "So go tell her. Tell her how much she means to you. How you can't face a day without her in your life. How the sun won't shine as bright without her." All the things I should've said to Asia, but didn't. Some tough villain I was, afraid of one tiny princess with poor aim.

Winslow frowned. "When'd you turn all gay?"

My fists clenched.

"I'm kidding," he said. "You're right. I must confess my love for Dru. If I don't, I'll regret it for the rest of my days."

"That a boy. Now go get your girl." I smacked him on the shoulder. He fell backward, smashing his head into the tree. The tree shook from the impact, sending leaves and bird feathers raining down on us. I glanced up in time to spot a bluebird fly away.

Poor Winslow wasn't so lucky. His gaze followed mine, but rather than watching a bluebird, he watched as a pinecone the size of a little pig tumbled toward him. It hit him square on the forehead. He let out a small squeak and his eyes rolled back as he slumped to the ground unconscious.

"Winslow?" I called. "Ummm ... buddy ..."

No response.

"Winslow?" I said again.

Nothing.

He'll be fine, I thought, glancing around the deserted forest. I shrugged my shoulders and slowly crept away.

Chapter 34

Later that evening, in the back room of the Three Blind Mice Tavern, I raised my beer mug in salute. A splash of white foam dribbled down the side. "A toast. To the groom."

"To the groom." My fellow bachelor party compatriots, four in all, raised their own glasses with a loud "hear, hear." I took a long drink, hoping to drown this charade in enough beer to forget the rest of the night. So far, it wasn't working.

Prince Charming lifted his glass filled with a frothy pink mixture, and a little sloshed over the side, leaving a pink stain on Charming's manicured nails. "Thank you all for coming." He glanced around the small table and smiled. "This means so much to me. To have you all here. My dear friends. When I think of all we've meant to each other . . ."

Friends? Not so much. Hell, the only person here who actually liked Charming was Charming. And maybe Bruce, the sheriff. Well, the king too, but he didn't really count. After all, I bribed him with a turkey leg to join the festivities.

I snuck a glance at Winslow. He glared back, his eyes burning. Guess he still held a grudge. I'd apologized for leaving him unconscious in the forest, what more did he want? Blood? "Winslow," I said. "Your forehead is bleeding again."

Not my fault, I assured myself. After all, how was I to know that during his "nap" a gaggle of bluebirds would take advantage of the troll-like butler?

Charming staggered to his feet, swaying slightly like Miss Muffet after one too many bowls of whey. "Tomorrow I will be a married man." He gave a small shiver. "But don't cry for me, my friends, for I gain something far more important."

A baboon-faced wife?

"Tomorrow I gain a family." He saluted the king, and then me. The king beamed while I felt slightly nauseous.

Winslow, on the other hand, looked ready to commit prince-icide. His eyes flashed red, and his mouth moved, forming words incomprehensible to the human ear. Winslow pushed his stool back and rose to his feet. "You don't deser—"

I cut him off. "Oh look. The stripper's here."

All heterosexual heads swiveled toward the door and the obese blonde shoving her way through it. She wore a tight black negligee that clung to her curves in an obscene manner. A cigarette jutted from her red, wrinkled lips. With a slight limp she sashayed to our table.

A villain at the bar let out a shrill whistle. "Hey, sexy grandmama."

I winced. For one thing, the stripper was far from sexy. Why waste my dough on Charming? It would be like taking a supermodel to Denny's.

The stripper arrived at our table. She was even worse-looking up close, sixty years old with stretch marks and an overbite that reminded me of Pinocchio's girlfriend, Woodchuck Sally. The stripper's eyes were much too close together, making her nose seem that much larger. That wasn't the worst part. Besides her sagging breasts, her breath reminded me why necrophilia held little appeal.

"Money up front," she said, exhaling putrid air.

"Here you go." I crammed two tens into her meaty palm. She counted each one. That took about five minutes. Maledetto public schooling, I'd bet.

Apparently satisfied, she pointed to our ragtag group with a sausagelike finger that smelled a bit like sausage. "Who's the lucky fellow?"

"Lucky" wasn't the word I'd use, but what the hell. Winslow glanced at the king, the king at Bruce, and Bruce to Prince Rotten, who was trying to hide under the table. I smiled, watching his struggle. "That's him." I pointed to the prince, who had taken refuge in the fetal position.

The old stripper yanked Charming to his feet, smashing his face into her boobs. "What's your name, sweetheart?"

"Ch...mmm...g," he muttered through mounds of flesh.

"Well, Charming, you and I are going to have some fun!" As she said those words, the jukebox kicked in. "Girls Just Wanna Have Fun" sprang from the speakers.

Bruce jumped up from his seat. "Oh, I love this song."

Before I knew what was happening, the tavern turned into an episode of *Maledetto's Got No Talent,* complete with a drunken egomaniac eating off the floor.

"Don't eat that," I said to the king, who was gnawing on a piece of questionable jerky. He spat it out and smiled. I shook my head and helped him to his feet.

In front of us, Charming sat pinned to a stool, the stripper gyrating above him. Tiny pink tassels attached to her melon-sized nipples swirled in circles as she moved in an almost hypnotic pattern. Charming whimpered, ducking his head to avoid taking a tit in the eye. I grinned. I never saw a more pained look on a man's face. It made my villainous day.

Of course, my happiness quickly turned into a nightmare when the old stripper turned her attention my way.

"You like what you see, sugar?" She smacked her round ass with her manly hands.

"Sorry, I'm gay," I said with a shrug. Sadly, she didn't look even mildly disappointed, and worse, Charming, who must've overheard our conversation, appeared thrilled. He smiled and shot me a wink. I grabbed a shot of whiskey from the bar, downed it in one drink, and gagged. And not from the whiskey.

The old stripper flashed her breasts at the king and smiled. He responded in kind, lifting his shirt to show off his flabby body and weak smile. Either he liked what he saw in the old stripper, or he'd developed some kind of twitch from the poison the queen had fed him for lunch.

From here, the bachelor party slipped over the edge and into complete chaos as the stripper removed layer after layer of clothes to the steady beat of eighties hair bands. I stopped watching the display once her prosthetic leg came off. A couple of blind mice cheered her on, but otherwise, the rest of the tavern watched in horrified silence.

When the show was finally over, the stripper took a bow, her breasts flopping to the floor as she collected the seventy-five cents in tips. Sixty of which was left by the king.

The king approached the stripper and smiled. "Why don't we go back to your place, luv?" the king asked. "Have us a good time."

"Okay, but I have to warn you," the old stripper paused, "I live in a shoe. I have kids too. And I don't know what to do. . . ." She trailed off as they headed toward the door. The king looked over his shoulder and winked.

"I need another drink," I muttered to no one in particular and headed for the bar.

Chapter 35

An hour and twelve shots of rye later, I wobbled from the bathroom back to my bar stool. Except for us hard-core villains, the tavern had cleared out, thanks in part to Bruce and Charming's karaoke duet of "Endless Love." Try as I might, I couldn't erase the ghastly vision from my mind.

"Another shot," I said to the barkeep. "Make it a triple."

The villain to my right nodded his approval. I knew he and the other three guys at the bar were villains, mostly because all four of them had already tried to steal my wallet, but I didn't recognize any of them. By the stench wafting off the nearest villain, I figured they were West Coast villains here on vacation.

I crawled onto my bar stool, blinking under the dim light as the room spun in five directions, none of which provided any insight into what I was still doing at the tavern when I should be resting up for the big day. Charming and Dru's wedding.

Sober up, my brain ordered. I needed to be at the top of my game tomorrow, not hungover, stinking of stale beer and cigarettes.

After all, tomorrow would be a busy day, thanks to too much alcohol and the stupid union. By my fourth shot this evening, I'd promised Winslow I'd stop the wedding. By my eighth, I'd agreed to be Charming's best man. Hell, by my thirteenth, I might propose to the black sheep at the end of the bar. I glanced her way. She baaahed in response.

There was one bright spot in the day to come. Asia. In less than twelve hours I would walk her down the aisle. I planned to take her into my arms, check her for weapons, and lock her in the nearest tower until death did one of us part.

Probably mine.

"You're Stiltskin?" asked the villain on my right.

I nodded. "Call me RJ." Here it comes, I thought. Villain #1 would either buy me a drink or punch me in the nose. The price of infamy.

"Told you, Smee," he said to the villain on my left. "You owe me a beer." Villain #1 then turned to me. "I'm Captain Cross-Stitch. This is my first mate, Starkley, and that's Smee." He motioned to the other two villains. Smee wore an eye patch over his left eye, Starkley over his right. Other than that I couldn't tell them apart.

Cross-Stitch, on the other hand, was a different story. With his shaggy hair, tattooed arms, and the long knitting needle where his left hand once was, he stood out in any crowd. The parrot on his shoulder and his peg leg didn't help him blend in either. The poor guy fit the villainous image for a pirate to a T. Odd since Maledetto was land-locked.

I nodded to the knitting needle and the intricate cross-stitch attached to it. "Pretty."

Cross-Stitch shrugged. "Knitting calms me."

Fair enough. Drinking helped calm me, but each to his villainous own.

"RJ." Cross-Stitch eyed me up and down. "What's a New Never City villain like you doing in Maledetto? Slumming it?"

It was my turn to shrug. I wasn't about to share my current union troubles. If these villains sensed any weakness, I'd find myself swabbing more than their decks. "Vacation," I said. "You know how it is. Sometimes you just gotta get away from the city. Clear your head."

"Not me." Smee frowned. "I'd give my left eye to be a New Never City villain."

I tilted my head to the side. From what I could see Smee's left eye was already missing, but I wasn't about to get in the age-old New Never City villain versus West Coast villain argument. The evil was always greener on the other side.

I snatched up my shot glass and slammed the fire-infused liquor. "Another round," I called to the bartender, waving my hand to my new friends. "And whatever they're having." Miss Muffet always said, "It's cheaper to buy a villain a drink than to pay for x-rays and a new set of teeth. So, RJ, buy me that damn drink and stop whining, the bleeding stopped."

Starkley rubbed his chin. "Stiltskin. Any relation to Natasha?"

Shit. Here it comes. I raised my left hand to protect my face and lowered my right to protect my family jewels. Natasha was both well known and *loved* in our villainous circles. On the day we married, many a villain swore vengeance against me. The sex was well worth it, though, even if our marriage wasn't.

I waited for Starkley to make his move. When nothing happened I lowered my left hand. "Natasha was my ex-wife." I tried to picture her pale face, blood-red lips, and black heart but her image faded, replaced with Asia's smile and quick laugh.

"Awww . . . shit, man," Cross-Stitch said, draping his knitting needle arm across my shoulder. The point jabbed me in the back. I winced, but didn't comment. He continued, "Natasha was one fine villain."

The other two villains as well as the bartender nodded in agreement. That she was. Even after our divorce I never doubted her villainous skills. At one time, she lived and breathed villainy, and the union. Miss Muffet called Natasha the best villain in the city; of course, she always ended that statement with, "until she married you."

The union had introduced us. I was on assignment in Greenwitch Village, stealing Girl Scout cookies from Brownies (Thin Mints only; for obvious reasons the union hated Thanks-A-Lots), when Natasha arrived to cover my shift.

Instead of taking a much-needed break, we spent the next eight hours talking and having sex in the bathroom of a Villains-R-Us. The talking took up about ten minutes. The only reason our marriage lasted as long as it had.

I slammed another shot as the bartender poured yet another round. Memories of Natasha and the whiskey left a sour taste in my mouth. Cross-Stitch raised his shot glass, the other villains followed suit. When my glass remained unmolested on the bar, Cross-Stitch gave me a nudge in the ribs with his knitting needle.

"Ow!" I rubbed at the wound. Blood stained my shirt a muddy red. Cross-Stitch nodded to my shot glass, and I sighed. "Fine," I said, lifting the glass with a wince.

"To Natasha," Cross-Stitch said. "May she keep the devil on his toes."

The other villains shouted, "Hear hear."

I closed my eyes and swallowed the whiskey without comment. Being married to Natasha had convinced me of one thing: The devil was one unfortunate bastard. I smiled at the thought and returned to drowning every brain cell in my head.

"RJ, you a union man?" Cross-Stitch asked a few minutes later.

My bloodshot eyes swung to his face. "I used to be." Which was true. Until last week, I would've died for the union, and had on occasion. But not anymore. Now I was my own man. Impotent, sure, but my own man. I laughed.

Who was I kidding? Lost in my thoughts, I missed Cross-Stitch's next words. "Sorry," I said. "What were you saying?"

"I asked if Natasha had a chance to talk to you before she . . . umm . . ." Cross-Stitch winced.

"Went ahhhhh and fell to the ground dead?" I tilted my head. "Is that what you're talking about?"

Redness stained Cross-Stitch's cheeks, whether from embarrassment or anger I wasn't sure. "Did she say anything to you?" he repeated, his tone urgent.

"Like what?" I asked. Warning bells clanged inside my pickled brain. Why was Cross-Stitch suddenly so interested in Natasha's final moments? Did he know who killed Cinderella? Was he about to reveal her murderer? Excitement swirled with alcohol in my stomach, turning me from just a drunk to an energized one.

"Like . . . that she was starting her own union." Cross-Stitch cast a furtive glance around the bar. "One with a 401(v) for all villains, not just the senior staff."

"And dental," Starkley said, flashing a mouthful of rotting gums and chipped teeth. "Don't forget the dental."

Smee added with a tap to his eye patch, "Vision too."

"Vision and dental too," Cross-Stitch added with an eye roll.

I blinked a few times. "What's this got to do with me?" Last thing I needed was to get involved with union politics. Over the years, a handful of villains tried to break the union without luck. Some, like Jimmy Hoffa-Cricket, were never seen again.

"We want you to take Natasha's place," Cross-Stitch said.

"Place?" What the hell were these guys taking about? I had my own apartment, why would I want Natasha's?

Cross-Stitch jabbed his needle my way. "We want you to be the next union boss."

Me? A union boss? I could barely tie my own shoes. I laughed, but quickly sobered when Cross-Stitch didn't join in. "You're serious, aren't you?"

He nodded, as did the other two villains. The barkeep looked unsure, and the black sheep looked better and better. I shook my head. "Another round for my friends," I said, hoping that if I got them drunk enough they'd forget this ridiculousness. I couldn't be the face of the new union, not with two black eyes, a lump on the bridge of my nose, and seven or so random bruises framing my visage.

"We need you," Cross-Stitch said. "All of villainy needs you."

"And I need another drink," I said, draining my fourteenth shot. "Barkeep?"

Chapter 36

The bartender cut me and my fellow brethren off after our eighteenth drink. "I'll call you a ride," he said, placing a cup of coffee in front of me. I shrugged, nearly falling off the bar stool. Maybe I did have one too many. I grinned at the black sheep with her tongue in my ear. "Hold that thought," I said and rose from the stool. "I've gotta take a leak."

"Baaahhhh," she said in response.

I was shitfaced, literally, as I'd just slipped on a wet paper towel in the bathroom and landed face-first in a suspicious trail of brown sludge on the floor. Stomach rolling, I rubbed away the smelly substance from my cheek and shakily got to my feet. I turned on the bathroom faucet, waiting for the water to heat enough to boil my skin. After all, how would I explain a sudden case of E. coli of the cheek, let alone explain a bout of mad sheep disease?

My eyes glanced into the mirror and I shivered. "Mirror, mirror on the wall...," I began.

"What the fuck do you want?" the mirror asked. I stumbled backward, smashing my head against the stall door. "Well?" the mirror asked again. "I haven't got all night."

"Sorry," I said. "Wrong fairytale."

I staggered for the door, bouncing off the bathroom

walls like a pinball. It took me a few minutes to find the exit, but once I did, I ran at full drunken stumble for the bar.

"Dudes," I said. "You're not gonna believe this!"

No response.

"Cross-Stitch?"

Still nothing.

"Hey." I shook Cross-Stitch's shoulder. "Wake up. You won't believe what just . . ." Cross-Stitch's head lolled to one side, blood leaking from his blue lips. "Ummm . . . Cross-Stitch? Are you dead?"

I didn't expect an answer from him or the other two villains, each with ten inches of arrow sticking out of their chests. Pink feathers littered the bar floor.

Fuck. Natasha's killer was back, out there waiting in the dark. "Call the sheriff," I yelled to the bartender. He ran out from the office, fuzzy black patches of sheep wool coating his bare chest.

"What happened?" he screamed. "Did you shoot them?" His eyes widened and he ran to the pay phone behind the bar. "Stay back," he warned me, the phone at ready.

"I didn't do this." I shook my head and took a step toward him. "It wasn't me."

"Uh-huh."

"I swear it." I stumbled closer. "Someone else killed them. The same person who killed Natasha."

"But you killed Natasha. The *New Never News* said so." He nodded to the newspaper lying on the bar top. Sure enough, the front page read, HUSBAND KILLS FORMER WIFE. CAN YOU GUESS HIS NAME?

"Come on," I said. "Do you believe everything you read?"

"Of course."

Fair enough. I stepped forward, intent on grabbing the phone in the bartender's hand and calling the damn cops myself. Two feet away, my foot slid in a puddle of what I hoped was only blood. I flipped in the air, landing on my head. The blow and too much booze knocked me out for a few seconds. Little pink birds swirled around my head, and my vision faded to black.

When I came to, the bartender still stood behind the bar, the phone clutched in his hand. He was dead, though, a pink-tipped arrow through his throat. A pink-tipped arrow meant for me. My clumsiness had saved my life. And not for the first time. Dumb luck, sure, but luck nonetheless.

I staggered slowly to my feet and limped to the phone. "Nine-one-one. What's your emergency?" the operator asked through the static of the phone.

I lifted the receiver. "No emergency. Not anymore." My eyes searched the shadows of the bar for a killer only to settle on Asia's pale face in the window.

She raised her hand and waved.

Chapter 37

"Come on," Asia said, pulling me from the bar and into the dark night. One lone star shone down on us, making Asia glimmer like a diamond freshly mined by a dwarf. She paused in our escape long enough to brush a lock of my hair from my face. "We have to get you out of here before the sheriff arrives."

"Why?" I rubbed my aching head.

Asia shook her head. "So you don't get arrested for murder, stupid!"

"Sweet talk's not going to work." I grabbed her hand. Her skin felt cold against mine. "Why'd you do it? Those villains had nothing to do with us. Why kill them?"

"What?!" She shook her head. "Are you insane?"

"Not that I know of, but maybe you are. That would explain a few things."

"Thanks a lot." She smacked me in the arm. "But I didn't kill anyone. Mary called me to pick you up, so I did."

"Mary?"

"The bartender. Mary. Short for Marion." Asia paused at my blank expression. "As in Marion had a little lamb?"

From what I could tell, Marion also had a little sheep on the side. But who was I to judge?

"When I arrived I saw you through the window and waved." She leaned closer. "How drunk are you?"

"Not drunk enough to hallucinate four dead guys." Yet drunk enough to believe Asia. Sure, she wanted me dead, and on occasion, had attempted to kill me, but why kill the other villains? Her aim wasn't that bad. "You did see them too, right?"

She nodded, her face pale in the moonlight. "Were they killed because they knew something about Cindi's death?"

Huh, I hadn't thought of that. It made sense, I supposed, or as much sense as anything else about this case did. Natasha knew Cindi's killer, and the villains knew Natasha.

A siren bellowed in the distance. Asia's face grew even paler. "Please hurry." She grabbed my hand and pulled me toward the street. "We have to get out of here."

"Okay, okay." I let her drag me to the king's bright blue moped, which sat parked at the curb, the engine still warm. I raised my eyebrow. She shrugged. "The cops haven't found my car yet. They're waiting for it to turn up in some villainous pork-chop-shop."

I winced, picturing all the vehicles I pilfered in the last ten years. And the two years prior to that I spent backpacking through Europe. "Asia," I began. "I'm so sor—"

"Shhh." She handed me a blue helmet that smelled suspiciously like the king, sort of a mixture of old man sweat and rotted meat. "We'll talk later. But right now, we have to get you out of here."

"You're the boss." I unsteadily straddled the bike.

Smiling, Asia threw her leg over the moped, nearly gelding me in the process. "Try to remember that," she said before slamming the bike into gear.

We jerked forward at the top speed of fifteen miles per hour. Rather than falling to the concrete below, I wrapped my arms around Asia's cold flesh and held on for dear life.

At ten minutes before midnight I stumbled from the shower, my wet hair plastered to my head and a towel wrapped around my hips. The cold water had acted much like a gallon of coffee on my intoxicated soul. I could now slur my words at an amazing speed.

"Asia?" I staggered to Cinderella's pink bedroom. I half expected it to be empty, but when I pushed the door open, Asia sat on the edge of the bed like some Victorian maiden, her arms wrapped around her chest. She glanced up at me through veiled eyes, her lips parted.

"Hi," she whispered.

"Hi."

She patted the quilt next to her. "Want to sit down?"

I wanted that and so much more, but I stayed where I was. Too much was at stake—my life, for one thing. "What's your game? I sit down and the bed explodes? A poison dart sticks me in the butt?"

"That wasn't quite what I had in mind." Her lips curved into a wicked smile. More beautiful than a stolen diamond and just as costly, she made risking my life worth it.

My eyes trailed down her fiery hair, past her slender neck, and into the rich round swells hidden beneath her shirt. The towel around my waist suddenly tightened. Asia shot me a knowing grin.

Fuck it. I ran to the bed, snatching Asia up into my arms, never wanting to let her go. Mostly out of fear she'd try to kill me if I did. "I've missed you," I said against her neck. Her skin warmed under my lips. I kissed a trail down her throat, to the slope between her breasts. She tasted as wonderful as I remembered, like the holidays. The good ones. Not the ones you had to spend with family.

"I want you," I said, pulling away to stare into her eyes.

"I wasn't sure you still would."

I gave a short, painful laugh. Not want her? I woke up every day for the last week wanting nothing more than to see Asia's face. Wanting to hold her in my arms. To kiss her red-stained lips.

Insecurity rose within me, partially from the booze, but mostly from years of mistrust and loneliness. I swallowed hard, brushing a finger over her parted lips. "Tell me you want me too."

Rather than waste her time with words, she yanked my towel free. Her fingers stroked the length of my erection, teasing and tempting me to lose control. But I wouldn't make that mistake. Not tonight. Not ever again.

I grabbed her wandering fingers. "Does this mean I'm forgiven? No more assassination attempts?"

She pushed at my chest, knocking me back against the bed, and straddled me. "Would you believe me if I said yes?"

I looked into her eyes, nearly losing myself in their depths. "Would you be telling the truth?"

"I guess we'll have to wait and see."

Using her body as leverage, I flipped her on her back and leaned over her. My fingers burrowed under her shirt, stroking the warm flesh of her breasts. Her breathing deepened. "I'm a patient man," I said, moving my hand lower. "But just so you know."

"Yes?" Her voice caught.

"Your time's up." My mouth took possession of hers, our tongues jockeying for position. Win, lose, or draw, the orgasm was worth the risk.

Chapter 38

Lying next to me in bed, Asia ran her finger along my sweat-slicked chest. My breathing had just now returned to normal, yet my heart still pounded like the tortoise following accusations of doping. Like birds of a feather, we lay flocked together, our bodies entwined. As great as the sex was—and trust me, it was mind-blowingly naughty—lying here with Asia in my arms was heaven. Or as close to heaven as a blackhearted villain like me would get.

"RJ," Asia began.

I gave her a small squeeze. "Hush, sweetheart. I know what you're going to say."

"You do?"

I nodded. "You don't have to apologize. I messed up too. I should've told you the truth about who I was at the beginning. I can't blame you for being mad. . . . Trying to kill me, on the other hand . . ."

"Pardon me?" Asia pulled away, her eyes searching my face.

Warning bells rang inside my head. What did I say? I was being gracious, damn it. "Baby," I cleared my throat, "what's in the past is in the past. We both made mistakes."

She gave a bitter laugh. "For your information, my only mistake was sleeping with an arrogant villain like you."

Shoving the covers away, Asia launched herself from the

bed. She jabbed her finger into my chest. "I wasn't going to apologize, you idiot. I was going to ask how black wool got inside your ear."

Shit. I dug inside my ear canal and pulled out a ball of fuzz. Asia frowned at the lint ball, her eyes narrowing with suspicion.

"It's not what it looks like," I said. "You see, I . . ."

"Forget it." Asia shook her head. "I should've known—"

The palace clock gonged, interrupting Asia's rant. Her face paled slightly as the clock continued to ring.

"What time is it?" she yelled.

I glanced at my watch. "Seven minutes after midnight. Why?"

"Shit," she said as she ran from the room, her naked body gleaming in the moonlight.

"Asia, wait," I yelled, but it was too late. My lovely, naked, and annoyed princess vanished down the corridor. I closed my eyes and inhaled the scent of her on my pillow. She smelled faintly of danger and pumpkin spice. I smiled, my skin still burning from her touch.

For a brief moment tonight, I found my happily-ever-after. Now I just needed to convince Asia of that fact.

My first thought upon waking was Asia finally succeeded. I was dying, and nobody could save me. My head felt like a lead weight, and my stomach seconded that assumption. Bile crawled up my throat, burning my esophagus with even the slightest of breaths. "Hungover" was too nice a word for what I felt. Even the toe jam between my little piggies hurt. I suspected, given half a chance, they would go wee wee wee all the way to rehab.

"Aaaaahhhh." I opened my eyes, praying for death.

"Morning, dear," a voice said from the bed next to me. I shook my head, not surprised to find yet another Maledetto family member in my bed.

"My lady," I said to the queen, ignoring the ringing inside my brain. "To what do I owe this pleasure?"

The queen twirled the end of one of her red curls. Dressed in a morning gown and slathered in age-defying makeup, she should've looked fresh as a daisy. Instead, the queen appeared as haggard as Baba Yaga after a rough night. Her face held a greyish tint and deep circles marred her eyes. A red pimple protruded from the tip of her nose, as did a few stray black hairs. Suddenly I noticed Dru's resemblance to her mother. Not a pretty sight.

"Where is he?" asked the queen.

"Who?"

"The king." Her voice hitched. "He never came home last night."

Right. I forgot the king's extra–bachelor party activity. The thought of him and the stripper sent waves of sickness throughout my body. Either that or the bottle and a half of booze I'd consumed the night before.

I sat up in the bed, holding my head and groaning. I vowed never to drink again. Since my liver doubted my sincerity, the bile filled my throat. I ran for the trash can by the door, missed, and ended up yakking on my bare feet. My eyes slowly rose from my naked toes, up my calves, to the nude juncture between my thighs.

"I guess what they say about villains is true." The queen motioned to my naughty bits. I blushed, quickly covering myself with my hands. Or trying to, because the queen was right, us villains had smaller than normal hands.

I crabwalked back to the bed and lunged under the covers. The queen smiled, but it didn't reach her eyes.

"My lady," I began.

She held up a hand. "Just tell me. Is she prettier than me?"

"Who?"

"The skank my husband is with, you dolt!"

I shook my head. "My lady. Your husband loves you."

If by love I meant "wishes you were dead." "He would never break his vows." The ones in which he swore to love, honor, and murder you in your sleep, I wanted to add, but given the crazy look in the queen's eyes, I refrained.

"Are you sure?"

I nodded, not sure about anything, let alone the old king's fidelity. He had left with the old stripper, after all. Then again, even the king of Maledetto could do better. Not much better. But a little bit better nonetheless.

"Well, in that case," the queen bounded from my bed and hurried to the door, her skirt tangling around her ankles, "I must prepare a 'special' breakfast."

"One fit for a king?"

She shot me a wicked smile and closed the door behind her loud enough to rattle my already aching head. I considered puking again, but decided it wasn't worth the effort. Instead I relaxed against my pillow and sighed.

A cool breeze swept underneath my door, and a familiar scrap of paper danced around before quietly falling to the floor.

Son of a witch.

Head pounding, I slowly rose from the bed and knelt next to the paper. Coffee stains and lipstick frayed the edges, but the signature was easy to read: Nigel de Wolfe. My missing receipt. The one Miss Muffet had stolen from my pocket.

What was it doing here? I snatched up the receipt. Had the queen dropped it in her hurry to murder the king? Or had it fallen from Asia's gown last night?

Chapter 39

Ten minutes later, my mind reeling with conspiracies, my aching head fell back down on my pillow. I let out a loud burp followed by a sigh. When the boozy fumes cleared, I frowned.

Today was Dru's wedding day. There was plenty of stuff for me to do even without the reappearance of my missing clue, namely, ruin said wedding, unmask a killer, and win my princess once and for all. Easy enough for a villain. Not so much for a hungover impotent one with the taste of sheep spit in his mouth.

I winced, remembering all the wooly details from last night. Someone had tried to kill me, again. I wanted to believe Asia. However, in the harsh morning light, her sudden appearance and a new stack of dead bodies didn't quite add up to innocence. And I knew my villainous math. In fact, that was my finest subject in school. That and home economics.

Then again, I'd lived through our lovemaking session with barely a scratch, which made me all the more suspicious. What was her game? Was she innocent or a reincarnated version of Mata Hari?

A knock at the door interrupted my musing. "Come in," I said, jamming the receipt underneath my pillow.

The door opened, and Asia entered, looking as beautiful

as always. The Devil's Eye hung off her waist by a gold braided rope. The jewels sparkled above the juncture of her thighs. The aching in my head gathered lower. Thankfully, the blanket covered my erection.

Asia swept into the room, her lips curving into a knowing smile. "Sleep well?" she asked.

"Like a baby." A drunken, confused, and horny baby, but a baby nonetheless. "You?" My eyes raked over her body, settling on her face. It appeared to be glowing, either a trick of the fairy light or something more. Something dark and dangerous. Something, as a villain, I truly appreciated. I shifted under the covers.

Asia's shoulders lifted in a vague shrug. "I came to apologize."

"To me?"

A frown marred her forehead. "Of course. This is your room, after all."

"I meant, for what?" Besides the obvious, like trying to blow me up, I wanted to add, but decided it might put a dent into our already awkward morning-after conversation.

"For a lot of things," she said. "But mainly for what happens next."

"Next?" The hair on my arms stood at attention. I had a really bad feeling about my continued good health.

I wrapped the blanket around me and rose from the bed. "Tell me what's wrong. It doesn't have to be like this."

She shook her head. "If I asked you to go, now, today, would you?"

"No." This wasn't only about Asia anymore. I owed it to my ex-wife and a gaggle of wannabe pirates to find Cinderella's killer. But mostly, I owed it to myself. I was more than RJ, villain extraordinaire. I was Rumple Stiltskin, damn it. A man with a mission. Nobody could take that away from me.

"That's what I thought." Asia opened the bedroom door. "Sheriff," she yelled. "Your suspect is hiding up here. He looks dangerous. You better bring the Taser."

"Huh?" I jumped from the bed and dove for my Levi's. "You called the sheriff on me? What about last night?"

"It was fun. Thanks."

Footsteps pounded on the staircase outside the bedroom. I yanked on my pants, sweatshirt, and combat boots. For once, the age-old laces versus Velcro debate ended without a tie.

Boots half-undone, I stomped to the window, avoiding my betraying princess's eye. From the window to the ground below looked to be about a three-story drop, not nearly enough to kill me, but just enough to bust a femur. Damn.

Asia looked on with a smile. "You can't escape."

"Watch me." I spun to face her. "Why, Asia? Why save me from the crime scene and then call the cops the next day? What can you possibly gain?"

She ignored my question and instead peeked into the hallway. "Oh, the sheriff looks pretty pissed. Is that a baton in his hand?" She winced. "I'd surrender if I was you."

"Thanks for the advice." I peeled the window open, years of paint popping free with a crack. A cool breeze swept inside the room, extinguishing the overhead fairy light.

I stuck my head out of the window, my stomach rolling from the height as well as last night's debauchery. The jump didn't seem that bad, if I landed in the soft bed of fertilizer next to the rosebushes. Of course, if I landed in the rosebushes, I was fucked.

"Don't do it." Asia tugged on my sleeve, real fear in her tone. "It's suicide."

Naw, at the worst, I would end up paralyzed from the

eyebrows down. "You didn't leave me much of a choice, did you?"

"It's for your own good."

Right. A long prison stretch for four murders I didn't commit sounded great. Hell, I could finally kick my addiction to freedom, and, hey, I might even find Mr. Right on the inside. "I see how you might think that, given the fact you've tried to kill me at least three times. But I'm sorry to disappoint."

"RJ, please. Think about the consequences."

That was something I should've done the first day when I found Asia sitting in my chair, huffing down my dinner. But I was too stunned by her beauty and sad sob story to question her real motives. And now it was too late.

I grabbed Asia's face in my hand and drew her mouth to mine. Our lips brushed, softly at first, mostly because I expected her to bite.

When my lips remained intact, I deepened the kiss. She wrapped her hands around my neck, our tongues, lips and teeth warring for supremacy. My sweet princess smelled of fine wine, promise, and pumpkin pie. Not a bad combination.

In fact, I'd started to crave her scent, like Jack Horner in need of a pie. Nothing felt right without Asia in my arms, which sucked since she proved yet again to be a treacherous witch.

Outside the door, the sheriff bellowed a warning: "Rumple Stiltskin, we have you surrounded. Come out with your hands up."

My hand slid up Asia's shirt, caressing the soft flesh of her breast. Her nipples hardened, poking me in the chest like tiny toy soldiers.

The sheriff pounded on the door. "You have until the count of three to surrender or else."

Asia's hand fisted in my hair, dragging my mouth from her lips. We stared into each other's eyes.

"One . . . two . . ."

A tear glistened in Asia's eye, rolling down her cheek. My fingers brushed at the single shiny drop. "One day, you'll push me too far," I said.

". . . two and three-quarters . . . ," the sheriff said.

Asia licked her lips.

". . . two and four-halves . . ."

Taking her hand, I pressed it to my heart. Our pulse beat as one, a little too fast, sure, but together. Forever.

"Three."

The bedroom door burst open. The sheriff and his battalion of deputies in paisley pushed into the room. Surprisingly enough, the sheriff did have a baton in his hand. Not an ASP like I expected, but rather a baton favored by baton majors everywhere. Its red and gold streamers danced in the breeze.

Asia glanced at the sheriff, and then at the open window with me hanging half out. She bit her lip, as if weighing her options. The sparkle that came to her eye suggested I was in serious trouble. Her mouth locked onto mine one more time, and she shoved my body over the window ledge.

Chapter 40

Like a newborn African swallow, I flapped my arms harder and harder, but no matter how hard I flapped them, I still hit the ground with the force of a meteor. My legs hit first, followed by my head. I must've blacked out for a second or two, for when I awoke, the sheriff was at the window, Asia clutched in his arms like a prisoner. Served her right.

"Stay right where you are," the sheriff said.

"No problem," I lied. Then I, of course, staggered to my feet and limped quickly away. But not too far away. I still had a couple of things left on my to-do list to accomplish today. Number one: Stop Dru's wedding, thanks to the stupid promise I made to Winslow the night before. Damn union curse. The poor bastard had asked nicely. What could I say?

Speaking of poor bastards.

Rounding the corner of the castle, I ran smack into Prince Rotten. He looked no worse for wear after last night's escapades, his blond locks coiffured in perfect order, his eyes clean and clear. I hated him even more. Charming raised a tuxedoed arm. "The sheriff's looking for you," he said.

"Yeah." I brushed at a glob of mud on my sleeve. "So I've heard."

"The wedding's in an hour."

I nodded.

Charming's eyes roamed over my stained, rumpled, non-tuxedoed wear. "Shouldn't you change? Maybe take a bath?" His lips curved into a smile. "I'd be happy to help. You are my best man, after all."

Shit. I'd forgotten that little fact. "About that...," I began, an idea forming in my fermented brain. "Wouldn't the sheriff make the best best man?" I kicked at the ground. "I mean, look at me." I gestured to my dirty, blood-smeared clothes. "It's your wedding...the one you've dreamed about since you were a small boy...I'd hate to ruin your big moment."

Charming gave me another once-over. "I don't know."

"Think about it." I nodded. "You standing next to Bruce at the altar, each of you dressed in black."

"Bruce does look good in a tux."

"Better than me." I shook my head. "I bet Bruce can do a hell of a Macarena too."

Prince Moron nodded.

"Well, that settles it."

"Settles what?"

I rolled my eyes. "Bruce will be your new best man. Now, why don't you go find him and tell him the good news? But remember, don't take no for an answer."

"Okay."

"That's the spirit." I slapped him on the shoulder. "Beg if you have to, but make Bruce drop everything for your big day." Even the search for an escaped felon and the subsequent arrest of said felon's ladylove.

"You're right," Charming said. He pulled me into a less-than-manly hug and copped a feel while he was at it. "You are a dear friend, RJ. I'm sorry for what I did."

I shoved him away, my eyes narrowing. "Exactly what did you do?" Was his apology a general one, like, "hey, sorry I ate your last yogurt," or something specific and much more sinister? Something like, "I'm sorry for slipping a roofie into your curds and having my way with you."

Please let it be the former.

Charming hung his pretty, blond head. "I . . . ," he sniffed, "borrowed your boxer shorts. You know the pair with the tiny stripes. I washed them and put them right back . . . but . . . I'm so sorry. Please forgive me."

I sighed. Thank God those boxers burned inside Charming's house. "I guess that makes us even, then."

He quickly glanced up, a happy puppy-dog expression on his face. "Oh yeah?"

"Sure." I grinned, patting his oblivious head. "I burned down your house. You borrowed my shorts. Tit for tat."

Charming frowned, taking a few too many seconds for my words to sink in. By the time he said, "Hey!" I was already limping inside the side palace door.

"Wait a minute," he called after me.

I didn't bother to turn around, but rather, limped at double speed through the kitchen door.

What a morning, and I'd only been awake for an hour. Now all I needed to do was fulfill my promise to Winslow and stop Dru from marrying the idiot prince. I felt kind of like the villainous version of MacGyver. Alone in a far, far-away land, I must save the world armed with only a paper clip and ten pounds of plastic explosives.

Damn, I wished for some plastic explosives. They made everything easier. A shame, but my limited brainpower would have to do.

This brought me to my plan to stop the wedding. I needed to find a disguise, sneak past the five deputies standing alongside the staircase, enter Dru's room, and convince her marrying anyone, let alone a gay prince, wasn't in her best interest. It sounded easily villainous, so of course, I was bound to screw it up. Stupid union.

My first stop was the library. Nigel's fur coat lay on the floor as always, smelling vaguely of wet dog and smoke. I lifted the pelt and pictured myself struggling up three flights of stairs with it on my back without drawing any unwanted attention. I'd be lucky to make it to the foyer before the king shot me.

I glanced around, searching the room for another disguise. I could always go as a lamp. The sheriff's men weren't all that bright anyway. Crossing the room, I yanked the lampshade from the nearest lamp and jammed it on my head. The metal prongs poked into my aching brain, causing me to moan aloud.

The library door opened and in walked a rabbi dressed in full rabbi gear, including a pink kippah. Probably not a Jewish standard, but who was I to judge. The rabbi walked farther into the room, seemingly unaware of my light fixture disguise. He muttered to himself, something about either Sanka or sanctity.

An idea started to form inside my head. An idea so villainous my body shook with excitement. I slowly slipped the lampshade from my head and stalked toward the rabbi like a bloodthirsty predator. Here comes RJ, I thought with a smile.

The rabbi failed to notice my approach, or the carcass on the floor at his feet. One minute he was standing there babbling about instant coffee, and the next, he was flat on his back, Nigel's pelt tangled in his feet.

"Damn." I ran toward him. Fate fucked me over again, or maybe it was the union. I wasn't sure which was which anymore.

I knelt next to the unconscious holy man and checked for a pulse. Lucky for him, it was there, strong and steady. Unlucky for him, by his third heartbeat, I had his pants off and was tugging the pink beanie off his bald head. Once the poor bastard was down to his underwear (Star of David boxers) and matching socks, I grabbed his feet and jammed him into the closet.

I quickly donned his apparel. It fit me much like an overweight shar-pei. My eyes swept over the pile of broken mirrors by the fireplace and my image reflected in the jagged remains. I grinned. The tilt of the beanie gave me a rakish appeal, almost like a beret, but without the French sneer.

As I straightened the rest of my rabbi wear, the library door opened again. This time the sheriff entered, Asia following meekly behind, her hands cuffed behind her back. He shoved her onto the couch. She landed with a thud, dust rising from the sofa. Anger flashed through me as I stifled a sneeze. Nobody but me manhandled my princess.

"Don't you say a word," the sheriff said to Asia. "Once I find your boyfriend, both of you will take a trip downtown."

Not that Maledetto had a downtown. It was more like a main street with a bronze statue of the king. A headless bronze statue that was questionably anatomically correct at best.

Asia glared at him, her eyes burning hot. I took a careful step toward the door, not wanting to draw the sheriff's attention. I paused, stunned by the sheriff's next words.

"When I catch Stiltskin, he's going away for a long time. Maybe forever." He grinned, his gaze fixed on Asia's face. "Will his ladylove wait? Does Princess Asia love a villain that much?"

My eyes shot to Asia, but she didn't comment.

"Ah," the sheriff said. "I can see it in your face. The villain has won your heart. A pity."

Asia slowly rose from the couch, staring unblinkingly at the sheriff. "It is you who should be pitied. You'll never catch RJ. He's not stupid enough to hang around here. He's probably in Mexicanada eating seal tacos by now."

I winced and resumed my trek toward the door and freedom. Just a few feet to go. Don't blow it now. Spending the next seventy years in prison held little appeal, but destroying Asia's faith in my villainy was far worse.

Almost to the door, I bumped into the edge of the headless lamp. It teetered, swinging back and forth on an invisible string like Pinocchio before crashing to the ground. I froze, my mind weighing the distance to the door. If I ran really, really fast, I'd make it to the door before the sheriff could blow my brains all over the library walls. I glanced down at my bum leg and frowned.

I was fucked.

"Sorry, Father," the sheriff said. "We didn't see you there."

Father? I glanced around, unsure to whom he referred. As far as I knew there weren't any little Stiltskins running around. The sheriff's eyes narrowed. Asia shoved herself in front of him and motioned to my rabbi outfit. Oh, right.

"You're forgiven, my son," I said to the sheriff in a pretty good nasal imitation of Fran Drescher.

The sheriff frowned and took a step forward. "Don't I know you from somewhere?"

"Impossible. Rabbi Obtuse lives in New Never City. He's only here for Dru's wedding." Asia's eyes were shooting daggers at me. "Rabbi Obtuse. Shouldn't you be going? Like now!"

Right. I fingered my beanie and bowed low. *"Dōmo arigatō."* As much as I longed to add Mr. Roboto, I refrained. Asia shook her head, probably wondering if my IQ matched my inseam. Which, to be honest, it only does when using the metric system.

The clueless sheriff bowed too. "Have a nice day!"

I nodded to him and opened the library door before turning around to face my princess. My eye caught hers, and I blew her a kiss. She flipped me off. An unladylike reaction for sure, but it sent a shiver of longing through my body.

Chapter 41

After leaving my princess and the moronic sheriff, I climbed the staircase, three flights in all, to Dru's princess-in-waiting room. Huffing and puffing, I knocked on the door. No answer. I knocked harder. Again nothing. However, the faint sound of crying reached my wooly ears. Pushing the door open a crack, I peeked my head in. "Dru?"

The room was dark and smelled of leg wax and burnt hair. In the corner of the bed, Dru lay curled into the fetal position, her thin arms wrapped around her body. A sob escaped her lips, sounding much like a unicorn with a cold.

I stepped closer. "Dru? Are you all right?"

"Go away," she said, her head burrowing deeper into her blanket. She looked so helpless and small that my heart gave a squeeze. Either that or my three-story climb caused a heart attack. I inhaled deeply.

Whew, empathy, not impending death.

Shit. A shiver ran through me. When the hell did I start caring about other people's feelings? I prayed this was merely a side effect of my union curse. If not, stealing candy from babies and replacing it with plastic suckers would lose all its appeal. And what about the holidays? I lived for stabbing old people with sharpened candy canes.

Dru sniffled, dragging me from my happy place.

"Oh, honey." I sat on the edge of her bed and patted her arm. "Tell me what's wrong. I can fix it."

She lifted her head, exposing her tear-reddened face hidden mostly by her unibrow that had grown two sizes bigger during the night. Her tears suddenly made sense. What kind of bride wanted to look like an ogre on her wedding night?

"Oh, Dru." Reaching for her chin, I held her face in my hands, wishing for hand sanitizer. Asia's kingdom for some freaking hand sanitizer.

Dru frowned. "What are you doing here?"

"I'm here to help you," I said.

"But, Rabbi, I'm not Jewish."

I pulled off the beanie, and Dru relaxed. "Oh, RJ. I'm so glad it's you. I need your help!" Her fingers dug into my forearm, leaving half-moon bruises.

Peeling her fingernails from my skin, I said, "Glad to help, but first, I need to tell you something." She started to interrupt but I waved her off. "No. We don't have much time," I said. "I need to say this, and you need to hear it."

"But—"

Again I cut her off. "Dru." I grabbed her shoulders and shook. Hard. Her eye rattled around in her head like a slot machine, finally settling in place. "Winslow is a good man."

"I—"

"Yes, he's ugly. Really ugly. I mean, like, ugly's uglier brother."

"That's—"

"But hairy, not-so-bright princesses can't be choosers."

Dru frowned, the tears in her eyes drying instantly as something else took hold. Violence. I saw the same enraged look in Asia's gaze a few minutes ago.

I held up my hand to thwart her disagreement. "Yes, he is a good man. And furthermore, he is in love with you."

"He—" she began.

"Not like Charming, whose one true love is a mirror or maybe gay porn ... anyway ... it doesn't matter. Dru," I took a deep breath, "you and Winslow are perfect for each other."

Mostly because no one else in their right mind would have either of them. There wasn't much call for unibrowed idiots with sibling rivalry issues, or stalker troll-like butlers in the personal ads.

Dru started at me, her mouth open, her eyes wide.

I waited for my words to sink in.

And waited.

And waited some more.

The palace clock gonged.

Below us, guests arrived for the wedding by horse and buggy (the Amish Maledettos). The clop of the horse hooves outside made Dru's silence inside almost bearable.

Finally, I couldn't stand it anymore. "Ugly got your tongue?" I asked.

"I—"

"Winslow's not a great catch. I know."

"He—"

"You're right. He's not a prince, and doesn't have a pound to his name." I tapped my finger against my chin. "Maybe you should rethink marrying anyone ... I hear the nunnery is accepting applications. . . ."

Her shocked expression turned murderous. "Would you shut up for one second!"

"Hey, I'm just trying to—" I began, ducking her fist aimed at my head. I jumped off the bed and backed away slowly, my arms raised to defend my genitals. Dru rose too, all signs of sorrow gone from her butt-ugly face.

"For your information," she spat, "any woman would be lucky to marry Winslow. He is warm, caring, and sweet."

He also smelled of catnip, but only when it rained. Probably not something I should mention now. After all, in less than one hour, Dru would marry Charming, and my promise to Winslow would be broken. I wasn't sure how my cursed self would react. I hoped like hell that I wouldn't declare my undying love to the butler, but who knew?

"If Winslow's so great," I grinned, "why are you marrying Charming?"

Dru choked back a sob and threw herself back on the bed. It groaned under her weight. "Because," she said, "Winslow won't have me. I'm ugly!"

Like Winslow was a prize. Didn't the deluded princess hear anything I said? "Are you crazy?" I asked. "Winslow would die for you. He told me as much."

Through tear-soaked eyelashes, Dru gazed at me with such hope that I felt queasy. "Do you really think so?"

"Believe it. I would never lie to you." I winced. "Okay, I would, but not until the union reinstates me. Even then, not about true love. Villain's honor."

The hope in Dru's face twisted into guilt. "But I'm going to marry Charming in forty-five minutes."

"So don't. Prince Idiot doesn't deserve you." I laughed. "Go find Winslow, and tell him that you love him."

"I do, you know."

Ew. "Yeah. I get it." Beast and the Troll, a fairytale for all ugly children. I walked to the door, throwing it wide. "Don't waste a second. Go find your butler love."

Dru nodded and struggled to her feet, her skirt swaying around her ankles. She glanced from the open door to my face and back again. "Are you sure?"

"Yes." I smiled my encouragement.

One glass slipper slid a step toward freedom, followed by its mate.

"You go, girl."

With the regal bearing of a queen, Dru sent me a nod of

dismissal and strolled past me and out the door. I let out a sigh of relief. I really, really didn't want to declare my love to a butler, curse or not. I had standards.

Mission complete. Winslow and Dru would live uglier ever after. I prayed when the time came they'd adopt. A goldfish.

"Oh, RJ?" Dru said behind me.

Shit. "Yeah?"

"Do me a favor." She halted. My heart hammered in my throat. Please no, don't say it, I begged. Nevertheless, the unsightly girl said it anyway: "Tell Charming I'm sorry."

Chapter 42

The next hour didn't go as planned. For anyone. Charming, dressed in his perfectly tailored tuxedo, stood in front of me at the altar of the Maledetto temple, smiling like a proud papa. He looked as clueless as the day we'd met. Flowers in all shades of white, from eggshell to vanilla bean, lined the aisle. I sneezed, sending the kippah on my head bouncing up and down.

"Bless you, Rabbi," Charming whispered.

"RJ," I said.

"Your name's RJ too?" Charming smiled. "My best friend is named RJ. What a coincidence."

I waved my hand to stop him, but he ignored me.

"I wish RJ was here. Not you, Rabbi, but my friend, RJ. But he can't be because he's on the run after murdering a whole bunch of people, including his ex-wife."

"I did not—"

"He tried to kill me too. Well, he tried to burn down my house while I slept." Charming paused in my litany of supposed evil deeds. "But he's really a great guy. You'd like him."

"I—"

"That is, if you ever have a chance to meet him. Since he's on the run from the sheriff after killing all those poor people, I doubt you will, but maybe someday . . ."

The king walked by us, effectively shutting up Prince Motormouth. The poor king looked rumpled and smelled of Bengay. He pushed passed us and took his seat next to a very angry queen.

She hissed, "You smell like feet."

The king blushed.

I shushed the unhappy couple, once again trying to tell Charming about Dru's decision not to marry him. The queen quieted instantly, a flush of red staining her already ruby cheeks. The king, on the other hand, started to rise from his seat, boiling me in oil with his eyes. I glanced around to make sure no one was looking and then lifted the beanie from my head. The king relaxed.

"Knew it was you," he whispered.

The queen rolled her eyes, but didn't comment.

The temple door opened. I shoved the beanie back on my head. The sheriff walked in, arm in arm with my princess. Asia wore a serene smile and a bridesmaid's dress of the brightest jade. The color matched her flame-colored hair and attitude perfectly. My legs started to move of their own volition. I took a step toward her, wanting nothing more than to scoop her into my arms and run, not walk, to the nearest tower.

Bruce's thick fingers curled around Asia's upper arm. Jealous rage filled me. Nobody touched my princess. My vision went red. My hands fisted. I would kill the sheriff, and then I would kill him all over again. And again.

Third time's a charm.

Asia giggled, and like an elixir, my rage dampened at the sound. Get a grip, I reminded myself. There was work to be done. First, I had to tell Charming that Dru ran off with the butler. And while he was recovering from the shock, I needed to find a way to free Asia.

Not to mention unmask a killer, which by this time seemed like an endless process. Hell, I was ready to throw in the towel, accuse Charming out of hand, and get the hell out of Maledetto. After all, Charming had likely committed some misdeed in his charmed life—definitely, if one considered stupidity a crime.

Asia and Bruce arrived at the altar. My eyes drank in the Popsicle-icious sight of her. My body hardened. Charming cleared his throat, a signal to start the Wedding March. The first tinkling of "I Wanna Hold Your Hand, but Nothing Else" began.

"Charming," I called. "Wait."

All eyes turned toward the back of the church.

Nothing happened.

The song ended.

Charming's smile faltered. He cleared his throat again. The organ player sighed, but did as ordered. Again, music boomed from the instrument. This time about half the people in the temple turned to the door.

Again, Dru failed to appear.

Asia caught my eye, nodding toward Charming. I shrugged. She shook her head, as if disgusted by the male species. "Tell him," she mouthed.

"I tried," I mouthed back.

She rolled her eyes. "Some villain you are," she said, and then cleared her throat to gain Charming's attention. He glanced her way, his smile growing wider. "I'm sorry, Charming." Asia grimaced. "Dru left."

"Left?" Charming tilted his head like a puppy. "Left what? I'm sure if we all try we can find whatever she misplaced." As his words trailed off, he dropped to his knees, running his fingers along the carpet. "Come on, help me look," he said to the wedding guests. They stared back at him in horror.

Only the ever-faithful Bruce willingly fell to his knees to aid Charming in his search. Unfortunately, Asia, handcuffed to the sheriff, fell to her knees too. The side of her tight bridesmaid dress split wide open, showing off pale perfect skin. Pale perfect skin of *my princess!*

I ran down the pulpit steps and lifted Asia to her feet, trying to block her exposed parts with my beanie. Thanks to Newton's Third Law and a pair of steel bracelets, the sheriff bounded to his feet as well.

"Hey, it's you," he said, waving his uncuffed arm in my face. "You are under arrest!"

I punched him in the nose.

In hindsight, punching the guy handcuffed to my lady-love wasn't the best move, for a couple of reasons. But mainly because the sheriff flew backward, landing three pews into the vestibule. Asia, of course, followed, her legs dangling in the air, her dress sliding down her body and over her head. Jade panties peeked out from between her long legs. I winced at her shrieks of anger, which grew louder as the seven dwarfs started to wolf-whistle in appreciation.

Asia righted herself soon enough with the help from a much-too-eager henchman. The sheriff struggled to his feet too. I glanced between the still-crawling prince, the bloody and annoyed sheriff, and my nearly naked princess. For once in my life, I wanted to stay, to save the day, to right the wrongs, even those I caused. Nonetheless, one look into Asia's burning eyes suggested I save myself from her wrath first and foremost.

"Now, Asia . . . ," I said.

"Get out of here. *Now.*"

And I did, thanks in part to her order and my own well-developed sense of self-preservation. I ran toward the temple doors as if the devil himself was on my rabbi tails. Of course, it was merely the sheriff and his brand-new stun gun, which only felt like the fires of hell chasing me. My beanie flew out of my hand, causing the sheriff to dive for cover behind a pew of elderly guests. This allowed me enough time to hop the prone, prostrating prince and make a clean getaway.

Sort of.

I ran from the church and into the forest, deeper and deeper, until nothing looked even vaguely familiar. Then, and only then, did I stop to catch my breath, which led to a small nap, and eventually the dream...

I was standing at an altar dressed in the finest tuxedo I could steal. Next to me, in a gown of shimmering white, Asia stood with a veil over her beautiful face. In my dream, I vowed to love, honor, and obey her until my death. The priest pronounced us husband and wife, and it was time to kiss my bride. I lifted the veil from her face, and screamed, and screamed, and screamed some more....

I awoke soaked in a cold sweat. The nightmare of Charming's moronic and oddly furry face underneath Asia's veil was one I wouldn't soon forget. A shiver ripped through me.

Picking myself up off my forest bed, I brushed at the pine needles clinging to my clothes, shedding them like the remnants of my dream. Impotent guilt, I thought. I failed to honor my promise to Dru to tell Charming about her abrupt departure, so the nightmare was union payback.

Still, a piece of me wondered if the guilt was my own. I could've saved Charming from the public embarrassment of being left at the altar. But true to my villainous self, I didn't. I smiled at the thought. Maybe my curse was finally withering.

"Fudge," I screamed into the silent forest. "Fork. Forget-me-not!"

Or not.

Damn.

"Did you say something about teeth?" a chick in a red hood asked from behind a tree. She looked no older than ten, dressed in scarlet and carrying a blood-soaked ax. Not someone to be messed with.

"Sorry. Must've been someone else." I smiled and took a couple of steps back. "You know how the forest can echo."

"My, what big feet you have." Her eyebrows rose.

"Yeah. Ummm . . . look, kid," I began and then took off running. I'd read the *New Never News* articles about a little red-hooded serial killer too many times to be her eighth victim.

I barreled my way through the forest, leaping over downed logs and ducking dive-bombing bluebirds. High-pitched, insane laughter followed me no matter how fast I ran.

"My, my, what big ears you have!"

I doubled my speed.

"My, my, what big eyes you have!"

Terror gave me added strength to run even faster.

"My, my, what short legs you have!"

I pulled to a stop. "Hey, my legs are not short. They're average for a man of my size."

"Average for a short man maybe." The crazy red-hooded bitch laughed. An ax flew over my head, missing my scalp by inches. It planted itself in a tree. Another burst of laughter followed.

Fuck it. Now wasn't the time to discuss the relativity of stature and the evils of the metric system. I took off running again, ducking and weaving through the Enchanted Forest like a big, not-so-nice wolf with a basket of fresh-baked goodies on his way to visit his nana.

No matter how fast I ran, the red-hooded chick stayed right on my heels. I had to find a place to hide, somewhere that the crazy bitch would never find me. Ah, there, on the right. The pond where I'd first met Dru.

Lungs bursting, I dove into a slime-coated pond with a splash. The water rippled and then settled, hiding me from my would-be ax murderer not yet tall enough to ride the

Tea Toddler at Feyland. Above me, her apple-cheeked reflection danced across the water, the shine of her ax glowing like a beacon.

Trust me, the irony wasn't lost on me. There I was, a world-famous villain, hiding from a little girl in red tights. Pathetic. No wonder the union gave me the boot.

Chapter 43

An hour later, shivering and covered in pond sludge, I dragged my body from the pond. Little Red had given up her murderous quest twenty minutes ago. But I'd stayed hidden in the weeds until I was sure the little serial killer wasn't lying in wait for my head on her plate. When the toad at the edge of the pond croaked the all-clear sign, I pulled myself from the muck with a wet squeak. Mud and slime dribbled off me in clumps.

My clothes, hair, and boots smelled like day-old fish. On the bright side, my dip in the pond had cured my hangover, not to mention a lingering case of villain's foot.

For the first time since Natasha took off with my worst friend, the Frog Prince, I actually felt somewhat sorry for the guy. A pond was no place for a man to live, amphibian parts aside.

Trudging to the shore, water and slime dripping from my every orifice, I considered the last couple of days. I was trapped in Maledetto, an unknown killer as well as my murderous princess stalking my every step. Not to mention being cursed to boot, but I'd had worse weeks.

In fact, when Natasha and I first married, we spent a week camping in the Enchanted Forest with Natasha's banjo-playing relatives. Trust me, the forest and Natasha's family were less than enchanting. I shuddered thinking about it.

It was time to take charge, to find Cinderella's killer and get the hell out of Maledetto. I sat down on the nearest toad-free log and contemplated my next move. I needed to return to the kingdom, at the very least to rescue my distressed and arrested damsel, and for a change of clothes. I guess I owed Charming an apology as well, for messing up his big day, even though it would kill me to give it.

Somewhere on my right, a branch broke under the heavy tread of a boot. I snatched up a toad, aiming its poison butt at the interloper. I wasn't going down without a fight. Little Red would see just how big and bad a villain I was.

Or not.

Through the brush, Charming's overly big and blond head appeared. Tears stained his cheeks, giving him a clownlike appeal. My guilt-o-meter increased half a point.

"Rabbi?" he said, stumbling my way. "What are you doing here?"

"Charming, it's me." I yanked the kippah from my head. "RJ."

"Oh, RJ!" He clapped his hands and ran toward me. "I'm so happy to see you."

I stepped back to avoid his hugging arms, but tripped over a log and ended up on my back, a toad ass in my face. The toad croaked once, excreted a yellow gooey substance, and hopped away. I wiped my face and sniffed my fingers, relieved when they smelled only of urine. Not my proudest moment.

I staggered to my feet, wiping my hands on the nearest bush, which turned out to be poison oak. My skin started to itch and blister instantly. It turned red and bubbled up two sizes bigger than a normal hand.

That wasn't nearly as bad as what happened next.

Prince Rotten yanked me into a bear hug, crushing me to him, his arms surprisingly strong, as was his breath. "Why? RJ, why?" he cried against my shoulder. "Why would Dru do this? To *me?*"

A swirl of answers crossed my mind, but my curse kept me from commenting. "Come on, mate." I patted his shoulder, more in hopes he'd release me than for comfort. "You didn't really love Dru. Did you? Admit it, you're happy she eloped with Winslow."

"What? She eloped with the butler?" He jerked away. "Dru choose that troll over me? Why? I'm a prince, for fuck sakes! I'm pretty. I'm a catch, damn it! What could he possibly have that I don't?" Humility? Kindness? A desire for women?

I raised my hand to stop Charming's tirade. "That's not the point. The point is, you're now a free man. No princess nagging at you twenty-four / seven. You can do what you want, when you want."

Or to whom you want.

The prince tilted his head as if considering my words. Then he promptly burst into full snotty sobs. "You don't understand. I loved Dru."

"No, you didn't."

"Well, I liked her."

I shook my head.

"Fine," he said. "But damn it, she was my last hope."

My eyes narrowed. In my short association with Charming, I never heard him utter a single unkind word, and now, he sounded much like a military general on the verge of surrender. Oddly, that didn't make me like him one iota more.

"I'm sorry," I said. "I didn't realize Dru's importance to your plot to dominate the world."

Charming grinned, all cunning gone as swiftly as it came. "The world?" He giggled. "No. I want something much smaller. I want to be part of the Maledetto family. A real member. Not just some charity case the king took in as a child. I want to be a part of a real family."

"And marrying one of the princesses would give you that." Well, I guess that explained his proposals to Asia, Cinderella, and then Dru. I almost felt sorry for the guy. Being an outcast was hard. I should know. I thought about what the queen had said, about Charming's lack of child-hood friends. About how the kids would laugh and tease him for being short . . .

"I was ten when the king took me in," Charming said, his voice trembling, "an orphan, with no place to go."

"That's rough."

He nodded, his eyes misting. "Don't get me wrong. The king did right by me. He raised me like his son. I want nothing more than to please him."

"So you asked Asia, the oldest daughter, to marry you."

He nodded. "The king worried Asia would never marry. Not with her . . . weight problem . . ."

What a fool. Was everyone in the kingdom blind? Asia's beauty came from the stubborn tilt of her head and the curve of her smart mouth. It was there in the way she beat a defenseless egg to death, or how she made love with one hot look.

Prince Moron continued, "I didn't want to marry her, not with all that blubber, but I proposed to please the king."

Violence boiled inside me. Poor Asia. She had suffered with Prince Twat much too long. I vowed to make it up to her. Not a day would go by without my listing her every attribute, starting with the tiny mole on the inside of her right thigh, the one as smooth and velvety as whipped cream on a slice of pumpkin pie.

"But then you dumped Asia for Cinderella," I said. "How'd the king like that?"

"I had no choice, really."

"Really?"

He nodded. "Cinderella was beautiful beyond compare and Asia . . . well, you know . . ."

I wanted to pummel him into prince pudding, but something held me back. Stupid union. One good smack would solve so many problems, not to mention make me feel a hell of a lot better.

"The king understood my need to marry his real daughter," he said, as if Asia was some kind of imaginary offspring. "And the king was happy for us. Cinderella and me. For a while." Charming's voice turned whisper soft. "Yet if I had a chance to do it all over again, I would never have proposed to her."

"Her?" Did he mean Asia or his pancake-sized fiancée?

"Cindi." He shook his head. "Please try to pay attention."

"Right. Sorry," I said, heavy on the sarcasm. Of course he failed to notice. "So why wouldn't you propose to Cinderella?" After all, she seemed like Charming's perfect match—vain, selfish, and stupid; add in a pinch of malice, and poof, a princess fit for a twit.

A frown marred Charming's perfect features. "Because Cinderella's dead, RJ. I can't marry a dead princess. What would people think?"

I bit my lip to keep from screaming. "I know that."

"So why'd you ask?" He shook his head. "Never mind. What am I going to do now? Cinderella's dead, and Dru's run away with a troll."

"Don't even think about it," I warned.

"What?"

"Asia is mine."

In an instant, his face transformed from sad to giddy. He clapped his hands together and danced around me. "What a great idea."

"No!"

"I'll propose to Asia."

"I'll kill you!"

"She's not fat anymore, even if her hair still resembles a carrot."

Somewhere in my cerebellum something snapped. I raised my hand and smacked Charming across the cheek. The slap echoed around the forest. Charming staggered backward, his hand rubbing his abused flesh. A red, deceptively small handprint stained his face.

"Why'd you hit me?" he cried.

"Are you serious?" I took a step toward him. "You're planning to propose to *my* princess, and you ask me why I smacked you? You're lucky that's all I can do." My foot lashed out, this time missing the idiot prince by a foot.

Tears glistened in his eyes. He sniffed, sucking in a string of snot. Unfortunately, it did nothing to detract from his princely appeal. The bastard.

I slapped him again for good measure.

Charming cried out and ran behind a large bald oak tree. He poked his head around the bark.

"Leave Asia alone." I wagged a finger at him. "If you so much as look at her I'll twist you into a Pollock painting." Art Forgery 101 had finally paid off. My villainous instructor would be so proud.

"Well, if that's how you're going to be," Charming said.

Damn straight it was. I would die for Asia, as long as she stopped trying to kill me. "That's how I'm going to be," I said, my arms crossed over my chest in a desperate attempt to intimidate.

"A pity," he said as he stepped behind the oak tree.

I started to frown, but before my lips could curve into the appropriate downward arch, a crackle of electricity buzzed from behind me.

Zap!

Fifty thousand volts shot through my body. I dropped to my knees. My brain seemed to short-circuit as a string of foul words stammered on the end of my wobbly tongue.

The sheriff stood above me with his freshly charged

stun gun. He juiced me again for good measure. Blood filled my mouth as my teeth sliced into my tongue. Rhythmically my limbs shuddered and my bladder threatened to give way.

A circle of toads watched my puppet show from a fallen log, mocking humor in their beady, bug eyes. Tiny bluebirds swelled in my vision, growing bigger and bigger.

Charming stood over me. "What do you think, Bruce? Should I go old school and get down on one knee when I propose to my sweet Asia?" He proceeded to do just that, his knee pressing into my spine.

"Both knees," the sheriff said. "She is a lady, after all."

"How right you are." Charming's second knee stabbed into my sciatic nerve, paralyzing me almost as much as the Taser had. Pain radiated up my nerve endings and into my brain like a freight train. I struggled for breath, grey spots dancing in my eyes.

"RJ," Charming said.

"Whhaaat?" I gasped.

"I do hope you'll come to the wedding."

Chapter 44

Sometime later, I awoke in the backseat of a patrol pumpkin, its red and blue lights flashing in a rhythmic beat. My hands, cuffed behind me, had long ago fallen victim to the Sandman. The tingling revived me somewhat. But my head still felt like a piñata the day after Cinco de Mayo, split open and empty. I moaned and blinked against the swirl of lights. The sheriff sat in the front seat filling out a stack of paperwork.

"Let's see," he said. "Impersonating a member of the clergy. Assault. Obstruction. And that's only in the last hour." His eyes met mine in the rearview mirror. "Oh, and let's not forget, first degree murder."

Dramatic pause.

"Eight counts."

"What?" I struggled against my bonds, quickly calculating the Maledetto body count. "I didn't kill anyone." Well, not recently, and definitely not in Maledetto. Unless one counted the toad I'd accidentally squished while escaping the red-hooded serial killer. But, come on, toad squishing was a misdemeanor at best.

The sheriff glanced inside his notebook. "Let's not forget, one count of attempted murder."

"Attempted murder?" I racked my brain for an intended victim. A name came quick enough. Charming. But wanting someone dead and attempting to kill them weren't the same thing. "I didn't try to kill anyone." Yet.

"Oh really?"

"Yes, really."

The sheriff scoffed. "Then explain the bluebird."

"What bluebird?"

"That one." The sheriff pointed to a bluish bird sitting on the hood of the patrol pumpkin. The bird looked innocent enough, if you overlooked its bloodstained beak. "That bird bit me." Bruce showed me his freshly bandaged arm. "I can only assume on your command."

"That's some assumption." I paused, nodding to the gold star pinned to his lapel. It shone brightly in the flashing red and blue lights. "Where'd you get your sheriff's badge? A cereal box?"

The sheriff blushed and fingered the star. Damn, I thought the patrol car smelled vaguely of Froot Loops. "Listen," I said. "I've never seen that bird in my life. I swear it."

He frowned. "And I'm supposed to take the word of a villain?"

Good point. "Open the door and I'll prove it."

"How?"

"I'll order it to fly away. If it's under my command it will." I swallowed. "If not, it will probably peck my eyes out. What have you got to lose?"

The sheriff nodded. "Fair enough."

The locks on the back door popped. I stared at the door handle. This was my chance to escape.

Or a really stupid way to die.

My money was on the latter.

But I had to try. A picture of Asia, beautiful in a stark white gown, burst into my head. Like a princess in a fairytale, tiny birds circled her head, threading pink ribbons through her long tresses. A slow burn grew in my chest, aching for my lovely lady.

A second image floated through my brain. Charming, dressed in a tux, his blond hair flowing in the nonexistent wind, stood next to my princess, his lips hovering inches from hers.

Hell no. I'd see Charming in hell first.

Before the sheriff could blink, in a trick as old as villainy itself, I slipped my legs through my handcuffed arms. With my hands now cuffed in front of me, I grabbed the door handle, mumbling a silent prayer or what passed as a prayer in the Church of Villainy. It went something like:

Now I do something really dumb, I pray it doesn't end with me pummeled into a villainous mulch. If I cry before I take, I pray no one sees it. Almond.

"Here goes nothing." I shoved the door open and slipped out of the vehicle and into the enchanted air. A cool wind swept across my still-wet rabbi costume. I shivered, but not from the cold. The bluebird tilted its head to one side, watching me warily. I took a step from the patrol pumpkin, leaving the door open just in case.

"Hello there," I said to the bird.

Squawk!

"Gretel, is it?"

Again, a loud squawk. I took that as the affirmative.

From inside the patrol car, the sheriff screamed and quickly shut the door, trapping me outside with the bluebird, a bluebird responsible for at least one death, and possibly two more. Unless Hansel and Missy had pecked themselves to death.

I swear Gretel smiled, her blood-soaked beak gleaming in the fading sunlight. I swallowed hard, but stood my ground, mostly because my legs refused to move.

"Nice to finally meet you," I said to the bird. "Would you be a good bird, and do me a favor?"

Squawk.

"See these handcuffs?" Using my chin, I gestured to my shackled hands. Gretel's beak bobbed. "Smart bird."

Squawk.

"Okay, here's the deal." I gave her my best "trust me" smile, all teeth and lips. "Pick this lock and I'll give you all the cocoa you can eat."

To a bluebird, my bribe equaled the golden ticket, except in this case Willy Wonka wasn't the man behind the scenes. Someone else was, someone who used the poor, innocent bird to kill Cinderella, Hansel, and Missy with cold-bloodied efficiency. And now my freedom, if not my life, were in Gretel's talons.

Gretel flapped her wings, as if debating my offer.

"Come on, sweetheart," I said. "Help a villain out."

She did, but with much more enthusiasm than I'd anticipated. Her talons locked onto my right arm, tearing into the flesh beneath. Blood ran down my arm, staining the sleeve of my shirt. I held in a scream, beads of sweat forming on my forehead.

With the precision of Goldilocks, Gretel picked the handcuff lock in record time. One minute I was a prisoner on my way to jail, and then next, I was a free man with one goal.

Stop Charming.

At any cost.

"Stop," the sheriff yelled from the safety of the patrol pumpkin. "Stop in the name of the law." A command I never quite understood.

Nevertheless, I did stop, just long enough to ask Gretel for one final favor. I motioned to the sheriff. "Don't let him out of the vehicle and I'll toss in a subscription to *Bird Fancy*."

Squawk.

"Yep." I nodded. "The one with the Toucan Sam centerfold."

Gretel flapped her wings, flying from my bloody arm to

the windshield of the patrol pumpkin. Her talons scratched against the glass with a terrifying screech. The sheriff screamed like a girl and raised his hands to protect his face even though three centimeters of glass separated him from certain death.

I tapped the glass with my knuckle. "You'll be safe as long as you stay inside the vehicle." I grinned at the sheriff. "Don't bother calling for help. Gretel's got friends in high places."

The sheriff glanced upward to the swarm of bluebirds circling overhead. He swallowed, his Adam's apple bobbing rapidly.

"Thanks," I said to Gretel. "I owe you one."

Without waiting for her answering squawk, I took off for the palace in search of a change of clothes and my one true love.

Chapter 45

"Son, I need your advice," the king said when I opened the front door of the palace. It looked like he needed more than advice. A shower, for one thing. He was still dressed in last night's bachelor party wear, his crown tarnished and slightly askew, and his eyes puffy and small under his sagging skin. "Please," he added with a hiccup.

"Not now, sir." Even if I wanted to help him, I couldn't. Asia was in danger of marrying Prince Rotten. And I wasn't having any of it.

I ran up the stairs, taking them two at a time. Three flights later, I arrived at Asia's bedroom. Not bothering to knock, I pushed the door open and gasped in surprise. Her room was decorated in what could only be described as the early villain period. Posters of wicked queens, evildoers, and old-school henchmen filled her walls.

But it was the picture over her bed that grabbed my attention most, a photograph of none other than yours truly taken years ago by a hack reporter at the *New Never News* following one of my villainous escapades.

I grinned, feeling oddly pleased by this turn of events. My sweet princess harbored a secret thing for villains. I still had a chance.

If I could find her.

"Asia," I called down the hallway. No answer. "Baby, where are you?"

Heart heavy, I headed for Cinderella's room and a fresh pair of clothes. As expected, sitting on the bed were a new pair of Levi's and a black T-shirt. Winslow might be getting laid, but he was still a damn good butler.

I quickly changed into my dry clothes, tossing my wet rabbi uniform in a pile on the floor. My head swirled with possibilities. Where was Asia? Was she with Charming? Was he at this very moment stealing my ladylove? I had one chance, and I had to act fast.

I ran down the palace stairs and right into the king, who sat slumped on the bottom step. My foot connected with his backside, and I did a flip in the air before landing on the floor, my head cushioning my fall. The king glanced down at me.

"That looked like it hurt." He shook his head. "You should watch where you're going. A careful man is a carefree man, as my papa used to say."

I blinked away a swirl of blue and pink birds from my vision. "I thought you never met your dad."

"He would've said that, son. I'm sure of it."

I rolled my eyes and staggered to my feet. "Sir, I need your help. It's very important."

"You're too late, boy."

No, I couldn't be. I needed Asia in my life. Sure, I'd survive without her smile, but I'd never be happy. And damn it, if my impotency taught me anything, it was that I wanted happiness. I wasn't willing to settle anymore.

"Asia said yes to Charming?" I swallowed over the lump lodged in my throat. "She's going to marry him?"

"What?" The king bounded off the step, his face turning purple like the capillaries lining his nose. "When'd this happen? I won't allow it."

I held up my hand. "Wait. Wait. Wait. What'd you mean when you said I was too late?"

"I was speaking metaphorically."

I raised an eyebrow.

"The queen asked for a divorce, son." The king sniffed and then used the end of his beard to blow his nose. "My marriage is over. I've lost the love of my life." He broke down in loud, racking sobs. Not a pretty sight. Snot rolled from his face like a booger waterfall.

I swallowed my disgust. "Sir, no disrespect, but isn't that what you want? To be free of the queen?"

"Hell no." The king flapped his arms in the air much like Gretel the bluebird. "What gave you a stupid idea like that?"

"Well, let's see," I lifted my index finger, "you tried to shoot her. Multiple times." My middle finger went up next. "You tried to snap her neck in a rat trap. And let's not forget the rocket in the tool shed."

The king smiled. "A Valentine's gift."

I gave up. "That's exactly what I mean. Women don't want death threats. They want to be loved."

The king scoffed.

"They also don't like it when their husband sleeps with a stripper."

"Oh, what do you know?" The king gave a bitter laugh. "Asia's run off with that twit Charming, and you're here, wasting time."

"What?" I grabbed the king's shoulders and shook him. "What do you mean Asia's run off? Did you see her leave with Charming?"

"Of course I did."

"Why didn't you tell me that in the first place?" I didn't bother to wait for his answer. Instead, I ran out of the palace, down the porch steps, and into the forest, my heart in my throat. I had to find Asia. I had to tell her that I loved her.

* * *

I ran deeper and deeper into the darkness. The forest had become a refuge for Charming's dastardly plan, or so I believed. The footprints helped, of course, two pairs of glass slippers by the look of them. Who else but a flaming prince wore glass slippers after Fairy Day?

Tracking the couple's trail didn't take long. In fact, I caught up with Charming and Asia after only ten minutes. They walked side by side, Charming's hand on Asia's arm. They looked like the typical happy couple on a forest jaunt. I didn't buy it for a second. Asia loved me; of that I was sure.

She just didn't know it yet.

The couple paused at a familiar wooden bridge. The same one I found yesterday when searching for Winslow. Charming smiled at my princess. He plucked a blue wild-flower from the ground next to the bridge and held it out to Asia.

Rookie mistake.

As soon as the flower touched Asia's soft skin, she began to sneeze. I shook my head and continued watching them from behind a large tree.

Charming quickly dropped the flower and handed Asia a Kleenex from the pocket of his tux. What kind of douche wore his wedding tux to propose to another woman?

Asia didn't seem to mind, though. She pointed to something off in the distance. Charming's eyes followed her finger. While he was otherwise occupied, Asia reached for the Devil's Eye around her waist and carved something into the wood of the bridge. She smiled at the finished product and patted Charming's arm to gain his attention.

They talked for a moment. Asia's smile grew with each passing second. Her fingers pointed at her heart and then to Charming's. He nodded and dropped to one knee. Asia's eyes widened and her hand flew to her throat. Charming spoke briefly, probably about how pretty he was, and then reached for my princess's hand. She shook her head. He nodded, his expression serious, eyes intent. The rat bastard. If he touched her, I would throttle him.

While I fantasized about wringing Charming's scrawny neck, the couple slipped away, continuing on their enchanted hike through the forest. I wasn't sure where they were going, but I'd follow Asia to the ends of the kingdom, her desire for Charming be damned.

The ends of the kingdom turned out to be a log cabin about two miles from the palace. It appeared old, built in the last century, with broken shutters and a crooked porch. Smoke curled from the chimney, as if the house expected visitors.

Was this Charming's plan? Lock Asia away in a remote cabin in the woods? I shrugged. As dastardly plans went, it wasn't the best. For this kind of thing, a tower worked best. High windows. Hard to escape unless you had an extra-strength weave.

Damn Rapunzel.

Charming entered the cabin first, holding the door open for my princess. She paused at the threshold as if deciding her fate.

"Asia, wait," I shouted.

Her eyes met mine. She smiled sadly. My heart swelled in my chest. She loved me. I could see it in her eyes. Those same damn eyes that turned around and headed inside with Prince Rotten.

Chapter 46

I pounded on the door of the quaint cabin. "Damn it, Asia, open this door right now." My fist banged harder against the wood. Splinters bit into my palm, but I ignored the pain. The pain in my heart took precedence. The ache grew stronger and stronger with every second the door stayed closed. Wetness gathered in my eyes, from the high pollen count, I assured my manhood. "Please," I muttered, smacking the door one final time.

The door opened as if by magic.

"Go away," Asia said, looking as beautiful and as sweet as ever. She'd changed from her jade bridesmaid's gown and into a stark white dress that looked suspiciously like a wedding gown.

My heart beat faster. This was my chance. Don't blow it, I warned myself. "Asia," I began. "I—"

"RJ, I don't love you."

"What?"

"I never will."

"But—"

She leaned in close enough for me to smell the sweet scent of her. "Go back to the palace."

"I—"

Her beautiful face hardened. "Forget about me. About us."

Blinding pain exploded in my chest. I was falling deeper and deeper into the abyss of unrequited love. There was no way out. No safety net. The pain was so intense I barely heard her next words.

"Run along, pup," she said, her tone as icy as Miss Muffet's after her third shot of whey. The look in Asia's eyes matched her tone. A cold, blank stare, as if we never shared a single kiss.

Unable to stand another second in front of the woman who was breaking my heart, I stumbled off the porch, my vision blurry, my throat raw. A lump the size of a pea even that other princess could feel swelled in my throat. I wanted to die. Right there on the spot. Even Natasha's betrayal hadn't hurt this much, and I'd given her half my 401(v).

I hate to admit it but I ran away. I ran as fast as I could. Legs burning, chest heaving, and still I ran. I ran and ran and ran until the pain in my heart faded. Then and only then did I stop to catch my breath. I sat down on the edge of the wooden bridge, my heart and head heavy.

Pup?

Had Asia call me pup?

What the fuck was that about?

My fingers clenched against the wood of the small bridge, the same spot where Asia had given her heart to Charming only twenty minutes ago. Splinters dug into my calloused flesh, but I barely felt them. Through a blur of tears, I glanced down at the one word Asia had carved in the wood.

Help!

Chapter 47

Two point six minutes later, I arrived at the palace, out of breath, legs burning. A kingdom record for sure, but I wasn't waiting around for Olympic gold. Nope, my goal was lead, and plenty of it. I dashed into the library and lifted the couch, searching for the king's rifle. No gun.

"Where is it?" I yelled, scanning the room for the weapon. But no gun appeared. Yet, in the corner of the room, something did catch my eye.

A bow forged of the finest iron.

A quiver of arrows lay next to it.

I scrambled over the couch to the bow and arrows. Lifting the weapon in my hands, I checked its weight. It was lighter than I expected, as if tailored for its owner. The steel bowstring gleamed with malicious intent, like a heavy-metal guitar at a country bar.

I grabbed the quiver of arrows, jammed it into my jeans, and headed from the library, pausing just long enough to stare down at the wolf pelt on the floor.

"Best served cold, huh," I said. "Not today, my furry friend."

The pelt didn't reply.

Bow in hand, I hurried from the library and out of the palace. It was time to face a killer, an annoyed princess

with trust issues, and my destiny. I hoped my destiny wasn't
to be killed by the killer or the princess.

Thanks to my impotency, things could go either way.

Backtracking through the forest, I again arrived at the
wooden bridge and paused to catch my breath. My heart
slammed in my chest with fear. Was I already too late to
save the day, let alone my princess?

Lifting the bow over my shoulder, I continued on my
hike through the forest, on the hunt for Cinderella's killer.

I approached the cabin a few minutes later, the bow at
the ready as I crept to the window and peeked inside. Asia
stood next to the fireplace still dressed in that awful white
gown, the Devil's Eye in her hand. She flipped it open and
peered inside. Her face hardened and her eyes grew a
darker shade of green. Damn Eye must be broken, because
it sure as hell hadn't warned Asia of the dangers surrounding her.

It also wouldn't save her, not this time.

But I would.

I scanned the rest of the room for any signs of danger.
The place looked like any other single-room cabin. A fireplace with an iron pot large enough to deep-fry a cookie
elf in oil sat against the far wall. A small bed stood opposite of the hearth. Two chairs and a matching love seat
filled the rest of the room.

Other than Asia, the cabin looked empty. No sign of
Charming anywhere. A voice I didn't recognize drew my
attention. I leaned in closer, my breath fogging the frosted
glass of the windowpane. This was bad. Really bad.

Unfortunately, I only caught the speaker's every third
word, but the meaning was clear, and far worse than I expected. I had to act, and quickly, before Asia suffered a
fate much worse than death. I hurried to the door, loaded
an arrow into the bow, and waited for my cue.

It came soon enough.

"Let them speak now or forever hold their peace," the strange voice crackled.

I kicked the door. It flew open, bits of wood spiraling in all directions, showering my intended target with a rain of toothpicks. I aimed the bow. "Don't move or I'll shoot."

Everyone moved at once.

Chapter 48

The roar of gunfire in the tiny room nearly deafened me. I threw my body to the side. The heat of the bullet grazed my forehead. For once in my life, I was damn glad to be on the short side of six feet.

"No!" Asia cried out, raising the Devil's Eye above her head. The glint of the blue jewel blinded me as it arched above me. The cold rage in Asia's face stunned me nearly as much as the barrel of the king's rifle pointed at my ribs.

The shooter aimed the rifle at the center of my forehead. "I hate you! Hate you! You ruin everything! Everything!"

"De Wolfe, I now pronounce you husband and—"

I fired the bow.

The arrow sprang free from its sheath.

Time slowed.

Prince Charming, also known as Junior—Nigel de Wolfe Junior, to be precise—dropped the king's rifle and grabbed his sternum. He staggered backward, blood welling from between his fingers. "Asia?! But why? I thought we were the perfect couple?"

Asia snorted. "You're gay."

"What? Gay?" he yelled, apparently more annoyed by her accusation than the large jeweled object known as the Devil's Eye sticking from his chest. "Whatever gave you that idea?"

Charming glanced down at his wound, and then at Asia. His lips curved into a frown. She raised her eyebrow, and he dropped to the floor.

"Nice shot," I said, nodding to the Devil's Eye sticking out of Charming's chest.

"You too," Asia said, pointing to my arrow embedded in the forehead of the rabbi I'd clobbered that afternoon, who was now dressed in borrowed, much too tight, skinny jeans and a black T-shirt with the words "Prince Star" across the chest.

"I was aiming for Charming." I hated to admit it, but my cursed tongue held nothing back.

Asia smiled. I took a step toward her, searching her for injuries. She looked okay. More than okay, really. In fact, she looked beautiful. Her hair fell around her shoulder in fiery waves and her cheeks were flushed.

Asia grinned. "Archery takes practice. Tomorrow I'll show you some of my moves."

"Tomorrow?" Hope swelled in my heart even as Charming's lifeblood seeped into my boots. "Does that mean what I think it means?"

She tilted her head to one side. "I'm not sure. What do you think I mean?"

I stepped over Charming's corpse and wrapped my arms around my beautiful princess. "I think you lied."

"About what?"

"That you don't love me." I nodded smugly. "I think you do."

"Really? What makes you so sure?"

"Oh, admit it." My lips moved closer to hers. "You can't live without me."

"Don't push it."

I kissed her then, our lips melding into a tangle of saliva and promise. After a brief period of groping, I pulled back to stare into the face of my ladylove. "There's something I need to tell you," I began.

She held up her hand. "Me first."

Against my better judgment I motioned for her to continue.

"I guess I owe you an apology." Her gaze dropped to the floor and Charming's dead body. "I didn't mean what I said, any of it. About us. About you leaving. I was just so afraid."

"Scared of Charming? Did he hurt you?" I wanted to kill him, but seeing as the bastard was already dead, I had but one option. I kicked his corpse in the bollocks.

"No." Asia grabbed my hand to stop me from another round of Charmingball. "I was scared for you. Charming threatened to kill you if I didn't marry him."

"So when I came to the door you told me to get lost," I smiled, "to protect me."

She nodded, tears gathering in her eyes. "I had no choice. It was either marry him so he could be king, or risk your murder."

The jigsaw pieces began to fit. Charming had wanted revenge against the king for the death of his father, the elder de Wolfe, but Junior had also wanted something else even more. He wanted to be king. And the only way to accomplish his goal was to marry one of the king's daughters.

But he couldn't marry just any daughter, as he found out after his first brief engagement to Asia. To be king by law, Charming had to marry the king's daughter, not stepdaughter—Cinderella. So he quickly broke off his engagement to Asia and proposed to Cindi.

"Cinderella really was in New Never City to see you." I grinned. "You weren't lying about that."

Asia frowned. "I never lie."

"Right."

"Fine," she said with a snort. "Cindi wanted to meet. She had something to tell me. Until a couple of days ago I'd thought she wanted to apologize for ending my engagement."

"But she really wanted to warn you about Charming." I nodded. "The Devil's Eye gave him away, didn't it? That's why Cinderella had it. She learned that Charming was the son of Nigel de Wolfe."

"Yes."

"And when Charming found out, he bought Gretel and used her to kill Cinderella." I pictured the handwriting on the receipt as well as on the paper I'd found in Cinderella's room and the wooden bridge. They all matched Charming's girlish scrawl.

"Yes."

"And with Cinderella out of the way," I said, "once I forced the king to accept you as his 'real' daughters, both you and Dru were in line to be queen."

"Yes."

I frowned. "So why did Charming propose to Dru instead of you?" For one thing, Asia was older, and therefore, she would be crowned before her younger sibling. But more importantly, Asia was stunning like a truffle among a bunch of Hershey bars.

Asia bit her bottom lip. "Because of you."

"What's that have to do with anything?" I frowned. Even I wasn't vain enough to believe my superior manliness intimidated Charming that much.

"I lied to him," she said as if the very words were unpleasant. "Told him that I couldn't marry him. That I was in love with you."

"Why?" My heart gave a squeeze. Maybe my princess didn't love me after all. Was I merely a Villain Toy? An impotent one at that.

"Because I didn't want to marry him!" She kicked his corpse. "I never wanted to marry him."

"Why did you accept his first proposal?"

She sighed. "You know why."

Honestly, I didn't have a clue, but I nodded anyway.

"You really don't have a clue, do you?" She laughed,

pausing in her game of Kick the Charming long enough to kiss me. I wanted to hold her forever, but she pulled away after a minute or two. "For years people only saw me as the fat one. And for a while, I saw myself in the same way."

Her tone, not so much her words, made my heart ache. It was filled with pain and loneliness, the same feelings that haunted me when I was a shorter lad. My fingers trailed the edges of her face. "Don't ever say that again," I said. "You are perfection."

She gave me a small smile. "In my fat state, the queen feared no man would ever have me. When Charming, a boy I'd known most of my life, proposed, it seemed like a miracle. To everyone else. How could I refuse? My parents were so happy."

"For themselves." My fists clenched. "But what about you?"

"The day Charming dumped me was the best day of my life." Her laughter filled the small cabin. "I was finally free. Free to do what I wanted. And what I wanted most in the world was to get the hell out of Maledetto and never look back."

Out of all the reasons why I loved this woman, she had just named one of the top five. Six if you counted her breasts as separate entities. The sooner we left the kingdom, the sooner I'd be back at my villainous pursuits, and Asia would . . .

Damn. What sort of options did a princess have in the big city? Damsel in distress? Mattress salesman? Poison apple tester? Maybe I could get her on in the union's mailroom. Naw, she was too sweet and maidenly to work for the union. They'd chew her up, spit her out, and then sell her regurgitated parts to McDonald's at half price.

No matter how much Asia loved me now, she'd eventually realize her mistake and run off with the first frog prince she met. I couldn't take that kind of pain. Natasha's betrayal hurt, but Asia's leaving would kill me. Literally. I'd be better off with her locked away in a tower.

"Listen, I can't . . . we can't—" I started.

"Don't flatter yourself." She grinned, flashing even, white teeth. "I lied to Charming to keep him off my back, but my plan backfired when you stole the Devil's Eye from him."

"How so?"

"Without the Eye I would remain forever fat."

I smiled, missing my pudgy princess. She looked good enough to eat. Of course, she was smoking hot now too. I reached for one of her fiery curls, running it through my fingers. Lust swirled inside me, nearly stealing my breath.

Smack.

"Not the time or the place." Her smile softened her admonishment, but not the slap. Damn, she packed a punch in her tiny fist. I rubbed my cheek and tried to pay attention to what she was saying.

"Charming believed no man, you included, could want fat Asia. Therefore, I'd never marry and he would rule the kingdom once Dru became his wife." She paused. "Then you stole the Eye. For me." Tears glistened in her eyes. She wiped them away with the back of her hand. "No one's ever . . ."

A lump rose in my throat. So this was what it felt like to be a hero. A part of me wanted to puke while the other half felt ten feet tall. Not a combination I relished, considering the splatter factor.

Asia composed herself. "Charming was furious after you stole the Eye. Not as pissed as he was when you burned his house down, but annoyed nonetheless."

"If I remember correctly, he wasn't the only one." I grinned, remembering a load of buckshot aimed at my testicles. Sure, Asia tried to kill me, numerous times in fact, but she didn't succeed, and really, in a relationship, that mattered most.

Her eyes narrowed. "I wasn't trying to kill you."

"Right." I winked.

"I wasn't!" She stomped her foot like a child; unfortunately, it landed in a puddle of oozing Charming on the floor. Blood splattered her slipper, turning the red ribbon black, the same red ribbon from the slipper in the forest. I bet if I compared the pointy heel to the hole in my forehead, there'd be a perfect match.

"Then explain that." I pointed to the slipper wrapped around her slim foot.

She glanced down, frowning. "Damn."

"Exactly." I shot her a big smile. "Caught red-handed."

"Not that, you idiot." Her foot lashed out at Charming's leaking body. "My favorite slippers are ruined. Thanks to him." She kicked the corpse again.

"Uh-huh." I laughed. "It's okay, my sweet, I forgive you for trying to kill me." Forgiveness felt oddly satisfying, almost like smugness but without the nasty rash normally associated with it.

"Forgive me?" Her lips pursed as if she swallowed a bad gummy bear. "That's real nice of you, Mr. Big Bad Villain." I'd thought so, but apparently Asia didn't share my opinion if her next words were any indication. "Too bad you're not the one who needs to forgive me." She motioned to the corpse at our feet. "He is."

Chapter 49

"Oh, baby." I reached for her arm, intending to offer comfort to my sweet princess. After all, she just killed a man. The first kill was hard, all those bloodstains and guilt. "You had no choice. It was him or you."

She shook her head. "You don't get it."

Probably not.

"I was trying to kill Charming, not you. An eye for an eye and all that. He killed my sister, so I killed him."

"If you knew he killed Cinderella, why did you bring me to the kingdom at all?"

"I wasn't sure who did it. Not then. Not until I talked to Hansel. But by then it was too late, you were already on the case." Her frown turned fierce. "And in the damn way."

I winced, picturing Asia's first murder attempt. The one in the forest. Charming stood inches to my left, a mere hairsbreadth away from death.

"But you shot *me!* Not him." I pointed to the wound in my side.

"Sorry about that."

My eyes narrowed. "And the bomb at Charming's house?"

"It was addressed to a villain among princes. Who'd you think it was for?" She shook her head. "You?"

"Well, yeah. I am the baddest villain around." I thumped

myself in the chest with my fist. A mistake, really. Rather than looking tough, the fist bump sent me into a coughing fit.

"There there." Asia patted my back.

Once my hacking ended, I wiped a trail of snot and tears from my face and glanced up at my princess. She was currently loading an arrow into the bow I'd dropped. Her fingers brushed the taut string. The bow vibrated in response. My blood warmed a few degrees when she plucked the string again.

"Ummm . . . sweetheart?"

She paused long enough to look up. "Oh, sorry. I was just checking the safety. We wouldn't want any accidents."

Right. The safety. I took a step back. "There's something I still don't get." Well, there were a couple of things, but Asia's trim butt bent over a deadly weapon made me forget the rest. "Why did Charming kill the guys at the tavern?"

"Well—"

"I mean, I get killing Natasha, she knew too much. The same with Hansel and Missy, but those villains . . . What did they know?"

"Yeah, about that," she began. "Charming didn't kill the villains."

I frowned. "Then who did?"

Asia lifted the bow into her arms, as if reaching for an old lover. Her eyes met mine. "I did."

Chapter 50

"Excuse me?" I backed up another step, like the half a foot that parted us would matter if she decided to fire the arrow currently aimed at my heart. "You swore to me that it wasn't you."

Her face flushed. "I lied."

"But why?" I was beginning to suspect my not-so-ugly princess was not-so-sweet either. Unfortunately, that turned me on all the more. There she stood in a blood-splattered white gown, her hair shimmering like firelight, and all I could think about was the color of her panties and the way her mouth tasted when she kissed me.

"I lied because I didn't want you to know the truth," she explained slowly, like she was talking to the village idiot. Her fingers tickled the bowstring, as if debating our continued conversation.

"That's not what I meant." My hands fisted. "Why did you kill the villains at the tavern?"

"Oh." Her frown twisted into a smile. "I wanted to."

I raised my eyebrow.

"Fine," she huffed. "They deserved it. Did you see what Cross-Stitch was wearing? A knitting needle for a hand. Really? What kind of villain knits?"

My face reddened. "In some cultures it's considered an art form." Just not this one. I took yet another step back.

Now we stood a good two feet from each other. I could smell the spicy scent of her pumpkin perfume. It reminded me of all the things I loved about my clearly demented princess. "Listen, we all have our pet peeves." I smiled. "Knitting is one of yours. I can accept that."

She bent her head coyly. "You can't believe how happy that makes me. Really. But that's not the point."

"Point?" Damn, I hoped her point was the figurative kind and not the kind that ended up piercing my gut with enough force to split a dwarf.

"The point is," she smiled, "I'm not the sweet princess you think I am."

Duh. The arrow pointed at my chest was a good clue, oh that, and admitting to four murders, not counting Charming's. 'Cuz if anyone deserved a cursed hand mirror to the chest, it was Prince Rotten.

"I've done some bad things," she said. Rather than regretful, her tone sounded smug. "Some things about me you might not like."

I closed my eyes, my voice wavering. "Princi Gone Wild? Please tell me the pictures are at least tasteful... and where I can get my hands on some..."

Asia laughed. "Not quite."

This was my chance to tell her all the things I meant to say earlier today. She started to answer, but I cut her off. "Before you say anything, I want to tell you something. Something I should've said a long time ago. This is important, so please, listen closely."

Her forehead crinkled with fear, matching the way my bollocks felt with her arrow still aimed at my chest. The temperature in the room suddenly plummeted. I glanced over at the dead rabbi's bloated body, and then at Charming's. This day wasn't turning out at all like I'd expected.

"Go on," she said. "I'm all ears."

I swallowed. "I love the way you smile and the way you kiss. I love your laugh."

"You do, do you?"

"Yes." I took another step back. "I love how you squint when you're angry . . . kind of like now."

"Is that all you have to say? That you love my laugh, and my kisses, and how my eyes look when you annoy me? Anything else, Mr. Big Bad Villain?"

"Ummm . . ."

"If you love all that, you're really going to love the way I shoot this arrow . . ." Her finger flexed on the trigger, but the arrow never flew.

I glanced down at my chest, just to check, and back up at my princess. The squint of her eyes morphed into something else. Sadness? Regret?

"I love that you tried to protect me." I winced. "Okay, I'm not thrilled with that part, but I understand. When you ordered me to leave, you had my best interest at heart. I get it."

From under a veil of eyelashes Asia looked into my eyes. "I've always had your best interest at heart, RJ. You must believe that."

"How can I doubt that?" I smiled. "No other woman would have bailed me out of jail after Charming framed me for murdering Natasha. But you not only bailed me out, you believed me when I said I was innocent."

"Yeah, about that," she winced, "Charming didn't kill your ex-wife."

"He didn't?" I frowned. "Then who did?"

"I did."

Chapter 51

"You killed Natasha?" I yelled. My mind raced for plausible explanations, but nothing came to mind. Asia wasn't the jealous type. Self-defense, then. Natasha was a union-trained villain. Maybe she threatened Asia, and Asia reacted like any normal princess would—with an arrow through the heart.

Or not.

I shook my head to clear it. "Why, Asia? Why would you kill Natasha? You hardly even knew her."

"I had no choice."

My eyes narrowed.

"Really. I didn't," she said. "You know as well as I do that when the union gives you a mission, you fulfill it." She winked. "Or else."

"You're a villain?" I shook my head, unable to comprehend anything, let alone the fact my girlfriend was a card-carrying member of the union.

She grinned. "Did I forget to mention that?"

"Yeah."

"Oops."

"But why kill Natasha? She was a union gal through and through." Until she started stealing paper clips from the union supply closet, oh, and then there was that whole forming her own union thing.

"For the same reason I killed the henchmen at the Tavern." She grinned. "No one likes a scab," she said, referring to those villains who worked outside the union. "She was trying to break the union. So I stopped her."

"But—"

"Plus, she annoyed me."

I couldn't argue with that. She annoyed me too.

"Protecting the union was why Miss Muffet was here, wasn't it?" Anger boiled inside me. Asia had used me, and not in the "I'll text you in the morning" kind of way. I felt . . . violated. Well, not really. But still. She could've told me.

"No. I asked Miss Muffet to come to Maledetto," she said. For the first time since I'd burst through the cabin door, Asia looked sheepish. Her bottom lip jutted out in a sexy pout. "I needed Miss Muffet's help, and so did you."

Right. The last thing I needed was that sawed-off curds eater's help. "What sort of help? Another impotency curse? Maybe a slight case of measles." I laughed, but then sobered when I noticed a red splotch on my arm. Damn Muffet!

Asia licked her finger and smeared the bloody splotch from my skin. "I asked Miss Muffet to steal the receipt. The one you found on Missy."

"Why?"

"To protect you." She took a step toward me. "I feared what would happen if you realized Charming had purchased Gretel. It's not like you could protect yourself. Not at that time."

My ego took the hit fairly well. I managed a stiff nod, while on the inside I cried like a little girl; neither reaction Asia seemed to notice.

She cleared her throat. "I asked Miss Muffet for another favor too."

"For my bollocks in a purse?"

Asia frowned. "Why would I want that when I've already designed a very nice evening bag for them?"

"Funny." But I wasn't laughing. "What other wishes did Muffet grant you? A corner office if you made me look like a fool? Three extra vacation days if I fell in love with you?"

"RJ—"

I raised my hand for silence. "Well, I hope your mystery favor keeps you warm at night." I spun on my heel and dashed from the cabin, bloody footprints and rage in my wake. Asia used me. That villainous bitch. Did she really even care about me, or was it all a lie? A thought that turned me on more than I cared to admit. I couldn't wrap my head around it. Asia was a villain. An evildoer. Just like me. We were two of a malicious kind. My heart beat faster in my chest.

"RJ," Asia said, "Wait. Please. I . . ."

I didn't look back.

I really should've.

Just as I was about to stop running from what I wanted most, an arrow whistled through the air. My leg exploded with pain. A shaft of a pink arrow protruded from me just above the knee. Rose-colored feathers swirled around me. I dropped to the ground, smashing my head on a rock. Sure, I'd been shot, stabbed, and bludgeoned by the best villains around, but damn it, never by a villainous princess I loved.

It sucked.

I grabbed a clump of grass and dragged my arrow-infested body a few inches. A trail of blood followed my torturous path down the cobblestone driveway leading from the cabin. No way in hell would I let Asia win. I was a better villain than that. I inched a few more feet. I'd see my princess in hell, hopefully naked, before she'd get the satisfaction of my surrender.

"You're not getting away that easy!" Asia yelled.

Her second arrow, overkill really, found its mark a few seconds later. The shaft managed to penetrate the palm of my hand without injuring a single tendon. Pain rocketed through my hand, and then my leg, before both went numb. A blessing, really, since the feeling in my heart intensified to nearly apocalyptic levels. Maybe my princess did love me just a little bit? Why bother shooting me, twice, if she didn't truly care?

With my uninjured hand, I wiped the blood out of my eyes and glanced up at the princess making her way down the cabin steps. The sunlight shimmered off her fiery hair, and a smile hovered on her lips. She was so beautiful. Demented and dangerous, sure, but gorgeous. She was everything I could ever want. My perfect villainous fit.

"Nice shot," I said.

"I was aiming for your head," came her reply.

"I'm sorry."

"Yes, you are," she said.

I grinned. Asia helped me to my feet, carefully avoiding the arrows protruding from various part of my body. I grabbed her hand and pulled her close to whisper, "I love you."

Her sigh echoed around the forest. "I know."

"Good." I smacked her butt. "But let's not spread it around. I have a reputation to keep."

Chapter 52

Two weeks later, I awoke to the smell of freshly assaulted eggs, spicy pancakes, and ground coffee. I glanced around, happy to see my old apartment again. My Pamela Hans Christian Andersen poster still hung above the bed, as did a newly framed picture of my not-so-ugly princess. In the photograph she wore a white wedding gown stained with rusty brown spots and a big smile.

I grinned, fingering the much-too-tight gold band around my own finger. "So you can never get it off," Asia said during our vows. To which I replied, "I think I'm going to pass out."

It was a beautiful ceremony, or so I'm told. I don't remember much of it. Blood loss does that to you. However, I remember every second of our honeymoon. Fat or skinny, Asia knew all the right moves. She had me begging for mercy by ten o'clock and out cold every night before midnight.

Except for the final night of our honeymoon, that night we made love for eight hours straight. "I love you," I whispered as we floated in that special place between orgasm and sleep.

"Back at you," she said with a loud yawn.

Exhausted, I fell into a deep sleep, my arms wrapped around my amazing wife. The woman I loved and trusted above all else. Until eighteen minutes later, when for some inexplicable reason, I awoke at 12:09 A.M. My wife was gone, replaced with what appeared to be a lumpy round object. I flicked on the light, shocked to find my arms around a large pumpkin, a very familiar large round pumpkin with freckles, to be precise.

"Asia?" I tapped the vegetable.

No answer.

"Sweet dreams, love." I turned off the lamp and went back to sleep. I must admit, spooning with a gourd wasn't as bad as one might expect.

The next morning, I woke up at dawn, Asia's slim body back in my arms. I shrugged and nuzzled the back of her neck.

"Morning," she said.

I lifted myself up on my elbows, staring down at her freckled face. "Morning, pumpkin."

The corner of her lip tilted up. "About that..."

That was one week ago.

One week since Asia explained about yet another curse, this one involving a pissed-off fruit vendor and a magic bag of beans. Asia, in her original cursed state, had gobbled the magic beans, leaving the fruity warlock angry enough to turn my precious princess into a part-time pumpkin.

The only cure, Asia said, was a giant's toenail, but not just any giant, the Jolly Green one himself. I'd nodded and flipped on QVC. Where else could one find super-sized toenail clippers at half price?

The doorbell rang, dragging me from my memories and my warm bed. I stumbled to my feet, tripping over the fresh de Wolfe pelt rug on my floor. A gift from the king. I shivered as Prince Charming's dead eyes followed me across the room. The doorbell rang again. I limped down the hallway to the front door.

"Coming," I said, pulling to a stop in front of the door. I opened it, expecting to see a Fey-Ex driver and a super-large pair of toenail clippers. Instead, the doorway was empty with the exception of a large envelope. I picked it up and gave it a halfhearted shake. No ticking sound. A good sign.

I checked the return address. One Union Plaza, New Never City. Damn. Another rejection letter for reinstatement from the union. I tore it in half and then in half again. Then I tossed the paper chunks into the air. They swirled around, finally falling like confetti across the carpet.

"You shouldn't litter," Miss Muffet said from behind my kitchen door. A cupboard door opened and closed. Silverware rattled. I swallowed a rush of fear and poked my head inside the kitchen. Asia was nowhere in sight, but Miss Muffet stood at the kitchen counter, a step stool underneath her ruby red slippers. What the hell was she doing here? And where was my wife?

"Nice shoes," I said for lack of anything better to say.

Miss Muffet smiled. "Won them in a poker game. That Dorothy can't bluff worth a damn."

"Not being inhospitable or anything," I lied, "but what the fudge are you doing in my kitchen?"

Her eyes narrowed. "I'm making breakfast."

"I see."

"Every villain needs a healthy start."

Was this Miss Muffet's way of apologizing for my impotency leave? Or for kicking my ass a couple of weeks ago? Was she finally going to reinstate me to active villain status?

I hoped so. This nice thing was getting out of hand. Asia took advantage of me at every opportunity. In fact, last night, by her request, I gave her a foot massage, then made dinner and love to her while wearing an elf's cap.

No way for a villain to live.

Miss Muffet motioned to the table. I took a seat, wondering again where my princess had gone. Since our wed-

ding, I ate every meal with her, mostly out of fear she'd try
to poison me.

Like mother, like daughter.

I glanced down at the spread in front of me. My stomach rumbled in hunger. Miss Muffet had outdone herself.
Piles of fluffy eggs, smoked sausage, and pancakes filled
the table. A glass of milk sat next to my plate. I felt like a
kid again, which made me all the more suspicious. Why
was she being so damn nice? Was this the favor Asia requested from Miss Muffet? Be nice to me until it drove me
absolutely insane?

"Try the pancakes," Miss Muffet said, shoveling a smiling pair onto my plate. Chocolate chip eyes dotted the
pancake and a swirl of whipped cream from a can acted as
a pancake mouth. The smell of fresh spicy batter rose up,
tickling my nostrils with delight.

My stomach growled. I drizzled them with syrup and
forked up a mouthful. "Thanks. Asia's not much of a
cook." I grinned. "But she is a whiz with an egg."

"So I hear."

I swallowed the pancake. The warm, gooey goodness
pleasured my taste buds, making my body hum with delight.

Wait a minute!

I spat the pancake out. It hit the kitchen wall with a wet
splat. "What kind of pancakes are these?" I yelped, kicking back my chair and wiping my tongue with a napkin.

"Pumpkin, of course." Miss Muffet smiled, gesturing to
the hollow pumpkin husk on the counter. A freckled
pumpkin husk!

"No!" I screamed, running to the counter to cradle the
pumpkin Asia tenderly into my arms. "How could you?" I
demanded of Miss Muffet.

Her forehead creased. "How could I what, dear?"

That was it!

I stormed across the room and smashed the pumpkin

shell across Muffet's curly blond head. She flipped off her chair, landing in a crumpled pile on the floor. She lay still, her neck at an odd angle.

I gazed down at the mashed pumpkin pieces in my hands and began to cry. Big, fat, girly tears. The pain in my heart intensified with each passing second. All our dreams were gone, disappeared in an instant of gluttony and pie spice. I'd eaten my wife! What kind of man could do such a thing? I was hungry, sure, but that didn't change the horror of what I'd done. I closed my eyes and cried.

"What did you do?" Asia's voice swirled around my head.

My eyes popped open. Non-pumpkin Asia stood in front of me, a look of absolute horror on her face as she glanced down at Miss Muffet's broken body. Pumpkin seeds stuck to her new red ribbon slippers.

"Asia?" I slowly rose from my chair. "Is that really you?"

"Who'd you think it was?" She frowned at me and then at Miss Muffet's body. "Oh, RJ, what did you do?"

"I thought . . . see, Miss Muffet . . . ," I stammered. What could I say? I'd bludgeoned my boss to death with a pumpkin I believed to be my wife. Hell, even my part-time pumpkin of a wife wouldn't understand.

On the plus side, my impotency curse was finally broken. Muffetmurder all but guaranteed that. And now there was an opening for a Villainous VP. Killing the former VP in a fit of pumpkin-splattered rage showed initiative, right?

Asia grabbed a mop from the kitchen pantry. "Get mopping. I'll hide the body."

I grinned. "No."

"What?"

"I don't have to follow orders anymore." I nodded at her shocked look. "My impotency is over. I am one hundred percent villain again. Thank God."

Asia bit her lip.

"I know, baby. It's a miracle."

"Yeah, about that," she began.

"No." I shook my head. "Don't tell me."

From the floor, Miss Muffet let out a loud groan and slowly staggered to her pumpkin-coated feet.

I frowned.

She tapped her head. "Metal plate, you dolt. I've taken harder hits to the head from a three-year-old."

Oops. I considered smacking her again, but ultimately decided against it, seeing as Asia stood within brain splatter range.

But Miss Muffet was far from finished. "You're not cursed, either. The union reinstated you weeks ago."

"What!?"

Muffet smiled, a sure sign I wouldn't like what she said next. "Oh, yes. Every little good deed you've done since you and she went to the kingdom was all on your own."

"That was the favor you asked Miss Muffet for? To return me to my villainous self?" Tears welled in my eyes. Asia really did truly love me. She'd given me the ultimate gift of evilness. When you cared to send your very best. I grabbed Asia's arm and pulled her to me. "I love you."

"I love you too."

"Enough!" Miss Muffet smacked me in the back of the head. "So, my boy, how's it feel to be an honest-to-goodness hero?"

"To be honest," I paused, "it burns."

"I'll bet."

I glanced up at Asia, who was trying to conceal her grin. "You knew all this time that I wasn't cursed anymore?"

"I knew."

I shook my head. "When I think of all the nice things I did . . . Jesus, I threw Prince Rotten a bachelor party, for fuck sakes."

"Yes. Yes, you did." Asia snorted with laughter, and

then quickly sobered. "You also told my parents they were welcome here. Any time."

The doorbell rang.

My eyes met Asia's.

"I'll get it," Miss Muffet said.

And we lived Happily Ever After.

Or not.

Keep reading for a special sneak preview
of j. a. kazimer's next f***ed-up fairytale,
coming soon from Kensington Books!

Prologue

Once upon a time (about twenty-two years, seven days, twelve hours, twenty-one minutes, and forty-seven seconds ago) in a land not so far away sat a forlorn frog, his lime-colored skin pale under his frogger's tan.

"Ribbit," he croaked halfheartedly, and then sighed, bored by his unending amphibianness. Days passed in a jaded blur of flies, hopping, and the occasional real-life game of Frogger. The most excitement he'd experienced in his seven and a half years of frogitude was a questionable wart. He groaned again, closing his bug eyes against the burning afternoon sun. Hours passed. The sun sank lower in the sky, shading it a princess-pink color.

The frog's nose twitched. Something approached. Something that smelled a lot like sugar and spice with just a hint of wet dog.

From the enchanted underbrush a child tumbled, a girl-child, clutching a tattered blanket coated with dirt and chocolate. The frog, surprised by his stubby visitor, did what frogs do. He croaked once and dove into the pond, sinking below the surface to avoid a confrontation with the seemingly sticky child. Frogs and their toadish counterparts were known for two things: double-sided sticky tongues and the ability to avoid any conflict. With the exception of the horny toad.

Those guys jumped anything.

The child bumbled her way toward the pond, nearing the hiding frog. Her blond hair burst from her head like a deranged troll, sticking up at odd and geometrically impossible angles.

The closer she got to the water, the more nervous the frog became. What if she fell in, he pondered in his pea-sized brain. Or worse, what if she didn't, and the frog was once again left all alone to live his fly-eating existence?

The question turned moot when the girl-child stopped at the edge of the pond, her purple lollipop eyes searching the watery depths. For what, the frog couldn't say, but his interest was piqued. *Could she be the One?*

Apparently finding what she desired, the child let out a small squeal, dropped her blankie, and jammed her hand into the murky water. The frog shook his head in disgust. If she was indeed the One, he was in trouble.

The girl shrieked again, yanking her arm from the water. A small golden ball emerged in her mud-coated hand. She smiled at the ball and stuffed it into her mouth.

Ew. The frog shivered with repulsion, and he was a frog who ate flies for three meals a day.

What was wrong with this kid?

No sooner had the golden ball passed the girl's lips than she began to choke. Great racking, silent coughs. Tears streamed down her cheeks as her lips turned the brightest shade of blue the frog had ever seen outside the reflection of his own eyes in the pond.

Panic set into the frog's tiny brain. Was the blanket-carrying, golden-ball-eating, sticky girl about to drop dead in front of his very eyes? What if she was the One and she died? What would happen to him then?

Blinded with terror, the frog did the only thing his frog

brain could think of. He jumped on the little girl, connecting with enough force to knock them both to the swampy ground in a heap of child and amphibian parts.

The golden ball popped free from the girl's mouth. It rolled down the embankment and into the murky water once again. The child watched it with a frown, which she then turned on her frog savior. Her fat fingers pointed at the pond. "Ball," she muttered with a yawn.

The frog responded with a ribbit.

The child frowned harder, her brow wrinkling under the curls of her hair. The frog paused to watch the child. There was something about her. Something that he wasn't sure boded well for either of them.

A second later, without warning, the girl scooped up her guardian-froggy-angel and stuffed his slimy body into her drool-coated mouth.

As soon as the frog touched her lips, thunder rumbled overhead. A flash of lightning lit the sky. With a shriek, the child abruptly dropped the frog. Her violet eyes widened two times their already bug-eyed size. Blackness quickly descended, turning day to night in the blink of a milky toad's eye.

As quickly as it came the storm vanished, leaving the little girl standing at the edge of the pond, a confused look upon her chubby face. She glanced down at the eight-year-old boy in front of her. A very naked, slightly greenish eight-year-old boy, who was standing in three feet of stagnant pond water where the frog had crouched only moments before.

The boy gazed down at his naked arms, legs, and boyish parts with surprise. Free, free at last from the dreaded curse, he thought with a grin. A grin that quickly faded under the little girl's gaze. She slowly looked him up and down, and shook her head, nearly poking out her own eye with the point of her dirty, clumped hair in the process.

The boy's face flamed red and he quickly covered himself with a lily pad. "The water's cold," he said like a million men before him.

The little girl smiled.

The Frog Prince frowned.

And they lived happily ever after.

Chapter 1

"Bullshit," I said to the gin-soaked fairy godmother standing next to me in the Royal Tux-We-R Shoppe. She shrugged her massive shoulders swaddled in pink chiffon. "Come on, Elly," I added. "No one lives happily ever after."

Whack! Elly smacked me in the back of the head with her wand and frowned. "Hush your mouth. I happen to know for a fact that fairytales do come true."

I rubbed my neck. "Not this one. I don't love her. I never will." The wand rose again, but I danced away, nearly colliding with an overly well-endowed mannequin.

"Then why do you want to marry her, Johnny?" She paused to look down her long, pointed nose. "In a week."

"Ten days!" Ten days. Ten frogging days. "And you damn well know why. And don't call me Johnny. My name's Jean-Michel. Jean-Michel. How many times do I have to say it?" I paused to consider my fairy godmother, a woman who'd spent the last twenty-one years of my life annoying me as much as fairyly possible. "Never mind. Are you sure she's the *One?*"

"What do you think of this? For your wedding tux?" Elly picked up a baby blue boutonnière from a rack of rainbow-colored boutonnières. "It matches your eyes."

Baby blue? Was she kidding me? If anything, my eyes were a manly indigo, maybe even sapphire in the right light, with enough beer. I shook my head. "Don't change the subject. Are you sure Lazy Beauty is the princess from the pond?" I shuddered, remembering my meeting with the sticky, drool-coated child twenty-one years before. She'd broken my curse, sure, but what eight-year-old boy wanted his first kiss to be with a drooling four-year-old? And it wasn't even a real kiss. The girl had tried to eat me!

Elly's voice drew me back to the present. "Of course I'm sure, Johnny." At my evil look she amended her words, "Jean-Michel."

"Okay then."

"I mean, really, how many twenty-five-year-old blond princesses with a frog fetish could there be in the city?"

"What?!" I snatched the matching baby blue bow tie from her large, almost manly hands. "Are you saying that you don't know if this is *my* princess? Are you crazy!"

Elly patted my arm, leaving red welts on my olive skin. "Relax. I'm ninety-five percent sure." She paused, her head tilting to one side. I wasn't sure if she'd stroked out or was thinking. Either way, I didn't want to interrupt. "Eighty-seven percent if we factor in her . . . affliction."

Affliction my ass. Medical textbooks had a term for the affliction where a seemingly healthy princess suddenly fell asleep at the drop of a tiara, not that I cared enough to remember it. In fact, to me, it was just plain laziness. Ah, poor tired princess needed a nap. What a hard burden to bear.

Her "affliction" didn't bother me much though. After all, I also spent the last twenty years of my life doing absolutely nothing worthwhile, or even a tad bit noble.

Just the way I liked it.

"We'll know for sure if she's the One after we meet with her this afternoon," Elly said with a smile. "Now try this on." She handed me a black tuxedo made by none other than Geppetto. The fabric felt stiff, almost wooden under my fingers, but I nodded and did as Elly ordered. Mainly out of fear. That godmother packed one hell of a curse.

"I'll be waiting right here," she said, motioning to a tuffet next to the dressing room. Oh goody, I wanted to reply, but again, my survival skills kicked in.

I was in bad enough shape without adding another curse. The one I already had was plenty. It went something like: Poof, you're a frog. Shazam, a princess, albeit a slight one, gave you a kiss. Then whammo, if you haven't lived "happily ever after" with said princess by the time you turn thirty (which I will do in ten days and six hours) you'll be turned right back into a frog.

Forever.

Hence my hasty marriage to a sleepy princess. I sighed and adjusted the sleeve of the fashionable tuxedo jacket. The blackness of the tux suited my olive skin tone and jet-black hair that I wore longer than was in vogue. But what the hell. I was going to be hairless and a lot greener in a few days. I brushed back a wayward lock of hair and smirked at the man in the mirror. He glared back.

"Mirror, mirror on the wall," I began. "Who is the finest damn prince of them all?" I didn't expect an answer, and was pleasantly surprised to hear:

"You are, sir."

I turned around, narrowly avoiding my servant, Karl, standing a hairsbreadth away. I stepped back and stifled a grin. Karl was dressed like a jester in my royal colors of green and white. He wore a jewel-encrusted hat and bells on his slippers. The poor guy looked ridiculous, but by the pride on his face the dope was clueless as to how much. A standard state for Karl. Eagerness, loyalty, and stupidity were all traits to admire, especially in a servant like Karl. He kept all my secrets, large and small, green and slimy.

"I have your tunic and leggings, sir," Karl said, holding up a pair of green leggings and an off-white tunic with a large letter *P* for "Prince" across the chest. As if the tights weren't bad enough.

I shook my head. "I'm not wearing that."

"But, sir, it's for your meeting with," he lowered his voice, "the One. You have to look your best."

"I'm still not wearing it." I gave a small laugh. "I don't care who I'm meeting. No man looks good in tights." Even a male specimen as perfect as myself. Poets wrote sonnets in my name. Women swooned at the mention of my manliness. What could one lazy princess possibly take exception to?

"But, sir—"

"Forget it." I motioned to a rack of dinner jackets hanging like the three little pigs on a rotisserie. "We'll compromise. Go pick out a jacket and I'll wear it to meet the princess." I grabbed his arm as he turned to go. "Nothing green," I reminded him for the thousandth time.

He nodded and practically danced across the room. I sighed and shook my head. Marrying Beauty was becoming quite tedious. First, I had to beg her father, the king, for her hand, then I had to submit proof of princelyship, in the form of three picture IDs and a birth certificate. Hell, it was almost easier to hop the New Never City border than spend five minutes with the tired chick.

I hoped all my trouble was worth it. If Beauty proved not to be the One, I was out of options. Still, the thought of marrying her—or anyone for that matter—grated on me. I should choose who to love. Who to marry. Who to bang for the rest of my days. Not some damn curse.

"Oh, suck it up." Elly swatted me with the edge of her wand. "You'll get married. Settle down. Have some babies. And forget all this 'I don't want to marry her' nonsense. You'll see. She is the *One*, Johnny."

"Excuse me," said a woman standing next to Elly. She was young, maybe twenty, with auburn hair and a sweet smile. I returned her smile, adding a wink for good measure. "Yes, luv?" I asked. "What can I do you for?"

She giggled prettily. Elly rolled her eyes. I waved off the annoying fairy godmother and took the young lady's hand.

"Is it true?" she asked. "Are you really him?"

I nodded, bowing low. "Indeed. I am Jean-Michel La Grenouille."

Her eyes narrowed. "Who?"

I rolled my eyes. "The Frog Prince, Mademoiselle," I said in a perfectly affected French accent. "The Frog Pr—"

Before the last syllable left my mouth, the girl grabbed my neck and planted a kiss on my lips. Her lips tasted of sugar and spice, but not a hint of wet dog or drool presented itself. A pity since my body reacted instantly, wanting more.

But she wasn't the One, so after five hot minutes of saliva and groping, I gently pushed her away, damning the hack reporter from the *New Never News* who first reported on my "quest" for love's eternal kiss.

Ever since that story hit the airwaves, women practically attacked me in the street, longing to be my One. I'd like to think that it was due to my winning personality and stunning good looks, but the curse's promise of riches beyond compare might have had something to do with their interest.

"Sorry," I said to the girl as I wiped a string of drool from my lips. She promptly burst into tears and ran from the shop, the imprint of my hand on the back of her skirt. I stared after her, thinking "what if."

Feelings I rarely allowed to surface did just that. My life wasn't my own. It never had been, nor would it ever be. Not until I was finally free once and for all from this curse.

Chapter 2

A half an hour later, Karl, Elly, and I arrived outside
Princess Beauty's bedroom. I fingered the tie around my
neck and frowned. This was it. I was about to meet my future bride, a woman who'd either ultimately save or de-
stroy me. With the way my luck was running, my money
was on the latter.

"Prince Jean-Michel La Grenouille." Karl announced
my arrival in a shout.

"Who?" asked the crusty-faced butler.

Karl sighed. "The Frog Prince. Not that he's a frog. Or
ever was a frog. He's just French. Not a frog!"

I closed my eyes and shook my head. Sometimes Karl
went overboard in his quest to keep my past a secret. I
couldn't blame him. Even my own father refused to accept
my early tadpole-hood. Instead of admitting it, he'd con-
cocted a French ancestry complete with noble crest. In his
mind, insulting an entire culture beat his only son's greenish past. I played along. Mostly.

"I repeat, he's not a frog." Karl bowed low and motioned me into the room. "Never was."

I stepped through the ornate doors of Lazy Beauty's
bedroom and frowned. Not at the wasted opulence of the
gold-plated ceiling or even the pink shag carpeting thick

enough to drown a blind mouse, but at the blond woman sleeping on the silk sheets of a four-poster bed. The woman wore enough flannel to make a lesbian jealous, not to mention a pink-colored bicycle helmet fit for a child.

This was the One?

Shit.

Plotting my escape, I gauged the distance from myself to the door. Window or door? I considered each. The door held the most appeal, since the risk of fracturing my leg as I flew through it was considerably less than option number two. I decided to keep my options—and the window—open, though.

One never knew.

Elly must've read my mind because she grabbed my arm and tugged me deeper into the room. "Well hello," Elly called to the princess. The princess didn't seem to hear her. Instead, she let out a loud snore. "My lady," Elly tried again, adding a finger wave. "Yoo hoooo."

When we reached the edge of the bed the princess shot up and screeched like the Wicked Witch of the East after the fall of the housing market. I jumped back, nearly toppling over Elly, who now lay sprawled on the floor, her wings twisted underneath her body.

"Wrong. Wrong. Wrong," Beauty shouted. "He did it all wrong."

I glanced around, unsure. Was Beauty sleepy and a wee bit crazy? The helmet was a pretty clear indication, but still.

Helping Elly to her feet, I raised a hand for quiet. Of course, Beauty continued to scream, her pale face growing red. The screeching sounded familiar, like that of the four-year-old girl. That made me less than pleased. I didn't want to marry this helmet-wearing crazy woman.

"What the hell is wrong with you?" I yelped after a particularly loud burst of squealing. Elly shushed me, and when that didn't work, she smacked me in the head with the sharp edge of her wand. I glared at her, but said no more.

"He did it wrong," Beauty sobbed again.

"Hush," an arrogant voice from across the room chirped. "It will be all right."

Squinting into the harsh glare of sunlight drifting through the windows, I tried to place the voice. There, in the corner by the bookcase, stood a cockroach wearing a top hat and a monocle. He twirled an umbrella and grinned.

"Jimmy?" Elly said in a whisper. "Is that you?"

"You know that . . . thing?" I asked, nodding to the roach. Elly got around, sure, but a cockroach? Then again, who was I to judge? I was about to marry a cranky lesbian in a helmet. Did they make white flannel wedding gowns?

Elly smiled at the roach and then turned to frown at me. "That's not a thing, but a who. Jimmy Cockroach. Marriage broker to the stars. If he doesn't find you suitable to marry Beauty," ever the drama fairy, Elly hesitated for a second before continuing, "we're screwed."

"A roach decides my fate?" I gave a bitter laugh. "You've gotta be fucking with me."

Jimmy glared at me as if he'd overheard our heated exchange. Elly bowed low. "My apologies, Jimmy. Jean-Michel's a bit nervous, as you can imagine. Meeting Beauty has been a dream of his for a very long time."

Now she got my name right?

"He did it wrong," Beauty repeated. "Wrong. Wrong. Wrong."

"What's she babbling about?" I asked the roach.

He heaved a long sigh. "There are rules, my boy. Undeniable rules when it comes to arranging a union." His voice grew higher as he warmed to the topic. "In Beauty's tale consistency is key. And you failed to follow the script. There will be no marriage."

With that decree, the little bastard jumped from the bookcase and disappeared into a hole in the wall. Beauty stopped whining and settled back against her pillow. In a few seconds a soft snore escaped her lips.

"What the hell was that?" I spun to confront Elly.

She frowned. "Shame on you, Johnny. You broke the poor girl's heart. Now she'll never marry you, and you'll turn back into a toad."

"Frog," I reminded her. "But that's not what's important here. What the hell happened? What could I have possibly done wrong? I didn't say a word to the chit."

Elly shook her head, sending her glittery silver hair bouncing in all directions. "It's not what you said; it's what you didn't do."

"Fine." I released a harsh breath. "Tell me what I didn't do, and I'll do it."

"Too late." The roach reappeared, this time wearing a greatcoat. "In Beauty's fable, her prince arrives and is stunned by her beauty, so much so that he drops to his knees." He shook his head. "You didn't. Hence you are not her prince. Now, if you'll excuse us, we have another applicant coming at three."

"This is ridiculous." I glared at the roach. "The king gave me his blessing last night. Beauty and I will wed in ten days. With or without your approval."

"Good luck with that." The roach snorted.

"Hey—"

"Good day, sir." He spun on his Kenneth Cole heel.

"Wait!" Elly yelled loud enough to wake the dead. The helmet-wearing Beauty let out another volley of snores. "Johnny will get it right. Just give him another chance."

Jimmy checked the small watch on one of his six legs and frowned. "Fine. He has two minutes. Go!"

I shook my head. "I'm not dropping to my knees. Not for you or any man." I winced. That had sounded much better in my head. "You and your lazy princess can bite me." I nodded to Elly. "We're outta here."

I started to walk away, but inside I was seething. Beauty was the girl-child from the pond. I was almost positive of it. She had the same blond hair; the same grape-colored eyes, and she smelled a little like wet dog. How many princesses could there be like that?

I couldn't just walk away. Not after I finally located my wayward princess. But I'd never bend, literally, to her will. I was the Frog Prince, damn it.

Thwack!

Elly's wand smashed into the back of my knee, and I dropped to the floor in pain. Manly tears burned my eyes, but I blinked them away. "What the hell did you do that for?" I yelled at the fairy godmother innocently picking lint from her dress.

"Do what, dear?" She batted her eyelashes.

I glared at her; a volley of curse words charged up my throat. But before I could utter a single one of them, a loud choked gasp filled the room.

My eyes flew to Beauty, who'd awoken in time to see me drop to my knees. Her lollipop eyes grew as big as stars. "You . . . ," she whispered, her voice tart as if she'd swallowed a lemon.

"I . . . ah . . ."

Jimmy Cockroach interrupted my rambling. He nodded and smiled. "To the happy couple!"